Masks *of* Murder

Published by j-Press Publishing
First printing, October 2003
10 9 8 7 6 5 4 3 2 1
Copyright © j-Press Publishing, 2003

Library of Congress Cataloging-in-Publication Data
Canby, C. C., 1937
Masks of Murder/by C. C. Canby
p.cm
ISBN 1-930922-04-3
I. Title.
PS3603.A535L58 2003
813',6--dc21

Book Design by Ronna Hammer

j-Press Publishing
4796 126th St. North
White Bear Lake, MN 55110

Masks *of* Murder

C. C. Canby

Acknowledgements

Special thanks goes to Officer John Ballis, now retired from the St. Paul, Minnesota police department, for reading the manuscript and providing expertise in police procedure.

Thanks, too, to Detective John Coffee for his valuable help in providing information about police operations at the White Bear Lake police department.

And a special thanks also to Detective Richard Salverda (RET), formerly of the Roseville, Minnesota police department.

These guys saved me from a lot of embarrassment again and again.

This book is for BrookLynn Karen von Gemmingen

Part One

Fall

1

S tanding by his mother's grave, hatless, in a navy-blue suit and loosely knotted blue-and-black striped tie, the little man shivered slightly in the cool fall air. His sister, mistaking the reaction as sorrow, searched his face then took his arm in hers. Conrad, Gary, Dorian and Linda had moved some distance away, waiting anxiously, as usual, until the little man decided to leave and get them back home. The other mourners, what few there were, had long since gone.

Five days ago the little man's sister had phoned him from their mother's house. Their mother was sick and wanted to see him, she had said. Though his sister hadn't told him so, he thought his mother must be dying. All he'd felt since he told his sister he would come was dread—not sorrow, but dread. The feeling sat like a leaden weight in the pit of his stomach all the while he was packing.

On the drive down the thought occurred to him that it might be better if his mother died before he got there. Seeing his mother again, after these several years with no contact, would bring it all back. Just going back to that house might bring it all back. He had managed to fashion his life somewhat back to normal—at least as normal as he thought it might ever get. Seeing his mother again was the last thing he needed.

It was for the sake of his sister that he said he would come. For her he would take the chance. She met him at the car when he pulled to a stop in the graveled driveway of his mother's home.

"I think she's dying," his sister said. "She just wants to see you."

He nodded. "I know." He kissed her on the forehead, as he had always done, and they walked arm and arm into the house.

His mother was sitting at the kitchen table, propped up by pillows, still in her robe, a cup, half full of black coffee, sat near her hand. Bluish smoke from a cigarette in an ashtray curled upward in a shaft of sunlight from the dirty kitchen window. Her half-closed eyes looked at him through a morphine fog at first, until she seemed to recognize him. They had hugged awkwardly, ritually, and he smelled the familiar cigarette smoke in her hair and on her breath. Except for the pillows and her cheap, thin terrycloth robe (a turquoise green, with red and pink bas relief flowers), it was as though the day he'd left this house for good (or so he'd thought) was preserved across time.

In the days that followed, what he'd feared would happen, did. His mother wanted to reminisce and as he shook old photographs out of a cardboard box, his life cascaded across the laminate surface of the kitchen table. In one of the faded Polaroids, he was a four-year old, sitting beside a Christmas tree holding a toy six-shooter, his eyes red and his face too bright from the camera's flash; in another, of a birthday party, he sat at a table in a paper hat, with cake and candles. Seeing these photos, a stranger would have commented on his happy childhood.

Then his mother pulled another photo from the pile that showed him squinting in the sunlight, standing by the then-tiny evergreen tree in the front yard with his "new daddy." His "new daddy's" hand was on top of his head. His bird-dog pup, "Bobo," stood in the background watching the family's other dog, "Lady," the cocker spaniel. At sight of the photo there was a lurch in his chest that nearly brought him to his feet and he felt prickly sweat on his forehead as memories flooded back:

"Daddy" is coming. He hears the heavy shoes plodding up the steps. They stop. He knows why. His "new daddy" is taking another drink from the bottle. If he drinks it dry before he reaches the top of the steps it will clatter down. His "new daddy" will have thrown it away. He doesn't hear the clat-

ter this time, but he hears the footfalls begin again. "Daddy" is coming. The door opens. "Daddy" grunts, takes another drink, sets the bottle on a table, removes his belt, folds it in half, then raises it to strike ....

It was all he could do to keep from jumping up and screaming. But he had become expert at controlling his inner passions. His reaction went unnoticed by his sister and mother. He sat passively, as if nothing had happened.

As in the past, try as he might, the little man couldn't finish the memory. He could only take it up again at the point when he would become aware of red welts and blue bruises on his arms and legs. Nor could he remember the actual whipping itself. He couldn't remember why he was whipped, either, except that he knew, somehow, he'd been bad.

Looking at those photographs as he sat beside his mother, her eyes glazing over from time to time, her body leaning uncontrollably until his sister pulled her erect again, the little man had tried to remember what he'd been like back then, before his new daddy had shown up. He wondered what he might have become, instead of what he was, and his heart broke.

Other memories came seeping back: memories of bullies, of a forlorn and lost kid always on the margins, of lying on his bed staring at the walls and ceiling instead of playing outside, dreading when his new daddy would come home. Lying on that bed staring at the same spot in the patterned wallpaper where, as a boy, he'd thought he could discern a face that seemed to always be watching him (it was still there), he'd tasted the tears again. But that hadn't been the worst of it.

█

Now, here, at his mother's graveside, the images and sounds of his past repeated themselves in the little man's brain and the emotions he'd felt back then recurred in full strength. From beneath the tent covering his mother's grave, the little man peered out at the sky, tears, anger, and hatred in his eyes. His diminutive body shuddered visibly. His small hands clenched into fists.

From a short distance away—standing with Conrad, Gary and Linda—Dorian's mouth set in a hard line, his eyes narrowed. "Here it comes," he whispered to Conrad. "Trouble."

Linda, standing next to him, scanned Dorian's face to be certain of his meaning, then shifted uncomfortably.

Gary raised his fingers to his lips and frowned at Dorian.

Conrad just stood there, towering above the others, watching.

"It always means trouble when he gets like this," said Dorian, despite Gary's admonition, "and I'll be the one to have to take care of it."

The tent swayed from a gust of wind. A loose corner flapped. Massive thunderheads, brilliant white, were piling higher and higher in a slow-motion, restless drama, as if vying for a limited space. The earth was tilting away from the sun, and winter would be coming soon.

The little man's mother had lapsed in and out of consciousness before she died three days ago. On the last day, she had awakened and, drawing his ear to her pale, thin lips, she whispered the news: his "new daddy" wasn't dead as they had thought. After years of silence, with no word of his whereabouts, he had contacted her again. He was alive. He was still out there ... somewhere.

2

Z eke Mallard was bent over, retrieving the bag of groceries in the back seat of his car when he saw Dorian's shoes. The big man looked sideways and started to turn, but it was too late. Shaking with fury, Dorian plunged the knife with all his might into Mallard's neck, just above the jawbone. He felt the resistance of bone and muscle, but the blade sank far enough. He tried to pull the knife out but lost his grip and it clattered to the floor. He staggered backward.

Mallard, wounded critically, grunted the primal grunt of pain as he jerked upward, then lunged backward against the open door of his Towncar, the bag of groceries falling from his arms. The door of the car sprang back from the man's weight, then forward, launching Mallard against the rear fender which supported him for a moment before he spun convulsively, facing Dorian, then abruptly sat down on the floor of the garage, his back against the left rear wheel.

Dorian, having regained his balance, stepped backward, watching. Mallard, stunned and confused, still sitting, looked down at the floor, his head tipping slowly, like a mechanical robot. A red stain was spreading outward around his collar. His left leg shuddered convulsively.

Dorian knelt down, peering into the big man's face. "How ya feeling, buddy? Ya got a little problem?" Dorian asked, pleased at the pun he'd made. Dorian was a miniature Frankenstein, his face square cut, with thin lips, piercing black eyes, hair slicked back over a protruding forehead.

Dorian stood up and approached the man once again, cautiously. He prodded the man's leg with his foot. There was no response. Even sitting, Mallard reached nearly to Dorian's chest. Dorian knealt down and retrieved the knife. The man rolled his eyes upward, staring at Dorian dumbly. His lips moved, as if he were trying to speak.

In a resurging rage, Dorian lashed out again, striking across the man's throat. Blood gushed and spilled down the big man's chest. Dorian jumped up and back to avoid the blood, but too late. It had splattered on his pants and shirt. He backed farther away, cursing.

The big man was now sitting like a drunk, head hanging on his chest, blood oozing from the corners of his slackened mouth. Dorian bent down to eye level again, surveying the big man venomously, his face cold and merciless. He looked down at the blood on his clothing and cursed again. He raised the knife once more and plunged it into the big man's leg again and again and was amazed that every time he did the man grunted, refusing to die.

Dorian stepped back, physically spent, his chest heaving, and watched. A short time passed. The man's eyes grew vacant, unseeing. Finally satisfied, Dorian turned to leave. It was only then that he noticed the badge and the gun, previously hidden by the big man's coattails. For a moment, he froze. A gun? A badge? Had he just killed a cop? "What's happened here? What's happened here?" he mouthed to himself.

He wheeled and strode down the driveway. Behind him, the big man sat motionless midst the spilled groceries. Dorian turned and cut across the lawn, running to his car, looking to see if there was anyone who might have seen what had happened. He didn't see anybody. He looked back at the garage, as if to make one final check, but couldn't see inside from that angle. It didn't matter. He had to get out of there.

He opened the trunk of the car, then pulled a red rag from his pocket, wrapped the knife in it and stuffed it behind and underneath the spare tire. He checked his clothing. He'd have to dispose of them. He checked again to see if anyone was around and thought he saw a movement in a car parked a short distance down the block. He watched the car for a few seconds—nothing. He got into his car, turned it around and drove back the way he had come.

Dorian had driven several blocks and was approaching the main thoroughfare when he met another car. He had the sun visor lowered and he stretched to allow it to cover more of his face. The driver was a woman. She appeared not to notice him. He watched in his rearview mirror as the car continued on.

∎

Andrew White's memory of Zeke Mallard, throwing him around and slamming him up against the car, brought his hatred to a new boil. The cop had whipped him like a mutt, right in front of Angelena, and he had to take it. The cop had enjoyed it, too. That motherfucker! No one could treat him like that white cop had treated him. Angelena would pay, too. It was her fault for encouraging the motherfucker. And she *had* encouraged him—flipped her ass around that white bastard like a bitch in heat!

White sat low in the car, a '97 Honda Accord EX. He'd stolen it only a few hours ago. It was a cool car, he thought, maroon-colored cloth interior, all the extras. He ran his hand across the nap of the seat. There was nothing in the car of any value, though, just some old golf scorecards and the dealer's manual, a few quarters in the change-holder and a pair of sunglasses. He would take the money and sunglasses and ditch the car after he took care of Mallard.

He sat with his back to the passenger-side door so he could keep low and still see out. He scooted down in the seat a little more so that his head barely cleared the dash. A cop like Mallard probably had eyes in the back of his head. This was a white neighborhood. Anyone who saw a black man parked in this neighborhood would get suspicious. He could barely look over the dashboard, but he could see Mallard's house well enough.

He went over his plan. He would try to catch the motherfucker by surprise. Catch him getting out of his car in the garage, maybe. It was going to be risky but he hated that motherfucker, hated his guts, and wanted him dead, and Mallard would probably be most vulnerable at that moment when he was just getting home, not suspecting anything. That cop was a big son of a bitch. He fingered the steel of the gun stuck in his belt, a .38 caliber. Mallard would be carrying something bigger, maybe a .44 Magnum, even. The bastard was big enough—or maybe a .357. It wouldn't matter, if he could surprise him. Who would be top dog then?

Reality hammered the young black man as he saw Mallard's Lincoln Town Car come into sight. His throat tightened. His heart took off like a jackhammer, and he got a terrible sinking feeling along with a rush of fear and panic. "Holy shit!" he said, out loud. "What the fuck am I doing here?"

The Town Car slowed and turned into Mallard's driveway. White could see Mallard plainly as he pulled in, the massive shoulders, the big meaty hands on the steering wheel. Mallard's head was even big, with a thick nose and lips, a full head of short-cut hair.

Mallard hadn't looked his way. White sat, frozen. His plan was already crumbling, coming down fast. He saw the garage door open. The Town Car went in and disappeared. He saw it all in a kind of slow motion dream.

White had already decided to pull out of his suicidal plan when another car pulled up to the curb just beyond Mallard's driveway and he saw a man get out and cut across the lawn in rapid stride, with a shiny object in his hand. The man looked in his direction for just a moment before he reached Mallard's garage but continued on without breaking pace. White saw the man go inside. He waited. Several minutes passed. He wondered what the hell was going on.

He saw the man come half-running out, the shiny object still in his hand—a knife; now White could see it more plainly. "What the hell?" White mouthed the words aloud. The man opened the trunk of his car, slammed it down, came around to the side, then looked up the street again, straight at White.

White scooted down lower, slowly, not wanting his movement to attract the man's attention—scooted down completely in the seat till he couldn't see anything. He heard an engine start and then the sound of it fade away.

White rose to his full height, cautiously, wanting to be sure that the man he'd seen go into Mallard's garage had left. The man's car was gone. He watched the house for a moment. He wondered again what had happened. Mallard had not closed the garage door yet. The visitor had seemed leery, on the lookout, and he'd certainly left in a rush. White started the car and eased it down the street in front of Mallard's house. He stopped and looked up the driveway into the garage. At first he didn't understand what he was seeing. Was that Mallard sitting down? White just sat there for several moments. There was something wrong here. The cop wasn't moving.

White opend the car door and got out. He stood looking. Mallard still wsn't moving. Slowly, cautiously, he approached the open garage.

"Holy shit!" exclaimed White. Mallard's body sat slumped against the rear wheel of his car, his eyes staring, blood drooling from his mouth. The scene froze White for a moment, then, reflexively, he whirled and ran to his car, jerked the door open, banging his head and elbow as he slung his body sideways into the front seat. He twisted the ignition key violently, starting the engine with a whir, then jammed his foot downward on the accelerator and the car shot forward, its tires squealing. He had to get out of there. Just up the block he saw another car approaching.

"Mother fuck!"

It was too late. The driver would see him. There was nothing he could do but continue. He slowed the car, hastily lowered the sun visor and tried to be as inconspicuous as possible. He eyed the woman driver as she passed. She appeared not to be paying him any undue attention. As soon as she had passed into sight of the rearview mirror, he accelerated the car a little more. His only intent now was to get the hell away.

Further down the road, when he believed he'd made it safely away from the scene, Andrew White thought back on what he'd just seen. Mallard was dead, no doubt about it. Someone, a little white man, had killed Mallard right there in his own garage as he himself had planned to do. What just happened he couldn't explain, but Mallard was dead. The big motherfucker was out of his life and he hadn't had to do a thing. White allowed himself to smile. Moments later, he began to laugh. "Holy shit!" he said. "Holy shit!"

3

"Zeke? Dead?" Detective Richard Lanslow dropped down on the edge of his bed, his elbow propped on one knee, forehead in his free hand, as if the words themselves had borne weight enough to crumple his legs. He was naked except for a towel he'd hurriedly draped around his waist. Water from the shower still dripped down his chest and shoulders .

"I'm sorry, Rich" the chief was saying, the emotion in his voice apparent even over the wire. "Got the 9-1-1 call from Christine about half an hour ago. Somebody killed him in his own garage."

Lanslow just sat there with the phone to his ear, stunned. "In his own garage? Who the hell ...?" His voice choked as he began to fully comprehend: His partner, his friend, the guy who'd been showing him the ropes for the past six months, his mentor, was dead.

The chief's voice came through the phone again with sympathy, "Sorry, Rich. Sorry."

"You're there now?" Lanslow asked, struggling to regain his composure.

"We tried to get hold of you on our frequency earlier."

"I ... ran some errands and ... just got home ... Zeke, dead. I can't believe this. I just can't believe this!"

"We need you over here ASAP, Rich."

"Yeah. Okay, Chief."

Lanslow straightened, dropped the phone into its cradle. He ran his long fingers through his wet, coarse brown hair. The water on his well-muscled body was turning cold. He sat there for a moment, trying again to absorb what he'd just heard—his partner and mentor, *murdered in his own garage.*

Rising, he dried himself hurriedly and put his clothing back on. Pulling on his coat, he wrote a note to Laura, his live-in fiancé, saying only that he would be home as soon as he could. He checked the pager on his belt. Somehow, he had turned it off. He cursed. He let himself out the door of their apartment, taking the elevator to the parking garage. He sped toward his partner's house, the blue light flashing on top of his unmarked car.

It was five o'clock when Lanslow arrived at Mallard's home. He had seen a lot in his seven years on the police force and had become relatively inured to most of it. He felt only dread, now. At this house, where he and Laura had eaten steaks from the grill and drank beer with Zeke and Christine Mallard, his emotions threatened to reduce him to a blubbering idiot.

The dwelling, a light green ranch, sat fifty feet back from the road, on top of a shallow knoll, the black-top driveway descending to the street. The lot was a quarter-acre rectangle like all the others in the neighborhood. A low hill, covered in mature oak trees, abutted the property to the west and south. The house faced north, toward an open, now empty school ground, containing several soccer fields.

Twisted yellow tape, waffling in the late evening breeze, had already established the police line. Squad cars were blocking the street in both directions, their red, yellow and blue lights swirling, cutting the early evening light, their radio messages rupturing the evening air. One of their own had gone down and there were cops all over the place. Two state troopers were directing auto traffic, such as it was, away from the crime scene at either end of the block. Most people in the area had still not arrived home from work, but a few neighbors stood staring at the scene while answering the questions of uniformed cops. Other officers attended the police line farther down the block to the west and east. Several women patrol officers were consoling one another, while a grim, hard look had captured the faces of the others. Crews from the media were setting up to do live shots, reeling cable from the satellite vans.

Lanslow fought to control his emotions as he walked toward the house. His training began to operate automatically. He noted that a crime-scene-investigation unit and the county medical examiner were already there.

They needed witnesses. He observed that the oak trees, still bearing most of their leaves, more than likely would cut off any view of Mallard's property from the houses on the hill above. He surveyed the low buildings of the school across the street. They were at least two-hundred yards away. It was possible, he thought, that some children or teachers in the soccer fields had been there when the murder had occurred. The fields were empty now, though, so there was very little chance that anyone from the school had seen anything. Only the neighbors to the east, perhaps some of those being questioned now, would be of any help, if they had, indeed, witnessed anything. As he approached to cross the interior line, a number of reporters shouted out questions. He ignored them.

At the line, the attending officer nodded to him sympathetically. "Sorry, Rich," he said.

Lanslow merely nodded.

"Chief wants to see you."

"I know. Where is he?"

The officer nodded toward the house. "Up there, in the garage. That's where they found Zeke."

Lanslow continued walking carefully along the curb and then up the inclined driveway, scanning for anything that might offer a clue to his partner's murder. Chief Bradbury was talking quietly with Detective Lieutenant Charlie Johnson several feet outside the door of the garage.

Several other men, whom he recognized as officers and detectives from neighboring jurisdictions, stood in the street, conversing among themselves. At this time of day, in late October, the sun was already fading. Bradbury's and Johnson's figures were silhouetted against the light from the garage behind them. Two police officers were holding a sheet stretched across the garage entrance to shield Zeke's body from the onlookers and the press. The chief caught sight of Lanslow and waited for him to approach.

"Sorry, Rich," said Johnson.

Lanslow stopped beside them. "Zeke is still here?" he asked.

"We're waiting for the ME to finish before we release the body," said Bradbury. "CSI is still working out here. They've finished inside the house."

"You've walked through the house?"

"Yeah. Nothing found there ... yet, anyway. The house was locked when we got here. It looks like everything happened right here in the garage."

Lanslow stepped around the sheet and took in the scene. The sight of his partner's body, slumped forward, his back against the Town Car, shocked him, even though he'd tried to anticipate it. He'd seen death before, but it had always been impersonal. This was personal. He just stood there, still disbelieving his own eyes. A light bulb flashed and for an instant Lanslow thought Zeke's body had jerked reflexively. He nearly retched. He became aware of Johnson and the chief watching him.

Swallowing hard, Lanslow again fought to control his emotions. Nodding to Dr. Hagen, Lanslow moved as close to Zeke's body as he could, stepping carefully to avoid the pool of blood and spilled groceries. His partner's face was frozen, the eyes fixed, staring at nothing now—not cloudy, though; Zeke hadn't been dead long enough for that. Lanslow just stood there for a moment, still disbelieving. Only a few hours before, they had been talking, joking, laughing. Mallard had been looking forward to the evening with his wife. Such evenings were rare. He'd told Lanslow that Christine had hinted of a surprise.

Kneeling carefully to avoid the groceries and fluids, Lanslow noted that his partner's throat had apparently been cut with a sharp force instrument. The entire front of Mallard's body was stained darkly with blood. Lanslow noticed several other large stains on the trousers and a pool of blood under Mallard's left leg. He could see several more wounds through gaps in the slashed pant's leg. Another pool of blood was coagulating beneath his buttocks.

"Where is this blood coming from, Doctor?" he said to Hagen, and pointed at the blood beneath Zeke's buttocks. The medical examiner was short and rotund, with a mustache that reminded Lanslow of a walrus.

"Got a wound in the back of his neck. Same weapon, probably a two-edged knife. Looks like he was stabbed there first, from the way he's fallen—then his throat was cut and then he was stabbed several times again, in the leg there. We'll have to verify that as best we can later, though."

Lanslow noted Zeke's gun, still strapped in its holster. The sack of groceries was lying slightly to the left of the body, its contents scattered about, the bag itself wet from a liquid, pooling on the garage floor. Lanslow noticed a can of chicken soup that had rolled across the floor, stopping against a garbage can, and a broken wine bottle, its contents spreading across the cement surface.

"What time?" Lanslow asked.

"The body was still warm when we got here, about average temperature. He probably hadn't been dead more'n fifteen, twenty minutes. Probably around 4:00 P.M. or thereabouts."

As he took in the scene, Lanslow was already trying to imagine what had happened. He envisioned his partner bending into the back seat to get his groceries, being attacked from the rear, being stabbed in the neck and then having his throat cut when he'd turned around to face his assailant. He had probably simultaneously dropped the bag of groceries. But why was he stabbed so many times in the leg? There was no obvious reason for that. Those wounds were wounds of passion, of hatred, anger and rage. What would be the motive for such anger? And who bore such malice toward the usually convivial and popular Zeke Mallard?

"What else so far, Doctor? Anything in the car?"

"Nothing unusual. CSI has looked it over."

Bradbury and Johnson had moved nearer.

"Anything else, Chief?" asked Lanslow, from his squatting position.

"Nothing, now. Brooks is taking a statement from Christine, and we'll be interviewing more neighbors."

Lanslow stood up. "Where's Christine?"

"We let her go inside," said Bradbury, motioning toward the door leading to the kitchen. "You can go on in. Either you or Brooks can go to the morgue. Then, you're on the case. You and Brooks and Charlie, here, and whoever else we need. Priority one."

4

Rivulets of mascara streaked Christine Mallard's cheeks from tears, her face had grown haggard, her blue eyes were pools of misery and grief. She was sitting on the couch, talking to Detective Sergeant Dean Brooks. When she saw Lanslow, she stood up and walked across the room to him. Lanslow put his arms around her and patted her back while she sobbed.

"Christine, I'm so sorry," he said, holding her tight and stroking the back of her head. Brooks, short and squat of build, with broad shoulders, rose from the couch and looked at Lanslow. He shook his head as their eyes met.

Lanslow held Christine at arm's length, looking into her eyes. He was struck by her fine beauty, even in grief. "Is there anything I can do?" he asked.

"No, Rich, thank you. Everyone is doing all they can. I just don't understand who could do this. Why? I just don't understand."

As usual in situations of grief, Lanslow felt himself at a loss for words. "We'll get whoever did it, Christine. We'll find out. And he'll pay. I promise you that."

"You bet, Christine," echoed Brooks. "We'll get the son of ... we'll get him."

"We've got to get you out of here, Christine," said Lanslow. "You can come and stay with us tonight."

"No. No. Thanks, Rich. I've got to call my sister. She doesn't know. I think I'll try to stay with her tonight." She wiped her eyes with a handkerchief.

"Is there anything else you need, Dean?" Lanslow asked, turning to Brooks.

"No," said Brooks. "You get some rest, Christine."

Christine Mallard looked at Lanslow's face again and suddenly broke into tears.

"I'm sorry, Rich," she said. "Zeke ... I was ... going to tell him ... " her voice trailed off. She sat down again, dabbing her eyes with the handkerchief, and blew her nose.

"Christine, let me call your sister. Give me her number and I'll take you over there," Lanslow said.

She nodded toward a cordless phone on the table beside the couch. "It's there. Just push M1. That's my sister's number."

Lanslow picked up the phone and pushed the buttons. Turning to Brooks he said, "Christine's sister doesn't live far from here, Dean. I'll be back in twenty minutes."

Brooks put his notebook away in a jacket pocket, nodding. "No problem," he said, "we're just about finished here."

I

Christine was silent on the short ride to her sister's home, dabbing at her eyes, staring out the car window. Lanslow didn't know what to say, as he cut in and out of traffic, sounding the siren in short bursts, the blue light flashing. He was afraid he'd choke up, anyway, if he tried.

"I'm pregnant, Rich."

She said it so quietly he wasn't sure he heard correctly. Lanslow knew she and Zeke had been trying to have a baby for years. He looked at her and she nodded. So, it had finally happened. And now, this.

"I just found out today. It's gonna be a boy, I know. Zeke wanted a boy.

I was going to tell him at ... ." She suddenly started crying, really crying, holding her head in her hands, sobbing, letting it all out this time.

Lanslow gripped the steering wheel harder. "Goddamn!" was all he could say.

Christine stopped crying and dried her eyes. "I was going to tell him tonight, at dinner. He would have been so happy." She blew her nose again. "Zeke's mother is in poor health. I don't know how to tell her."

Shit! Lanslow thought. He just was never any good at consoling people in grief. "I can do it," he said lamely, dreading the prospect, but ready to help, nevertheless.

Christine smiled wanly. "Thank you, Rich, but I'm the one who should tell her. I have to do it."

The porch light was on at Christine's sister's house, a large, two-story home with tall, Tuscan-like pillars supporting the roof over the entry-way. Irene and Randy Moser were lawyers, a fact that Zeke had often mentioned with a tinge of jealousy as well as more than a little derision. As soon as they pulled into the drive, Irene came out and ran to the car. It hadn't been easy for Lanslow to tell her what had happened, listening to the horror in her voice, then the pain as she began to comprehend. He watched the two women as they walked slowly into the house, Irene holding an arm around Christine's shaking shoulders, helping her up the steps. Randy came to the door, holding it open for the two women. He waved feebly to Lanslow, but didn't come out. It was just as well. Lanslow didn't have time to talk. He pulled out of the driveway and headed back to the scene of the crime.

▌

"Goddammit!" said Lanslow again, out loud to himself, as he gritted his teeth harder. He became aware of tailgating the car ahead of him and for a moment wanted to pull the driver over just for the hell of it. "Settle down," he told himself, and tried to relax the muscles in his neck and back and loosen his grip on the steering wheel.

"Senseless," he said to himself, out loud again. "Absolutely senseless." He flashed his red and blue lights and gave the car ahead a short burst of the siren, then sped on by.

He grieved and remembered. Before Zeke made detective they had been partners. Three years later he had made detective and they again became partners. They had seen about every crime together one could think of—domestics, burglaries, stolen cars, robberies; they'd broken up bar fights, been together at the delivery of babies. You name it they'd done it—except they'd never had a homicide. Now, they had one, but his own partner, the man who'd become almost another big brother to him, was the victim.

The day Ned, his real older brother, had died in an auto accident played itself out again: the call in his dorm room from his parents; the shock; the utter grief; the days of numbness following. These old emotions, like tributaries, flowed into the roiling emotions stirred by Zeke's death. They threatened to drown him.

But it had never been the Lanslow family's way to wallow in grief or in the past. This attitude was his father's, and Albert Lanslow insisted on it, imposed it upon his sons and even his wife. Richard Lanslow learned that it was the way of his aunts and uncles, too, on the Lanslow side, who'd carried it down from the grandparents. It was not that he and his father and mother hadn't felt the death of his brother fully, as any other family would. Ned's death had nearly destroyed their sanity and there had been tears of anguish and grief—but only for a time. So now, in the family tradition, he stanched the flow of his tears that he had only allowed in the privacy of his car. He began to search for some footing upon which to get on with it.

The problem was, unless Zeke had made some enemies he didn't know about, the murder just didn't make any sense. He doubted that the forensic technicians would be able to help much. That remained to be seen, though. They had performed miracles before. If the technicians couldn't come up with anything, however, or if they had no witnesses, the investigative team's first task would be to find someone who had a motive for killing Zeke Mallard.

Lanslow began to think about who would be on the team. It would be he and Dean Brooks, primarily. He didn't know Brooks that well, even though the detective had been with the department longer than either Zeke or he. Brooks had always been in the investigative division. He knew that Dean had been born in the Midwest but for fifteen years had worked in the Los Angeles Police Department before joining the White Bear Lake department. White Bear Lake (most residents simply referred to it as "White Bear"), a northern suburb of St. Paul, Minnesota, had a population of fewer than thirty thousand. When asked why he had taken the "step down," Dean had said he'd grown tired of the hassle and wanted to "take things a little easier," and "get back to my roots." Brooks had lost his edge, now, as the scuttlebutt around the department had it, and was just cruising toward retirement. Zeke Mallard had even made some fun of him behind his back. It was the one time that Lanslow had seen a side of Zeke he hadn't cared for. Were there other things in his partner's life he didn't know about—things that had led to his murder?

■

Chief Bradbury was standing at the end of Zeke's driveway when Lanslow returned. Beside him were two uniformed officers with leashed German Shepherds sitting next to them. It was nearly six o'clock, fully dark now. The crowd of onlookers had grown, and the officers at the police line were having to keep a sharp watch. More press, too, had arrived. The darkness emphasized the sea of revolving police lights, the exploding flashbulbs of the cameras. Lanslow recognized several reporters he knew, still scrambling for live shots. To his surprise, Zeke's body was only now being loaded in the medivan to be taken to the morgue.

"Why has it taken so long to move Zeke?" he asked, as he approached Bradbury and the dog handlers.

"CSI wasn't finished, Rich," said Bradbury. "We're going over everything twice, or more if we have to. Forensics is our biggest hope on this one, so we're going to do it right." He nodded toward the K-9 officers.

"This is Officer Kline and this is Officer Kincaid, from St. Paul." He pointed to Kline's dog, and then to Kincaid's. "And this is Corky, and that's Mercedes."

"Find anything?" Lanslow asked the officers. Kline shook his head.

"Mercedes followed a scent a little way into the street, then lost it," said Kincaid.

"How'd the dog get a scent?" Lanslow asked. "Do we have a piece of evidence?"

"Mercedes is an air-scenter," said Kincaid.

Lanslow nodded, looking at the dog. He'd heard of these dogs. Humans slough off thousands of dead skin cells that float in the air as they walk or move about and it is these cells that give the dogs a scent to follow. The dog had fixed its big brown eyes securely on Lanslow and was following his every move.

"Have Brooks and Johnson finished up in there?" Lanslow asked Bradbury, nodding toward the garage where the two officers were walking about.

"Go on up, see what you can find," said the chief. "We've done our walk through, but we're going to go over the garage, yard, driveway and the street again with magnifying glasses if we have to."

"Okay, Chief."

Lanslow walked on up to the garage. "How're we doing, Dean?" he asked, as he approached the detective, who was jotting something in his notebook.

"We're finishing up here, Rich," said Brooks.

Lanslow removed his own notebook from his coat pocket. He looked around the garage. Shovels and rakes hung from nails along the side. Carpentry and other types of tools sat on shelving in the back. There were cardboard containers stacked on a platform built on stilts, under which Zeke had parked his Town Car. A stationary exercycle, covered in plastic, sat alongside a bright red snow blower. Underneath a workbench, there were bags of ice-salt and birdseed, and a small electric generator. The sight of Zeke's golf bag and clubs leaning against the wall in the back corner suddenly brought another lurch of emotions. Zeke had induced him to play the game a couple of times that summer and the results had been hilarious. The memory drowned out the grief for a moment, but it returned. "Come on," he told himself, "you've got a job to do." Lanslow began to write in his notebook.

"Zeke's gun was still holstered," he said to Lieutenant Johnson, who had moved within his peripheral vision. "He must've been hurt real bad, gone down fast, not to be able to get his gun out."

"The weapon must have been a real doozy," said Johnson. "The guy almost took Zeke's head clear off. If the wound in the neck is what I think it's going to be, then even a big guy like Zeke couldn't stay on his feet." Johnson shook his head.

"Zeke's wallet is still in his pocket, too" said Lanslow. "Christine said nothing was missing inside the house or in the garage."

"This wasn't a robbery," said Johnson. "I don't think Zeke caught someone in the garage."

"They're doing the autopsy right away. Someone's got to go to the morgue," said Brooks, looking at Lanslow. "You up to it, Rich? I can go."

"I'll do it, Dean. He was my partner."

5

Conrad threw up his hands, his shaggy mane of blonde hair falling down his back. His arms dropped back to his sides with a thud. "It's gotten completely out of hand," he muttered. "Things have just gone too far." He stalked the room like a caged lion looking for a way out, growling way down in his throat. He stopped, facing Gary. "He killed a cop! Do you know what that means, Gary? Do you know what that means?"

"It's not entirely Dorian's fault, though," ventured Gary, somewhat timidly. Gary was short, of medium build, with a weak chin, a sallow face and a little overweight. He watched Conrad apprehensively. He understood their respective roles: Conrad was the leader, the manager, the CEO; he, Gary, was Conrad's sounding board, the consigliere, his chief advisor. When Conrad failed to erupt as he usually did when challenged, he continued: "You have to agree."

"That may be," Conrad said, his gaze riveted on Gary, his brow wrinkled with worry, "but he didn't have to go that far. It'll only bring us all trouble. They'll be after us."

"Maybe not," said Gary, acutely aware of the tremendous difference in their physiques. "Dorian says no one saw him, and there's no link between Dorian and the cop."

"He's not going to be able to get away with these things forever," said Conrad. "He's gonna mess up someday and we'll all be in trouble."

"Really, it's the little man's fault," Gary offered. "He always seems to be at the center of all our troubles. He overreacted again and Dorian was just protecting him, and us, too. Maybe we need to get rid of the little man?" The statement was a question, but as soon as he said it, he knew he'd overstepped.

Conrad wheeled on Gary, the ire on his face mingling with shock. "Don't be stupid, Gary! You know we can't do that. He's frail and inadequate, but we depend on him, just like he depends on us. You know it and I know it. Anyway, since when have you started taking up with Dorian?"

Gary ignored the insinuation, because it certainly wasn't true. "Okay, I agree," he said. "So, maybe we should get rid of Dorian?" He knew he'd overstepped again, but he wished that they could get rid of Dorian, and Linda, too, for that matter. Those two have always been a pain in the neck, he thought.

"Gary," said Conrad, with unconcealed condescension, "is that all you can come up with? You know that's impossible. Dorian is quite necessary from time to time. Like you said, most of the time he's just protecting us, even though he goes off on his own, sometimes—he and Linda."

"Well, what the hell do we do, then?" demanded Gary, exasperation overcoming his prudence, suddenly exiting his role as the wise advisor.

Conrad resumed his pacing. "Look, I think you're right about the little man being the center of all this. We all get into trouble when he just goes off half-cocked. I'm trying to understand him a little more. And I'm trying to reach him. He won't even talk to me, now, though. So, for the present, we have to concentrate on Dorian. You should try to talk to Dorian, Gary. You have the talent to do it. If anyone can persuade him to change his ways, it's you."

"You know how it is between us," said Gary. "Dorian can't stand the sight of me and I can just barely tolerate him. Why can't you talk to him?" His fervor surprised even himself.

"You've seen how we interact," said Conrad. "I have no more influence over him than I do over the little man."

"Well," said Gary, "we all have our troubles. I can't see it getting any better until the little man's temper is reined in, somehow. That's the key to controlling Dorian, too. If we don't, Dorian will just try to protect him and stir up more trouble in the process."

Conrad stopped pacing and shook his massive head slowly. "We're in serious trouble, now. Something is going to have to be done ... and soon."

6

Another shower seemed to remove most of the odor Richard Lanslow had carried with him from the autopsy room at the morgue. When he crawled into bed at two o'clock, he was exhausted but knew he probably wouldn't sleep. He tried not to rouse Laura, but she stirred and rolled over, mumbling, and put her head on Lanslow's chest. "So late, hon," she said, "why so late?"

"Zeke's dead, Laura. Zeke was murdered this evening."

Laura Riggs sat bolt upright in bed, her figure a dark silhouette against the sheer curtains, back-lit by the lights from the parking lot. "My God, Rich! Who?"

"Don't know. We don't have any suspects—yet. We just finished with the crime scene."

"Christine. What ... how's Christine?"

"I took her to her sister's. She's taking it hard, but she'll be okay."

"Rich, I'm so sorry. So sorry, hon." She stroked his forehead. "How are you doing?"

"Okay, I guess ... for just having lost my partner, who was also my best friend. All I feel right now is anger at the son of a bitch who did this." The words made it rise again, the anger, and he clenched his fists, feeling the tenseness in his legs and shoulders. He tried to relax.

"How was he killed?"

"Stabbed. Throat cut. Right in their garage. Looks like the bastard caught Zeke from behind as he was unloading his groceries."

Christine's hand flew to her mouth in horror. "His throat was cut? Christine was there, at home?"

"No, we think she got there only a few minutes after Zeke was killed.."

"She discovered him there? In the garage? My God, how terrible!"

"Yeah. She saw him as she pulled into the driveway. She said she could tell Zeke was dead. Called 9-1-1 from her cell phone."

"Why would anyone want to kill Zeke? Was he robbed?"

"No. His wallet was still in his pocket. Christine said nothing appeared to be missing."

"Then why ... ?"

"That's the big question. We just don't know. I was at the autopsy. They didn't find anything, other than the knife wounds. Not yet, anyway. We'll get a more complete report later."

▮

At the eight o'clock press conference Saturday morning, Chief Bradbury stood at the podium, his face grim. There was a crowd, a number of off-duty and reserve officers as well as Detectives Lanslow, Brooks and Johnson. The mayor and city manager, faces sober, stood off to the side, along with members of the city council, awaiting Bradbury to begin. Reporters, with pens and notepads, and photographers with cameras at the ready, were all there. The room was hushed except for the click and whir and flash of the cameras.

"As you all know, one of our veteran officers, Detective Zeke Mallard, was murdered last night," said Bradbury. He surveyed the men and women assembled, his eyes grave and steely. "We all mourn Zeke's death. We can only extend our deepest sympathies to his wife, Christine, and promise her we will do whatever it takes to catch the coward who did this. We have established a task force and Detective Charlie Johnson will be lead detective on the case. He will be assisted by Detectives Brooks and Lanslow and other officers as needed. We will give this case the priority it deserves and I know that we all, every one of us, will do our best to help these detectives and the rest of the task force in any way we can, to solve it. Now, here's what we know ... ."

■

Jack Matthews, professor of sociology and criminology, woke up tired and sore Saturday morning and couldn't figure out why. Tired was usual, physical soreness wasn't, except when he exercised. His exercising was so sporadic it always made him sore, but he hadn't exercised in over a week, so it wasn't that. Was he already getting old in his early forties? "No way," he said, trying to convince himself.

The cat had awakened him. He'd forgotten to feed her before he went to bed and now she had aroused him at 6:00 A.M., her whiskers brushing his face lightly as she delicately smelled his ear. He stroked her gently and she purred, turning round and round, arching her back against his hand. She then sat in a beautiful cat-pose and looked directly into his eyes.

"Okay. I'll get up," he said, stretching to get the kinks out of his legs. As he arose, even his back and arm muscles felt sore. The cat jumped from the bed and disappeared in the semidarkness.

"Oh, God," moaned the figure beside him. Maureen raised her head and eyed him sleepily. "What time is it? What are you doing?" she asked.

"Cat's hungry," he said. "Think I forgot to feed her last night."

"Screw the cat," said Maureen. "What time is it?"

"A little after six. I should feed her."

"Oh, God," she said again and rolled over, taking the covers with her.

Matthews went to the refrigerator, the cat rubbing against his legs. Early daylight cast the room in a soft haze. He poured himself a glass of orange juice and drank it down, peering out the kitchen window. The sun's morning glow was a soft pink through the needles of the white pines bordering his driveway.

"Yeah, okay, okay," he said, hearing the cat's soft meow. "You're gonna get yours." He pulled a can of cat food from a top shelf of one of the cabinets, opened it, knelt and spooned half of it into the cat's dish. He then filled her water bowl with fresh water.

He climbed into bed again but couldn't sleep. Maureen had gone back to sleep, breathing deeply beside him. He felt a headache coming on so he got up and went into the bathroom. He shook two Excedrin pills from the bottle into his hand, knowing that the caffeine would for sure not allow him to get back to sleep, but he took them anyway. The pills were the only thing that seemed to help, if he took them soon enough.

Back in bed once more, lying there with arms folded behind his head, he listened to the early morning sounds emanating from outside. Maureen hadn't stirred even when he had gently rescued enough of the blanket to cover his feet. The cat now lay at the foot of the bed, purring.

Matthews lived in a modest house, a ranch with a walk-out basement. He had lived alone after the divorce from Elizabeth, until Luke, his son, had decided to stay with him while attending the University of Minnesota. Before Luke had moved back, they had only seen one another a couple of times over the years. Matthews might as well have still lived by himself, though, for all he saw of his son, even now. He tried to remember when they had last said hello to one another: at least three or four days. "Probably sleeping with his girlfriend," thought Matthews. "Like father, like son," as the old saying went. But he was not complaining. Matthews was just glad Luke, now age twenty-five, had finally turned his life around and was pursuing his education.

Matthews listened to the clock ticking next to him. "Ticking my life away," he said to himself, testing the soreness in his muscles. It was 6:10 A.M. He thought about yesterday. Where had the time gone? Following his afternoon class he had been really tired. He had attempted to grade some papers, but grew disgusted at the very first one. He was finding it more and more difficult to wade through the worse-than-mediocre ramblings of his freshman and sophomore students. It had occurred to him that he might be burning out. There it was again: a sign of his aging. He had refused to entertain the possibility and decided to call it quits and go home. Maureen would be coming over later, and in the meantime he had to run some errands.

The next thing he knew, Maureen was there, jostling him awake, and he was still sitting in his recliner in his study, a book open beside him. Seven o'clock, and for the life of him he couldn't remember falling asleep. But he must have slept for an hour or so before she had arrived. He had even showered and gotten dressed into casual clothing.

So it had happened to him again. Just like before, he thought. He shook his head, perplexed. The clock still ticked his life away as he stared into the semidarkness. "Must be what it is ... getting old," he said to himself, though he still refused to believe it.

When Maureen had awakened him he actually hadn't recognized her at first. He remembered her staring at him with a look he'd seen before, as though she was seeing a stranger. "New shirt?" she'd asked, unable to hide a little wrinkle in her nose, and he looked down to find himself wearing a rose-colored shirt with flower designs, a shirt he couldn't remember wearing before, a shirt he didn't even particularly like. "Just thought I'd try it out again," he said, lamely, thinking that he'd deal later with how in the world he'd ever decided to put it on in the first place.

His memory of the evening after that picked up with him and Maureen having a light dinner, some television, then to bed and sex. From then on, his memory was fairly clear. The sex with Maureen had been good—slow and gentle. He listened to her deep breathing and just for the hell of it, as if he were a kid again, he tried to synchronize his own breathing with hers. Maureen took deeper breaths than he did and took longer to expel them. She was a runner, ate right, healthy, firm legs, firm body, even at forty-four. She tried to get him into running but he couldn't understand why anyone wanted to go through the torture.

Maureen had returned to school at a later age to change her career after her divorce. She had been a student in his introductory sociology class. Before their affair, she'd told him during an office-hour chat that her interest was to become a sociologist and to help people. He'd told her that if she wanted to help people she should get into psychology or social work, not sociology. He knew, now, that she hadn't wanted to become a sociologist at all; she had wanted a relationship with him. His advice hadn't deterred her from continuing to take his courses, even though she did change her major to psychology. She always sat in the front row and kept crossing and uncrossing her shapely legs. One thing led to another and....

He slid gently out of bed to see if the morning paper had arrived. Slipping on his sweats and sandals, he went out to the mailbox. The morning was brisk, definitely an October morning. Matthews's front yard was well endowed with mature trees, many of which he had planted and tended gently himself. The reds and golds of the maples against the evergreens sometimes sent Matthews into an almost trance-like stupor, as did the shimmering yellows of the aspen and birch. He stood at the end of the drive for a few moments, relishing the colors, softened now by a gauzy mist. The cool air on his bare chest and shoulders was delicious up to a point, then he shivered.

Walking back up his driveway to the front porch he glanced at the headlines. The sniper was still terrorizing the District of Columbia and the surrounding area. Interestingly, there appeared to be no pattern to the victims killed, as yet. It was an interesting case, grist for the criminologist's mill.

Then, another headline near the bottom of the page caught his attention: "White Bear Lake Police Officer Slain." He was still reading the account of the murder when he walked into the bedroom, and Maureen was sitting up, propped against the headboard, petting the cat.

"I thought you were sleepy?" he said.

"Misha won't let me sleep, along with some other people I know."

"Misha isn't a person," he said.

"What?"

"Never mind. You remember the young detective, Lanslow, on the faculty at Bremer?"

"I don't think so."

"He came to the house last summer for the book signing. He's the adjunct in the office at the end of the hall, teaches a night course in law enforcement."

"Oh, yeah. The tall, handsome one. What about him?"

"His partner was killed last night. Knifed right in his own garage."

"For God's sake! Who did it?"

"They don't know yet, apparently."

Matthews sat down on the edge of the bed. Maureen scooted across to look over his shoulder. There was a large photo of the slain detective. Matthews recognized the name of the slain officer, Zeke Mallard, as Detective Lanslow's partner.

Even before Lanslow became an adjunct faculty member at the college, Matthews had gotten to know him briefly through his own consulting work with the White Bear Lake department. Matthews also did some mentoring of the young instructor when he had signed on at the college, and it was through Lanslow that he had come to know of Zeke Mallard, though he had never met the veteran officer.

He read the details of the murder over again even though they were skimpy. The murder had probably occurred too late for the newspaper to get much detail into the morning's press run, or maybe the police weren't giving out much information. It would be SOP for them not to, Matthews knew, unless such information might be of help in catching the killer. He was anxious to talk to Lanslow about the case when he saw him at the college again.

7

After the press conference Lanslow sat hunched over his desk, once again going through the reports that had come in. He ran his fingers through his hair over and over. Finally he stood up and stretched his arms above his head, then began bending over, touching his toes. Bags beneath his eyes testified to a restless night. The last time he'd looked at the clock before falling asleep it had read four-thirty. He had awakened a little after six, and tried to go back to sleep but couldn't. He was back at the station by seven-thirty.

Lanslow was aware of Dean Brooks glancing up at him from time to time as he went through his calisthenics. The sergeant sat at his desk going through a separate stack of reports. They had moved Brooks's desk to a position directly in front of Lanslow's. Brooks had said moving his desk would make it easier for them to talk, but Lanslow was skeptical. When he was going through a case file, the last thing he wanted was to talk, and, too, it was just a little strange having someone sitting directly in front of him all the time. His fears were somewhat alleviated by the fact that Brooks was mostly hidden by desk trays and stacks of paper and binders. Brooks's desk looked like a landfill. From time to time, though, Lanslow had gotten a glimpse of the sergeant detective, wading through the reports. Like Lanslow's, his face registered the strain of yesterday's events.

After about ten toe touches, Lanslow sat back down and returned to the reports that had been filed late or faxed in. He had been going over them rapidly. According to the ME's preliminary report, most of which Lanslow had already learned during the autopsy (he'd had to leave the room and vomit), the shape of the sharp-force object with which Zeke had been killed was yet to be positively determined, but it appeared to be a seven- or eight-inch double-edged knife. The first wound had been, as they suspected, in the neck; the second, according to the report, had probably been to the throat, and the third set of wounds had been to the left leg.

Brooks, across the expanse of the two desks, emitted a low whistle. Lanslow looked up. "What?"

The sergeant held up his copy of the ME's report that Lanslow had just finished reading for the second time. In the other hand he held photos of Zeke Mallard, slumped against the Lincon Town Car. "What a fucking terrible way to die!" He laid the photos on his desk and studied the ME's report again, apparently unaware of the emotions he'd aroused in Lanslow. "Says here that either one of Zeke's wounds could have killed him, but he wouldn't have died right away. He would have known." Brooks hadn't even bothered to clear a place for the reports he was reading and his elbows rested on another stack of papers. He was still looking down at the report.

Lanslow grimaced. "Yeah. I know." He continued leafing through the other reports, as sketchy as they were. So far, the Minnesota Bureau of Criminal Apprehension's CSI unit had not found a single shred of evidence pointing to a suspect. The garage and the rest of the house were clean. They had found blood on leaves of grass in the yard. Tests were still out on that. No witnesses had come forth.

"K-9s didn't find anything" said Brooks, suddenly, either to himself or Lanslow. Lanslow couldn't tell for sure. "They picked up a scent but it ended in the street," he added. Again, Lanslow couldn't tell whether Brooks was talking to him or to himself.

"I talked to the K-9 guys. They said they hadn't found anything," said Lanslow, deciding to test whether Brooks was talking to him.

"It tells us something, though," said Brooks, looking up. "Our perp was probably in a car. Must've followed Zeke home or was waiting for him. The distance from the curb to where the trace ended was just about a car's width. He could have parked a car there, on the south side of the street, and his scent would have ended where he'd gotten into the car and left."

Lanslow had read the report. "That's true," he said.

Brooks looked back down to the report and continued reading. A moment later he said, "No tire tracks on the street," and Lanslow looked at him curiously. Did Brooks know he'd already been over the reports? Brooks didn't notice Lanslow looking at him.

"They found some black rubber marks on the street's north side," Brooks continued, unaware of Lanslow's stare. Brooks was scratching his chin. "That might mean our killer turned around and headed back west, in the direction from where he had come, assuming he had parked on the south side to begin with. Or, maybe ..." Brooks looked up to see Lanslow staring at him.

"Do you always think out loud?" asked Lanslow.

"Yeah. Always done that," said Brooks, sheepishly. "It bothers the hell out of Alma. How about you?"

"I guess I can get used to it."

"It helps me to keep things straight. Otherwise, everything just buzzes and gets jumbled up in my head, you know?"

"Whatever works," said Lanslow, thinking he was beginning to understand the scuttlebutt on Brooks.

Lanslow continued his reading. He knew their attempts at reconstructing Zeke's murder were pretty much speculation at this point. The only hard evidence they had were samples from the rubber tire marks, now in the lab in St. Paul. But these samples would tell them little; they could have been from any car, and although several patrol officers had been assigned to canvass the neighbors around the crime scene again to gather any additional evidence, those reports wouldn't be coming in until later in the day.

"Let's try another tack, here," said Brooks suddenly, just as Lanslow had settled into another report. "You were close to Zeke. Who do you think might want to kill him? Anyone in the family? How about Christine? Did she and Zeke get along?"

Lanslow tried to get on track with Brooks since it seemed he was going to have to anyway. He'd gone over this line of thought already. Lanslow remembered the grief in Christine's voice in the car and he hadn't been able to get her 9-1-1 call out of his mind since he'd heard it. "Christine and Zeke got along fine, as far as I know. She's pregnant, you know." He knew that Brooks probably didn't.

"Oh, shit! I didn't know that." Brooks appeared genuinely concerned.

"I just don't think Christine could have done this, Dean" said Lanslow. "First, Christine probably wouldn't have the strength to use a knife like that. And, second, even if she had, where was the murder weapon? How would she have concealed it so quick between the estimated time of death and her call to 9-1-1?" A search of the premises and her car, with Christine's consent, had yielded nothing.

Brooks nodded. "She could have hired someone," he said, though Lanslow could tell that the detective himself didn't put much stock in this even as he said it. "How about insurance?"

"Zeke never mentioned it. It'll have to be checked further." Lanslow pulled out his notebook and scribbled a reminder.

"Another angry relative, maybe?"

"We have to check that out, too, but I don't put much weight on it. The only relatives living in the state are Christine's sister and brother-in-law. They were both at work."

They both knew the next line of questioning: A third party? Brooks went back to his reading.

Lanslow's suspicions had already moved toward a non-relative. Maybe the murder had just been one of those purely random events. Circumstances surrounding the crime tended to rule this last notion out, though. Random murders didn't occur in people's garages, he thought. The stab wounds to Zeke's leg suggested passion—and that suggested someone who had it in for Zeke. The most likely would be somebody Zeke had arrested who wanted revenge. They would have to check out Zeke's past collars to see if they could find a likely suspect.

Lanslow dropped the sheaf of reports to his desk and held his head in his hands, covering his eyes.

"How'd you ever get into law enforcement?" asked Brooks, watching Lanslow again.

Lanslow uncovered his eyes and looked across the desk at Brooks. "Oh, I tried a lot of things in college," he said. "Couldn't make up my mind. Dad wanted me to follow him in physics, and I tried that, but I couldn't handle the math. Took a course in law enforcement and liked it."

"Physics! Oh, man! Pretty smart man, your dad, I'll bet."

"The smartest."

"I couldn't take college," said Brooks. "I wanted some action and I was gonna go into the Marines, but a buddy of mine, an ex-marine, showed me his nose one time, just pushed the whole damned thing over to the side of his face, said that's what they'd done to him in boot camp. He didn't have a bone in his nose any longer, they'd knocked it out. So I changed my mind. Went into the Air Force and became an air police-man."

Lanslow frowned. "Knocked the bone out of his nose?"

"That's what he told me. You got a master's degree, didn't you?"

"Yeah. I was going to teach full time."

"You like teaching?" asked Brooks.

"It's okay. Not everything I'd expected. That's why I'm still a cop."

"They don't pay cops shit, but at least it's not boring," Brooks said.

"Teaching isn't boring, it's putting up with administrative crap that wears the hell out of me," said Lanslow, thinking about the little office and the one file cabinet he shared with three other adjunct faculty members and the effort he had to go through just to get his exams typed and copied.

"That's true anywhere you work," said Brooks, matter-of-factly and returned to reading a report. Lanslow picked up the first responder's reports he'd started to read, eyeing the detective over the rim of the paper. He wondered if Brooks was feeling him out somehow. Sometimes when other cops learned he had a master's degree their attitudes toward him seemed to change. Someone had once referred to him as "Joe College." Lanslow wondered if Brooks felt the same way.

The first officers had arrived within five minutes of Christine's call to 9-1-1 at 4:17 P.M. Zeke, Lanslow knew for sure, had left the station at 3:15 P.M. Lanslow himself had left shortly thereafter. The bag that held Zeke's groceries was from Kovac's grocery store, as was the receipt that was found in the bag. The receipt had a time of 3:47 P.M. Zeke had more than likely been last seen alive in the grocery store where he'd purchased the groceries. He'd probably purchased the groceries, gone to his car, then directly home—only about a ten-minute drive—where he had been killed. All in a matter of less than an hour. Christine had arrived shortly thereafter and found him dead.

Lanslow pulled out the statement Christine had completed earlier that morning. It said she had left for work at about seven-thirty Friday morning. She'd been at work all day and had gotten off in the afternoon to visit her doctor's office, then around 3:45 P.M. had driven directly home. She reported meeting one or two cars as she got close to her house, but she couldn't remember anything about them, other than she thought they were dark, rather than white or some other light color. Statements taken Friday evening from most of the neighbors for blocks around had yielded no leads.

Lanslow read further, noting that Zeke and Christine had planned on a special evening; she had called him early in the day to make sure he wouldn't forget to bring home some things from the grocery store. Lanslow had seen these items among the spilled groceries at the crime scene and in the photographs, as well as the bottle of wine, broken, its contents mixing with Zeke's blood. Lanslow even remembered Zeke taking the call earlier in the day. Zeke had mentioned that Christine had sounded unusually upbeat over the phone. Lanslow now knew why. Christine was pregnant and was going to tell Zeke that evening. The thought occurred to him that it was curious that Christine had asked

Zeke to purchase the wine, her being pregnant. In her jubilation, had she been willing to take the risk? Or maybe Zeke had anticipated something celebratory? He made a note to ask her about it.

"We've got to go to the grocery store, Dean," said Lanslow. "Zeke was probably seen there last before he died. We need to check our time-line and see if there was anyone in the grocery store who remembers anything."

Detective Brooks looked up and nodded. "Absolutely," he said. "Let's go."

The store manager was able to match Zeke's receipt with the store's receipt, so they knew for sure this was the store where Zeke had purchased his groceries. Furthermore, the receipt gave the register number where Zeke had paid his bill. Lanslow showed Zeke's photograph to the checkout clerk who'd been at the register where Zeke had purchased the groceries, and she said she might have seen him, but wasn't sure. A boy who carried out bags for customers thought he might have seen the detective, too.

On a Friday evening, the store had been busy and the clerks and manager on duty were vague about whether they remembered seeing Zeke Mallard, when shown his picture. The store did not have surveillance cameras. No one had noticed anything unusual. Zeke had apparently paid with cash, so there was no further record of the transaction. The receipt had read 3:47 P.M. Shortly after that time, Zeke Mallard had left Kovac's bearing a bag of groceries.

Then Lanslow thought of the bottle of wine. Since Kovac's did not sell wine, Zeke must have stopped somewhere to purchase that, too, either after or before he had purchased the groceries. The wine bottle had been in a separate bag but there was no receipt.

On a hunch, the detectives visited the liquor store located just down the sidewalk from Kovac's. After explaining what they needed it took the manager only a few minutes to find a record of the sale. A store receipt showed that at 3:27 P.M. a purchase for the same brand of wine Zeke had brought home, and on the store's surveillance tape, with about the same time showing, there was Zeke, big as life, joking with the clerk, as he made the purchase. The tape showed another person in the store, but the image was of a man farther back, wearing a hat, apparently looking over the collection of German wines, his head barely revealed above the storage rack. When Lanslow had the tape replayed, it appeared that the man might have been looking directly at Zeke Mallard. The man's face was only a white blob on the blurry black and white film. Zeke had not taken the receipt from the clerk, as far as they could tell. It seemed clear that Zeke had walked out of that store, proceeded to Kovac's, paid for his groceries at 3:47 P.M., then driven home to his death.

8

Sunday morning, Jack Matthews could just make out the splendor of the day through the multicolored stained glass of the church windows, back-lit brightly from the sun's rays. In a prim suit, Maureen sat beside him on the hard seat.

The professor shifted on the unyielding surface. The speaker was affirming the "gloriousness" of the day that God had made, especially for them, on this wonderful Sunday. "Glory" and "glorious" also seemed to be two more of his favorite words. The thought occurred to Matthews that he'd never heard the preacher make reference to the nasty days that God had foisted on the congregation from time to time, the rainy, wet days, with a thirty-mile-an-hour wind ripping hats off heads and turning umbrellas inside out, or the snow-driven days at fifteen or twenty degrees below zero, when the cold crept its way into the very marrow of one's bones. Maybe such days were the work of the Devil? Only the good days were works of God? And how about the hardness of the pew? Was that the Devil's work, too?

Matthews smiled inwardly at his sacrilege. He shifted his position again. Maureen glanced at him curiously, then turned back to the words of the speaker. Maureen seemed impervious to the hard pew. Matthews glanced over, studying her profile surreptitiously, the high-boned cheeks, the slender neck, the curve of her mouth. He wouldn't be here, in church, except for her. Religion and sociology didn't mix, except when sociology made religion itself an object of study. For Maureen, religion was an important part of her life. For Matthews, sitting in church on Sunday mornings was a concession of his valuable time.

The preacher's monologue became a drone and Matthews's attention drifted. As usual, he became absorbed in speculation. It was curious, he thought, shifting again on the pew: Maureen, an intelligent woman—pursuing a master's degree in psychology, even—seemed to abandon reason when it came to religion. When he would point out to her what he saw as religion's logical absurdities, she would merely shrug, even though Matthews was sure she could see them, too. Psychologists referred to the human capacity to hold conflicting attitudes as "cognitive dissonance." For Matthews, however, the application of a technical term to the phenomenon didn't help explain it.

A conversation he'd had with Harvey Schroedl, a sociologist colleague at the college, and Leo Morganthaler, an anthropologist, came to mind. They had been talking over beers at a Duluth pub before retiring to the hotel in which the convention they were attending had been held.

"It's simple," Harvey had said. "Humans are the only creatures in the world who are inauthentic."

"What the hell do you mean by that?" Morganthaler had asked, his long beard nearly dipping in his beer glass. Morganthaler looked like a lumberjack. He even held his pants up by suspenders.

"Animals can't be anything other than what they are," Said Schroedl. "Humans can be anything they want to be."

"You sound like a goddamn army commercial," said Morganthaler.

Harvey Schroedl reminded Matthews physically of W. I. Thomas, a pioneer sociologist at Chicago back in the 1930s, bald head and all. Matthews had heard Harvey's spiel before. It was Schroedl's mantra.

"Harvey sees all the world as a stage," said Matthews.

Morganthaler picked it up. "And one man in his time plays many parts."

Harvey had smiled indulgently and ordered another round of beers. "It's the distinctive human trait," he had said.

They had continued jousting with Schroedl, he and Morganthaler, as much out of the fun of seeing Harvey growing apoplectic as anything else. But Matthews, in fact, agreed generally with Schroedl's viewpoint. Their discussion had more or less deteriorated with succeeding rounds of drink, drifting over the various points of the spectrum of social problems: war, racism, abortion, poverty, global warming. It ended with health insurance and the outrageous premiums of the HMOs they belonged to.

The voice of the preacher interrupted Matthews's train of thought. They were to stand for a hymn. He listened to the voices, discordant and uncoordinated. From across the aisle, a known strong-in-the-faith member's voice could easily be heard above the rest as he sang out with sonorous gusto, as if to publicize his unswerving certitude. From the rear, directly behind them, a woman's off-key voice competed earnestly.

Matthews himself did not sing along. He glanced across the aisle at the "strong-in-the-faith" member of the church, who was going blind from a degenerative disease. Matthews wondered if the man ever thought about why God had allowed such a thing to happen. How could this man reconcile his condition with the doctrine that God was all-loving? He knew what the answer would be: God works in mysterious ways. Or, perhaps, he would be referred to the lament in the *Book of Job:* "Why is light given to a man whose way is hid, and whom God hath hedged in?" The standard answer: life is a test of faith and obedience.

What a comfort, Matthews thought, not to have to think things out, not to have to wrestle with trying to explain the paradoxes of human existence, to put it all down to the struggle between good and evil! It explained a lot, this matter of comfort. It was the basis of irrational behavior of all sorts—not just religious behavior. Take the case of Officer Mallard's murderer: A knowledge that such an act was wrong, even the belief that it could lead to everlasting damnation, apparently was not enough to overcome the force of emotion that must have been behind the act, as it had been described in the media. And he

was sure the police hadn't revealed all the details, even. It was emotion, Matthews was sure, that had played the major part in the killing
of Zeke Mallard.

Matthews felt a poke in the ribs. He became aware that they were
supposed to be praying. Matthews bowed his head in hypocrisy as
the preacher's voice came to his ears, then faded away and became
a meaningless hum. "Our gracious, heavenly Father, we thank you for
this glorious day and for the time we have with you this glorious morning. We ask that you bless us, Lord, and shine your light down upon us.
We ask, especially, that you ..."

It had taken only a few minutes for all his thoughts to pass through
Matthew's brain. They were replaced by thoughts stimulated from his
secret study of Maureen's countenance, thoughts of their relationship.
He had decided some time ago that he loved her. He was there, in
church, for Maureen, just as she was there, in his life, for him. Someday
he would propose.

░

Sunday found Richard Lanslow still struggling with Zeke's death, though
the initial shock had subsided somewhat. Laura had gallantly taken
upon herself the task of easing her fiancé's distress and had prepared a
breakfast of scrambled eggs, potatoes and bacon. He'd tried to help but
had just gotten in the way. Laura sat him down firmly at the dining table
and placed a cup of coffee and the paper in front of him. As soon as he'd
finished breakfast, however, he rose from the table, gathered his plate,
glass and silverware and deposited them on the counter by the sink. He
walked to the closet to get his coat.

"I don't understand why you can't stay home today," said Laura. "What
can you do on a Sunday?"

"I think I'll pay Christine a visit. You can come along if you want."

"Why do you want to see Christine? I talked to her yesterday. She
seemed okay."

"She might be able to come up with something new. Besides, I think I owe her a call, just as a matter of courtesy. There are some reports I want to go over, too."

"You can't let it go, even on a Sunday?"

They hadn't been living together long enough for Laura to learn of the hectic nature of a police detective's career, where a so-called normal life would be abnormal. As he pulled his coat from the closet he wondered again, as he had many times since they'd met, if Laura would be able to take it. If not, they were going to learn, now, and fast. It was one reason he'd wanted them to live together, a kind of pretest, as he saw it. He'd already seen too many marriages fail among his fellow police officers.

"I thought we might take a walk at the nature center this afternoon," she said.

"Listen, hon. I've told you about this," he said, as mildly as he could.

"I don't see why ..."

"Zeke was my friend as well as my partner, Laura."

Laura looked at him steadily, questioningly. She shrugged. "Yes, you're right. It would be so nice to have you around, though, just to relax a little."

"I don't intend to stay long. You're not going then?"

"I want to finish what I'm doing here. Then I should get some milk and bread from the store."

"I'll pick them up on my way back."

"Oh, great. I'll be able to get a letter off to Mom, then. She'll be wondering."

It was true, Lanslow thought. Sarah Riggs would be wondering about his and Laura's relationship. Lanslow knew that he was not exactly Sarah's choice of a husband for Laura, though she had never said it outright, of course. He guessed that his future mother-in-law thought Laura—an elementary school librarian—was marrying beneath her. Never mind that Lanslow held a master's degree and taught a night class at the college. To Sarah, Lanslow was merely a policeman. The day she had learned that he and Laura were cohabiting and planned to be married hadn't been pleasant for his fiancé. Sarah had wept profusely over the phone to Laura and, of course, Laura became upset. She and her mother were close.

Lanslow thought of his own mother and father, now living in an Arizona retirement community. They hadn't met Laura yet. He'd sent them pictures and their letters expressed their joy that their young son was settling down, that someday, soon, he might marry and they might become grandparents. Not so with Sarah Riggs, who was divorced, her ex-husband dead. She wanted Laura to herself. Eventually, however, Sarah had seemed to grudgingly accept the situation, hoping against hope, Lanslow supposed, that it wouldn't work out.

He stepped into the hallway and started to close the door but hesitated, listening. The clatter of the dishes as Laura cleared the table seemed a little louder than necessary.

9

In his office on Monday morning, Jack Matthews looked at his image in the mirror. He saw a tall, middle-aged man, medium built, with hair graying slightly at the temples. He was wearing bifocal glasses and a tweedy sport jacket. The button-down collar of his shirt showed just above the neckline of the Cashmere sweater. He thought he looked every bit the scholarly professor. Sometimes he even felt that he was. He had the diplomas to prove it, at least, holding BS, MS and doctoral degrees in sociology, with an emphasis all the way in criminology. The college where he lectured wasn't Harvard or Princeton. Still, for someone who'd come from the wrong side of the tracks, so to speak, he couldn't, he supposed, complain.

A large figure appeared in his office doorway—long beard falling practically to his chest, reading glasses halfway down his nose, the Ojibwe carrying-basket hanging down his back filled with the skulls of *Australopithecus Afarensis, Homo Erectus, Cro-Magnon, Homo Neanderthalensis,* and *Homo Sapiens.* Leo Morganthaler, the anthropologist, all six-feet-five of him, stood there, stopping by after his class, on his way to his office down the hall.

"I see you've been trying to corrupt the creationists, again," said Matthews, leaning back in his executive chair, grinning. His office was small, no more than ten feet square. Along the back wall, behind his desk, was his library, holding the books he needed while he was here at the college.

His more extensive collection was in his study at home. His second floor office window allowed him to look out through the limbs of a tall tree to the college's massive parking lot. On his desk was a phone, and his "in" and "out" and "on-hold" trays. On a table beside the desk was his computer. To his left, against the other wall, was a four-drawer file cabinet in which he kept his lecture notes, his research notes, and his exams. The cabinet was locked, of course.

Morganthaler set the basket down just inside Matthews's doorway and took a seat. He reached in the basket and took out the skulls, placing each in its evolutionary order on the floor in a semicircle around his big feet, as if laying out the implements at an alter for worship. This was a regular occurrence, from which Matthews got great pleasure, because he knew what was coming. Leo loved his skulls. He loved to point out the subtle differences between them. "I had two students walk out on me today," he said. "Don't know whether they'll be back or not."

"I wouldn't sweat it. I had a young lady tell me she was dropping my course right after my lecture on demographics last week; said I was teaching abortion."

The anthropologist laughed. "I wouldn't give a damn," he said, "if they just don't go to the Dean. Fewer papers to grade." He picked up the skull of *erectus* and rolled it over and over in his hands, the tips of his fingers exploring the crevasses, curves and protuberances.

"I don't think we have anything to worry about even if they do," said Matthews.

"Maybe. But the student is king around here."

Matthews had found Leo to be the only member of the social and behavioral sciences division, other than Harvey Schroedl, that he could talk to seriously on matters concerning the social sciences. Matthews supposed this was at least partially due to the similarities between their disciplines—often called "sister disciplines"—anthropology, the study of man; sociology, the study of society. Not a whole lot of difference, except perhaps in abstraction and methodology. But there were other affinities between Matthews and Morganthaler: a certain outlook on life, a need to probe beneath surface appearances, a wonderment of existence and being.

There were a few other division members that Matthews had found somewhat approachable, though not nearly like Morganthaler: Harold Peterson, the psychologist, self-styled renaissance man; Anna Marier, another psychologist, of the behaviorist persuasion, willing to discuss, but insisting on reducing everything to stimulus and response; Harriet Milham, a historian, too Catholic and not even realizing it, and too serious, as well—not a funny bone in her body, but still somewhat open to intellectual discussion, even with a sociologist. At least that was true until Matthews had once joked in Harriet's presence that he had defined history to his students as "just one damned thing after another," a definition which was, of course, not original with him, but she hadn't seen the humor. They hadn't had an intellectual discussion since.

The other faculty members Matthews had dismissed, each in turn, as hopeless "teachers," mere purveyors of The Word, their focus not on the creation of The Word, but the superficial transmission of it. Matthews recognized in this dismissal his own arrogance and elitism, and he chose it without remorse.

Morganthaler put *Erectus* down and picked up the skull of *Homo Sapiens* in his right hand, then the skull of *Australopithecus* in his left. "Quite a difference, don't you think?" he said, looking from one skull to the next. Indeed, the skull of *Australopithecus* was tiny compared to that of *Homo Sapiens*, its frontal lobe a mere swelling compared to the bulge of the wise man's. Matthews recognized the question as preamble to deeper discourse.

"Over here," continued Morganthaler, hefting *Sapien's* skull, "we have everything we think of as truly human. Here," he lifted the skull of *Australopithecus*, "we have the merest of human beginnings."

"We've come a long way," said Matthews.

"Have we?" said Morganthaler.

▌

Police officers and officials from all over Minnesota and even from the bordering states came to Zeke Mallard's funeral on Monday. The media were there, *en masse.*

Richard Lanslow stood with Christine at the gravesite, the mounds of shoveled earth covered with green fabric. He had tried without much success to comfort her when he had visited Sunday afternoon. They had taken a walk and he asked her about the wine. "It must have been Zeke's idea," she had said. "He knew we were celebrating something. I wonder if he had guessed?"

Now, through the eulogies and the rest of it, he was trying again to comfort her, but once more he felt his inadequacy at such things. He felt especially inadequate in this instance because his thoughts and perceptions were on other things. Christine leaned against him (oblivious of his inner ineptitude) and that seemed to be of some help to her.

The day was bright in a way that occurs only in the fall in Minnesota. The angle of the sun, much shallower now in October, provided a clarity and lightness that doesn't exist in the summer months. The gold and yellow of the aspen, maple and birch leaves shimmered in it, and the red of the oak leaves provided a deeper touch of color. The air was crisp. The discharge from the honor guard's rifles smacked against the sky.

From the very first, through the prayers and even the muffled sounds of weeping, Lanslow had been curious about a young woman he'd picked out in the throng. That he'd done so was no accident. Lanslow and the others on the case had been on the lookout for anyone suspicious. Though there were many he didn't know in attendance, there were few young women alone, weeping as this one did. She tried somewhat to hide it, but the handkerchief was too obvious. She was an unlikely candidate for murder, Lanslow thought, but why was she here, and so obviously distraught?

Lanslow caught Detective Brooks's eye and nodded in the young woman's direction. Brooks nodded in return, signaling his understanding, and began taking up a better position to watch her as covertly as he could.

The final oration was short, the casket was lowered into the grave and it was over. Zeke Mallard, Lanslow's mentor and friend, was gone. A grief-stricken Christine leaned even more heavily against the young detective's shoulder as he accompanied her to the car. The photographer's cameras flashed and whirred.

As he closed the door and went around the rear of the car to the driver's side, Lanslow turned to see if he could get a glimpse of the young woman again. She was nowhere to be seen. But neither was Brooks.

■

Following his afternoon class, Jack Matthews pulled the newspaper from his briefcase and scanned the headlines. The funeral was the big story on the front page. A color photo of the procession of police personnel marching solemnly behind the hearse was next to Zeke Mallard's official photo, again bordered in black. Inside, where the story continued with additional articles, was a picture of Christine Mallard leaning against Richard Lanslow's shoulder. The main article said that the murderer of officer Zeke Mallard remained unknown.

Matthews had been following the case with a great deal of interest, not only as a criminologist, but because of the young detective whose photo he now gazed at, mentioned as Zeke Mallard's partner.

The phone rang. It was Luke.

"Hi, son, how are you doing?" said Matthews, when he recognized Luke's voice.

"I'm doing okay, Dad. I got a favor to ask."

"What do you need?" Matthews felt the concern in Luke's voice over the phone.

"I think Annie is in trouble. I think I'll try to go back and see what the problem is."

"What kind of trouble?"

"I'm not sure. She called, and she didn't sound good. I don't think she's over Mom's death yet. I'm a little worried about her."

Matthews had met Annie, Luke's half sister, only a few times, despite the fact that the family had lived only about a five-hour drive away in southern Wisconsin. Luke hadn't talked about her much other than to imply from time to time that she had given the family trouble, even before Elizabeth, his former wife, had died. According to Luke, a rift had developed between Annie and her father, even before he had mysteriously disappeared when Annie was fifteen and Luke was nineteen.

Elizabeth's new husband, as Matthews remembered him, was a big man, with a bearish demeanor as well as attitude. Luke had complained that he drank too much and ran a strict house. Matthews took Luke's lamentations and accounts with a certain skepticism, seeing as how Luke could very well be prejudiced, but he could understand that such a situation could develop, given the stepfather's and Luke's temperaments.

As far as the relationship between Annie and her father was concerned, Matthews had never considered it any of his business. But between the stepfather and Luke? That was a whole different matter. Matthews hadn't liked the man either, although their infrequent meetings had been superficially cordial over the years, each sparing the other their true feelings. The man seemed incredibly dull and low-cast to the professor, and he could only wonder how Elizabeth could be attracted to such a man. But perhaps that had been the problem in his and Elizabeth's marriage, when he thought about it: maybe it was he and Elizabeth who were mismatched?

"Has Annie done something?"

"She wouldn't say, exactly. She was crying. Anyway, I don't have enough money for a flight back. I don't want to miss too much class, so I don't want to drive. I was wondering if I could get a loan. I'll pay it back."

By a "flight back," Luke meant to the east, to Pennsylvania, where Annie was attending a small religious college. Like Luke's, Annie's decision to go back to school had been later than usual.

"Is this really that bad, Luke? Of course I'll give you the money, but why won't Annie let you know what the problem is?"

"She probably didn't want to worry me too much. I should go back."

"She's nearly twenty-one, an adult now. Can't she take care of herself?"

"I think she's still grieving over Mom ... I need to see her, too, Dad."

Matthews paused. Luke did sound worried. Matthews wondered if Luke was over his mother's death yet. Of course he wasn't; probably never would be. And neither would he be, for that matter. "Well, okay. I'll be home as soon as I can, then. I can stop at the bank or write you a check. How much do you need?"

"I'll need cash. I won't have time to cash a check. I'm going to try to get out later tonight. I think it'll be around five hundred or so, to get a seat this late. I can make up the rest if I need to."

Matthews found himself (feeling guilty for doing so) suspicious of what Luke was telling him. "Hmmm ... well, I'll have to pick some additional cash at the bank on my way home," he relented. "I'll be home in about an hour, then."

"Thanks, Dad. Sorry. I have to do this. I'll pay you back."

❚

Since his mother's funeral, since learning that his "new daddy" was still out there somewhere, the little man's days had turned into tunnels of memories, leading him downward and backward in time, opening old wounds he'd thought healed. A voice he hadn't heard in years swam out of the past. He began to feel as if he was crazy, the voice mocking him—and sometimes he didn't want to go on like this, with the voice hounding him, coming out of nowhere, with the memories invading his consciousness to where he sometimes couldn't separate the real from the unreal.

He stood at the light, waiting to cross the street. The drivers of the cars whizzing by him wouldn't have a chance, he thought. All he had to do was jump and it would be all over. They couldn't possibly stop before it would happen.

It was the rush hour, people were anxious to get home. The cars' colors blurred before him, their speed dizzying, their sound deafening. The day had turned gray and a cold wind whipped at his clothing.

"Jump!" said the voice.

His body leaned forward perceptibly toward the street and the oncoming cars, then he rocked back. "Who said that?" he inquired, pivoting his head from side to side.

The young man standing next to him stared at him curiously, edging away somewhat.

"Just do it!" said the voice. *"Get it over with. Jump!"*

"Pardon me," said the little man to the young man standing near him. "Were you speaking to me?"

"Afraid not, mister," said the youth, as other people gathered at the street corner, waiting for the "walk" sign to come on. The young man stared at him curiously.

Such energy, thought the little man, as the stream of automobiles poured by him; all those people, the wind, the sound, the movement. Was the voice an emanation from the cosmos? Telling him to join it? Would that, finally, be his unity with God, to jump and to be thus obliterated by the swirling energy of the universe, absorbed by it? It was tempting.

"Go ahead," said the voice. *"It'll be over then."*

"I don't want it to be over," he whispered to himself. I don't think I do."

"Yes, yes, you do. It's all too painful," said the voice. *"Jump!"*

The little man suddenly jerked himself out of his trance. What was he doing here? How had he gotten here?

The light turned. People began to walk across the street. He followed. He'd have to find his way home—if he could just figure out how.

I

After the funeral, over Laura's protestations ("You need the rest"), Lanslow had returned to the station from their apartment. Brooks came into the station at five o'clock. Lanslow was sitting at his desk, feet up, going over the reports of interviews with neighbors. "What's with the girl?" Lanslow asked.

Brooks plopped heavily into his chair, pulling his notebook from his pocket. "Her name is Angelena Rosario. She lives on Hopkins Street in St. Paul. I followed her to the address, over on the east side."

"Oh, yeah. I know where that is. Near the tennis club?"

"Yeah. She went there straight from the funeral. It's a working class neighborhood, mostly Hmong, some Hispanic and black. The place is an apartment building, just down from the club."

"You didn't talk to her?"

Brooks lowered his notebook and looked at Lanslow. "Didn't think it was a good idea to do it right away before I did some checking."

"Yeah, you're probably right," Lanslow said, realizing he might have put Brooks off.

"She drives an '82 Dodge Dart, black, Minnesota license plate DMZ144. Nothing on it, not even a traffic ticket. Nothing on her."

"You think we should check her out some more?" Lanslow jotted down Brooks's information.

"Sure. I watched her place for a while. Doesn't look like a strong lead, but it might not be a bad idea to talk to her."

10

To his surprise when Lanslow got to the station early on Tuesday morning, Brooks was already there. Small, light snowflakes were drifting down lazily, a few at a time, from a gray, cloudy sky. According to the forecast, there would be no accumulation. Too early for snow, thought Lanslow. Too damned early.

He and Brooks had gone to talk to Angelena Rosario Monday evening but she wasn't home. The apartment building was completely dark and no one answered their knock at the door. They had returned to the station to write their reports and finish going over the latest reports.

Brooks looked up from behind a sheaf of papers, chewing on a doughnut. He looked tired. "Want a doughnut?" He motioned toward a clear plastic tray of powdered-sugar doughnuts. His face looked like someone had pressed two big silver dollars beneath both eyes.

Lanslow declined. "You look like you need a little more sleep, Dean."

"Thanks, partner. You don't look so hot either."

Brook's reference to him as his "partner" surprised Lanslow. He hadn't made that transition quite yet even though it was technically true. For him, Brooks was as much on probation as he was. "Anything new?" he asked.

"Nothing, yet. I just got here a little while ago. Our best bet is a former collar. I'm getting the names together now."

"I think we should follow up on this Rosario woman, too," Lanslow said.

"Right. Go ahead. No use in us both going, though—just for an interview. I'm going to get some help putting this list of former collars together."

❚

Lanslow turned his unmarked car off Interstate 35E onto the University Avenue exit ramp, then turned left, traveling east back under the overpass, past the Union Gospel Mission. The skyline of St. Paul seemed eerily cold against the gray sky, a whitish mist lingering across the topmost floors of the skyscrapers. It had stopped snowing. Three transients, bags slung across their shoulders, their dirty clothing from another fashion era, crossed the street to the Mission, weaving their way through the heavy traffic. They had probably just exited a freight coming from someplace north, on their way south, stopping now at the Mission for a hot meal before continuing their journey away from the coming Minnesota winter. May be too late, thought Lanslow. He allowed them to pass, then continued over the bridge above the railroad tracks to Desoto Street, past the tennis club and from there to Hopkins Street. He checked the time: 9:00 A.M.

The building where Angelena Rosario lived had once been a three-story home. Now it was carved into apartments. A chain link fence, acting as a barrier to the paper trash lining its base, bordered the tiny yard. Apparently the boarders parked their cars at the curb on the street. A black 1982 Dodge Dart sat next to the curb, license plate DMZ144.

A young black man in baggy pants and coat jive-walked by as Lanslow got out of his car, eyeing the young detective curiously for a moment, then, as if he knew a cop when he saw one, hurried on up the street. Lanslow unlatched the gate, noting the sign on it that read "Beware of dog," and walked up to the porch and knocked.

∎

The older, fox-faced woman who answered Detective Lanslow's knock examined his badge, then told him she was the owner of the building. She introduced herself as Imogene Gorham. A smoking cigarette hung between her fingers. A black Doberman sat behind her, drooling.

"Do you have an Angelena Rosario living here?" asked Lanslow.

"Uh huh. She's upstairs," the woman said, with the gravelly voice of a smoker. "I think she's here. She in trouble? What's she done? I won't have no troublemakers."

"She's not in trouble, ma'am. Just some routine questioning."

"It's about that cop that got killed, ain't it? I've seen him and her. He picks her up, then drops her off later and leaves. I recognized him from his picture in the papers."

Lanslow looked at the woman, eyebrows raised. "You've seen them together?" he asked.

"Oh, yeah. Several times. She don't work for the police, so I figure there's got to be something goin' on there. He ain't just dropping her off from work. Paper says he was married. Ha! That picture of his wife, in the paper, she was all broke up. I'll bet she didn't even know."

"Have you seen them together a lot?"

"Oh, yeah. Many times. She's been stayin' here 'bout a year, maybe a little less. I seen her with another man at first, a black man. He don't live 'round here. Then this policeman showed up. 'Bout six months now, I'd say."

"Do you know anything else about her and the detective? Anything other than seeing him pick her up and drop her off here?"

"I don't know nothin' 'bout him. I know she told me she works at a Val Mart store out in White Bear Lake. She pays her rent. I think today's her day off."

Lanslow lowered the small note book he'd taken out of his pocket and looked directly at her. "When the detective picked her up, were they gone for a long time? Was it usually during the day or night?"

"Seems like he always picked her up in the afternoon. They'd come back, mostly, in the evening. Sometimes at night, not real late, around nine or so. Lately, seems like it was later. One night she didn't come back 'til the next morning. So there you go. Duh ... doesn't take much to figure that out, now, does it?" She eyed him curiously. A thought occurred to her. "Now don't take me wrong, officer," she said, "I ain't the nosy type, but this ain't a yuppie neighborhood, neither, you know what I mean? I gotta protect my property."

"Of course, ma'am. What about the black man you said you saw her with? Was he her boyfriend?"

"Oh, yeah. After the cop came into the picture, she and that black guy were into it most all the time. Had an argument one night, right outside the gate. He was goin' after her somethin' terrible. Know what I mean? Rantin' and ravin'... must have gone on for a half hour. I was 'bout to go out and break it up, but she finally came in."

"Do you know this man's name, ma'am?"

"Uh uh. He ain't from 'round here. Ain't seen him for a while, neither."

"Well, you've been very helpful, ma'am. Is there anything else you'd like to tell me?"

She shook her head. "That's about it. As I said, I ain't the nosy type, but I keep track of the comings and goings 'round my house."

"Well, ma'am, thanks for your help. I'll just go on up and talk to Miss Rosario now, if that's okay. I may want to talk to you again, later, though"

"Sure. But that's about it. I told you all I know." She reached down and grabbed the dog's collar as Lanslow entered. She pointed to the stairs. "You can go on up. She's in the last room on your left, just across from the bathroom."

Lanslow climbed the stairs, aware that the woman remained at the foot watching him. Startled by what he'd just heard, he walked up the stairs slowly, trying to compose his thoughts. When he reached the top of the stairs, he walked to the end of the hall, as the woman had directed, and knocked on the door.

▍

Angelena Rosario was a small woman, with big, dark brown eyes and smooth brown skin. Her hair was jet black and hung to her shoulders. Her mouth was wide, with a full, pouting lower lip. She wore a pair of light blue jeans that clung tightly to her well-shaped hips and legs, and a red blouse, open just enough to reveal a tantalizing cleavage. She appeared to be in her early twenties. At the sight of her, Lanslow began to understand how his partner could be mixed up with such a woman, as he now suspected Mallard had been. At the same time, the image of Christine made him wonder, too, how his partner could make a choice. Christine's was a mature beauty, an appreciating beauty, forged from marital history, the ups and downs, the good times and bad. Rosario presented the beauty and appeal of the young, of the vital, the erotic, the strange and different.

"Miss Rosario?"

"Yes?"

"Miss Rosario, I'm Detective Lanslow of the White Bear Lake police department." He held out his badge. "I wonder if I could ask you a few questions?"

"Yes. Come in. I've been expecting you. Zeke talked about you often."

Angelena's small apartment was clean and neat. It consisted of two small rooms, reconstructed into an efficiency apartment. One room, the larger, had been divided by a curtain that was now closed. Behind the curtain, Lanslow guessed, was the bed; in front of it was a small love seat that acted as a couch from which to watch the small television that rested on a chrome-plated stand with wheeled legs. Just off to the right of the entryway, a smaller, open room held a refrigerator and an apartment-size gas stove. Next to it was a cabinet with a built-in sink. A two-door upright cabinet held the kitchenware. There was no bathroom. Occupants of the building apparently shared the bathroom across the hall from Rosario's room.

"You don't look anything like I'd pictured you, Detective," said Rosario. Her voice carried only slightly the accent of a person who primarily spoke Spanish. Lanslow caught the scent of a sweet perfume.

"How long have you and Zeke ... known each other?" Lanslow asked, scanning the apartment once again. He couldn't help but wonder what might have, probably had, gone on in that bed behind that curtain.

"A few months. We met early last spring. I work at the Val Mart store in White Bear. That's how we met."

"Ms. Rosario. I'll get right to the point. Obviously, a mutual friend, and my partner, has been murdered. What, exactly, is ... was ... your relationship with Zeke?"

"We were in love," she said simply, lowering her head and wiping the tears forming in her eyes with a Kleenex plucked from a box sitting atop the TV. She looked at him and repeated almost defiantly, "We were in love."

Lanslow could only look at her. After a moment, he said, "All right, Ms. Rosario. I'm sorry, but I must ask you a few more questions. Does Zeke's wife know about this relationship?"

"I don't think so. Zeke didn't think so. Zeke ... we ... didn't want to hurt her. Zeke was going to tell her, though. He was going to get a divorce. We were going to get married."

Lanslow couldn't believe what he was hearing. It was beyond him how he could have so misread his partner, could not have known. He wondered if what Zeke had told Angelena Rosario was true—or if he was just trying to keep her in bed. Lanslow shook his head. He was becoming more and more convinced that no one could know another person completely. He wondered how well he knew Laura, the woman who was to be his wife, the woman he was now living with, sleeping with.

"I can probably save us both a lot of time, Detective," said Rosario, interrupting Lanslow's thoughts. He looked at her expectantly.

"My former boyfriend, Andrew, hated Zeke. He threatened to kill him and me, too, if I didn't break off our relationship."

"Andrew ... ?"

"White. Andrew White. I broke up with him but he keeps calling, coming over. I wouldn't put killing past him. It wouldn't surprise me. He's crazy."

"Crazy? What do you mean?"

"Just crazy. He thinks he can do anything he wants to, no matter who it hurts. He does strange things. Violent things. I'm not sure why I ever took up with him. I felt sorry for him, I guess. He worked for a while at Val Mart, where I work."

"Where does Mr. White live? Around here?"

"No. He lives on Dale street in St. Paul. That's all I know."

Lanslow paused for a moment as he jotted down Rosario's information in his notebook.

"Does Mr. White own a car, Miss Rosario?"

"No, I don't think so. He didn't the last time I saw him, a couple of weeks ago."

"How would he get to work?"

"He usually rode with Albert. Albert worked at the Save-U-More store across the street fromVal-Mart."

"Albert? What's Albert's last name?"

"I don't know. I only talked with him once or twice."

"Did Zeke know about Mr. White?"

"Oh, sure. He roughed him up after he wouldn't stop bothering me. Right after that, that's when Andrew told me he would kill us both. I believed him. Zeke said not to worry."

"Can you tell me anything else that would help me find Andrew White? Does he live in a house, apartment ...?"

"I think he lives with his mother. Her name is Roberta White. That's all I know."

"Okay, Ms. Rosario," Lanslow said, as he looked this woman over one more time. "Thanks for your help. I'll be wanting you to make a formal statement for us, later. I'll call you and let you know, okay?"

As he left Angelena Rosario's apartment, Lanslow was still astonished at what he'd learned. His partner, whom he thought he'd known so well, had a secret life. Mixed with his astonishment, though, was an adrenaline surge. He hadn't expected such a strong lead so soon. Had he found Zeke's killer so quickly?

11

It had taken only a call to dispatch to locate a Roberta White, resident of an address on Dale Street in St. Paul. A check by dispatch on Andrew White had revealed that the young man had no record.

Turning on to Dale Street, he'd thought about getting hold of Brooks to come along but, against his better judgment, had decided not to. Brooks hadn't shown much inclination to conduct interviews that morning, and Lanslow was a little irritated about it. This was not a good way to start off their relationship, he thought, but right now he didn't have time to deal with it.

The houses along Dale Street had once been the homes of upper middle class families but had now been largely transformed into multiple family dwellings. Most of the houses sat back from the busy street, with small narrow walks running to the porches.

It was nearing twelve o'clock when Lanslow checked out with his dispatcher, telling her to notify St. Paul of his location and that he would be trying to locate a party who might have information on Zeke's murder. He parked his car about a half-block from the address he'd written in his notebook. The less time any occupants knew he was coming the better the chance they'd still be there when he knocked.

The house was a three-story brick structure, with a long front porch upon which several straight-backed wooden chairs sat, pushed against the exterior wall. Wide wooden steps brought Lanslow to the top of the porch and he approached a wooden screen door. He knocked, rethinking his decision not to call Brooks.

The front door opened a bit and a young man's face stared at him for a moment, then the door slammed and Lanslow heard running steps inside. Lanslow made a quick, calculated decision. He bolted around the side of the house and sprinted to the rear, arriving at the backyard just as a young black man burst through the door and bounded down the steps, heading for the alley. Seeing Lanslow, the man whipped out a pistol and fired. Lanslow heard the zing of the bullet as it flew past his ear. He fell to one knee, pulled his gun from its holster and yelled, "Police! Halt!"

For one moment Lanslow held the young man's form in the gun's sights, just as he'd practiced over and over at the range. Involuntarily he felt his trigger finger tightening, but he gained control and backed off. He had never shot anyone, and didn't want to start now, except as a last resort. Not even Zeke's killer. And he didn't know that this running man was Zeke's killer, for sure, or even whether he was Andrew White.

The suspect didn't break stride. He was a small man. Wiry and fast, he was already thirty yards away. The man disappeared into the alley.

Lanslow finally reached the alley in pursuit but just as he had him in sight once again the man cut left and disappeared behind a garage with overhanging tree branches and a half-dozen or more garbage cans pushed against its rear wall. The limbs of the tall oak trees in this older neighborhood formed a canopy that created an almost eerie dark shade below, enhanced by the gray weather. A dog somewhere down the alley began to bark.

As Lanslow reached the point where the suspect had disappeared, he called the White Bear Lake dispatch on his cell phone, advising of his location, that shots were fired and giving the direction in which the suspect had fled on foot. Dispatch would, in turn, request back up from the St. Paul P.D. Soon there would be St. Paul squads all over the place.

As a siren wailed somewhere in the distance, he peered around the garage into a backyard, but saw nothing. The area was a patchwork of houses with small storage buildings and garages abutting the alleyway.

He proceeded into the yard, but there was no sign of anyone. Making his way along the driveway next to another three-story house, he looked up and down the tree-lined street but could see nothing in the dim light. At that moment his cell phone rang.

"Detective Lanslow. This is Sergeant Smith of the St. Paul police. Can you hear me?"

"I hear you Sergeant."

"Where are you now Lanslow? We have several squads approaching the reported address."

"I'm on the street east and behind the address. The suspect is a young black male, fleeing the scene in a southeasterly direction. He's armed. He took a shot at me. I'm proceeding on foot, south, down the street."

"Okay, Lanslow. We'll be sending squads up and down that street and we'll block off the area. Let us know if suspect flushes."

"You got it, Sergeant."

Lanslow proceeded cautiously down the street with drawn gun. People were beginning to come out of their houses and stare at him, then turn quickly and close their doors. Some distance down the street he saw a man at his front gate, gesturing wildly. He ran toward him, holding his badge in his hand so the man could see it.

"What's the matter, Sir? Did you see a young man running this way?"

"He stole my son's bike!" said the man, pointing down the street. "He went down there."

"All right, Sir. Please get back in your house. We'll have more police here soon."

Lanslow trotted down the street, gun still drawn. At that moment two squad cars approached, each from the opposite direction. They each halted not far from where Lanslow had stopped, waiting. He still had his badge in hand.

"You're Detective Lanslow?" asked a uniformed officer, emerging from his squad car. "I'm Sergeant Adams."

"Yeah. A man reported a stolen bike. I think the suspect is on it. He was running in your direction."

"We didn't see anyone. He must have cut across one of the lawns."

"I'm going to poke around here some more."

"Okay, Detective. We have a K-9 unit on the way, too."

"Sure, but he's on a bike. May not do any good."

"We'll try it anyway, Detective."

"All right. I'm going to try to talk to the kid's mother, too."

Brooks had arrived at Andrew White's house within a half-hour after Lanslow's call. Both men, along with Detective Ed Sallow of the St. Paul police department, stood near their unmarked cars parked in front of Andrew White's house. Sallow was a big, burly man whose coat and shirt appeared to be near bursting from around his body. They still didn't know if Andrew White had escaped, and a house-to-house search was being conducted. The police wouldn't stop soon. If White was still around, they would catch him. But Lanslow didn't hold much hope of that.

"Rosario was Zeke's girlfriend?" asked Brooks, incredulous.

"Yeah. And her former boyfriend, Andrew White, threatened to kill Zeke and her if she didn't break off the relationship."

Brooks just shook his head in disbelief. "I'll be damned! Who'd a thunk it? How long had this been going on?"

"Several months now."

"You didn't know?"

"Not a clue. I'm as surprised as anyone. Maybe more."

"What about this White?" asked Brooks.

"This may be our guy. He has no record, but he took a shot at me, and he has the motive. I talked to his mother after the guy got away. I got a picture."

"We've put out an APB," said Sallow. "We've got him on a bunch of counts ... if we can find him."

"He got a good shot at you?" said Brooks.

"Oh, yeah. I heard the bullet whiz by my ear."

"Did the bullet hit anything?" asked Sallow.

"No. Don't think so," said Lanslow.

"We'll have to check everything, anyway," said Sallow.

Brooks shook his head again. "You say you've questioned the mother?"

"Oh, yeah. Roberta White has confirmed the young man was her son, but other than that she's not been too helpful. I managed to pry some names from her, though, of friends of White, boyfriends and girl-friends."

"Well, that's a start," said Brooks. "You shoulda called me, you know."

Lanslow nodded, chagrined, but he was in no mood to discuss it.

Later, Sergeant Adams drove up in his squad and, as Lanslow had suspected, told them the K-9 unit had followed a trail to a point in the neighborhood where, according to the owner, a man matching the flee-ing young man's description had stolen his son's bike. They'd found the bike several blocks away, but White was gone and the dog couldn't pick up a trail.

"He could've gotten away clean out of the area," said Adams. "We'll continue searching until we're sure." He turned to Detective Sallow. "Anything else we need to do here, Detective?"

Before the detective could answer, Lanslow said, "We need to take a look at Mr. White's room and the rest of the place."

Brooks gave the young detective a reproving look, then turned to Sal-low expectantly, since they were now in his jurisdiction. "You okay with that, Ed?"

Sallow looked at Sergeant Adams. "You've secured the area? Nobody leaves or enters," he said.

Adams nodded.

Okay. We'll need a warrant to search these premises if the mother won't give us permission," said Sallow, turning back to Lanslow and Brooks. "We'll have to check, then I'll call in and get it started. You guys can come with me and we'll see what we can find."

"Absolutely," said Brooks.

"Thanks for the backup, Sergeant," said Lanslow, as Adams got into his car.

12

Mrs. White looked on as the detectives poked about her son's room. She had refused permission to search the house and other areas of the property and was obviously distressed and displeased that they had obtained a warrant. A large woman, she leaned against the door frame, arms folded across her huge breasts, her mouth set in a curve of contempt.

"Did you know your son had a gun, Mrs. White?" Brooks asked, as he pulled out a dresser drawer. Like Lanslow and Sallow, he had put on latex gloves. He pulled out a small cardboard box and opened it. Inside was a pair of sunglasses lying on top of a stack of several one-hundred dollar bills.

"My son is a grownup, now, Officer. I don't have him tied to my apron strings no more." Brooks showed her the contents of the box and her eyes widened just perceptibly before she regained control. Lanslow could tell she was worried.

"How old is your son, Mrs. White?" asked Lanslow. He paused over a small table that appeared to serve as a desk. Pulling out a drawer, he spied a small stack of white, postmarked envelopes, secured by a rubber band.

Roberta White paused for a moment, watching Lanslow. "He's ... twenty-three, now. Almost twenty-four."

Lanslow picked up the envelopes and removed the rubber band. They smelled like the perfume in Angelena Rosario's apartment.

"Now, see here!" exclaimed Roberta White. "You have no call to pry into my son's personal letters like that."

"Sorry, Mrs. White, but we do," said Sallow. "Your son took a shot at Detective Lanslow, here, and he made a threat against Officer Mallard—and, as you know, Officer Mallard was murdered last Friday. Your son is implicated in his murder, Mrs. White."

Lanslow thumbed through the letters. "Does your son own a car, Mrs. White?" He placed the envelopes in an evidence bag and handed it to Sallow.

"No, he don't," she said.

"Where does your son work? Does he have a job?"

"No, he ain't workin' right now. He picks up odd jobs."

Brooks opened a closet and found it full of clothing on hangars and shelves. "Pretty expensive clothing for not having a job," he said, examining a couple of shirt labels.

"He had a job at Val Mart, in White Bear Lake, till a while ago. They didn't treat him right, there. They gave a white boy the assistant manager's job, even if Andrew had been there longer."

"Mrs. White," said Sallow, "we're going to have to take some things of Andrew's for analysis in the lab. We'll give you a list of the things we take and we'll return them as soon as we can. Okay?"

"Sure," said Mrs. White, shrugging her shoulders. "You *boys'll* do it whether I like it or not, anyway. Andrew's got nothin' to hide. You'll see." She frowned as Detective Sallow held up a box of .38 caliber cartridges he'd plucked from a dresser drawer.

When they had finished their search, Sallow instructed one of the uniformed officers to place police crime scene tape across the door of Andrew's room and he watched as Mrs. White locked it at his request. He warned her as tactfully as he could to stay out of it, reminding her that it was a crime scene.

█

By six o'clock, they were back at the station. Charlie Johnson leaned far back in his chair, propped his feet on the desk, folded his hands in back of his head and peered at Detective Lanslow, grinning at him from across his own desk. "Sounds like you guys had quite a day," he said.

"You might say that," said Lanslow.

"You think we have our man?"

"Everything points to him," said Brooks. "Motive, means, and probably the opportunity."

"Why else would he shoot and run?" asked Lanslow.

"Okay," said Johnson, "but we need to find him, get him in here. Right now, the evidence is circumstantial. We'll need something stronger."

"St. Paul is looking for fingerprint evidence from the stuff they got from his room and they'll check it against the Bureau's data," said Lanslow, nodding. "We know White has no record, but we'll check further. Any other CSI reports come in today?"

"The blood on the grass is consistent with Zeke's. Must have dropped from the murder weapon as the perp made his way to the vehicle. The weapon was probably an eight-inch job, double-edged. This is one thing that doesn't fit with your suspect, Andrew White. Why would he use a knife? He shot at you. Why wouldn't he shoot Zeke?"

"Maybe he thought a gun was too easy for Zeke," said Lanslow. "The girl, Rosario, said he threatened to kill Zeke out of jealousy. Maybe he wanted Zeke to suffer."

"Yeah, maybe. Anyway," Johnson continued, "CSI says the angle of the neck wound suggests Zeke was attacked first from his right side as he was bending over the back seat of his car. Apparently he turned around and dropped the bag of groceries. Then he was slashed across the throat, then stabbed in the leg. No fingerprints in the garage other than those of Christine, Zeke, and Zeke's brother-in-law, Randolph Moser, which were on some tools that, according to him, he borrowed once. CSI found no prints we couldn't confirm. Lots of fingerprints in the house, but it didn't look like anyone had gotten into the house. They'll be checked out. All the blood was consistent with Zeke's. Nothing else, no hair, fibers, nothing. No footprints. No witnesses, we know of. No one seems to have seen anything suspicious. Nothing back yet on the rubber marks in the street."

"Randy was at work when Zeke was killed. I already checked that out," said Lanslow.

"The brother-in-law? Yeah, I know. But we have to check everything. He could have hired someone. You know him better than anyone else around here. Anything?"

"I don't know him that well," said Lanslow, "but Zeke never said anything bad about him. Just the usual contempt for lawyers."

"Well, looks like Mr. White is our prime suspect right now, then. All we can do is hope we can find him and bring him in. You got any contacts in that area? I don't." Johnson looked back and forth between Brooks and Lanslow.

"'Fraid not," said Brooks. "Never really worked in St. Paul."

"None," said Lanslow.

"Okay, you'll just have to work on it," said Johnson. "Any more ideas?"

"We need to do a little more talking to Rosario," said Brooks. "And we need to talk to White's friends. He can't stay hid forever."

"We need to go through White's things" said Lanslow, "see if there's anything else of interest."

Johnson looked at his watch. It was nearing seven-thirty.

"Okay, Rich. We'll hit this thing fresh, tomorrow."

After Johnson and Brooks left, Lanslow knew he should leave, too. Laura would be waiting. With the intention of just a quick glance through, he picked up the stack of envelopes and letters (he'd obtained copies from the St. Paul police) from the evidence pack on his desk. Idly, he picked up the letter on top of the stack. It was addressed to Andrew White, from Angelena Rosario. He began to read.

■

"Luke flew back East to see Annie?" asked Maureen.

"That's what he said," replied Matthews, stroking his chin. He laid the newspaper he had been reading on the dining table and stared out the window. A picture of Richard Lanslow and Christine Mallard at Zeke Mallard's funeral was on the page. Darkness was setting in and he could see only the shadowy trunks of the large oaks in his front yard.

"So, what did Luke say Annie wanted to see him about?"

Maureen sat down at the table across from Matthews and wiped her hands on a dishtowel. A pile of sliced potatoes lay on the cutting board on the kitchen counter. The smell of cooking meat filled the air. She sometimes did this, cooked for them during the evenings, stopping off at Matthews's house after finishing her research assistantship duties at the university. Cooking dinner like this didn't imply anything further about the evening ahead, necessarily. They didn't even need to talk about it. She might stay; she might go on back to her own apartment. Whether she did or didn't usually just worked itself out.

"He didn't say, or at least I can't remember if he did. Something about her and her mom. He sounded worried." Matthews didn't mention his own concern about Luke. It was something he didn't want to talk about right then. He was trying to digest the details of Zeke Mallard's homicide that he'd read in the newspaper.

"Worried about Annie and her mom?" queried Maureen, surprised. "Is Annie still grieving?"

Matthews was aware of her watching his face over the rim of her coffee cup before setting it back down on the table. He knew Maureen believed that he was still not over Elizabeth himself, and she seemed compelled to probe the depth of his feelings now and then, even after Elizabeth's death. Secretly, he was pleased at her jealousy. It proved her feelings for him.

"I don't remember Luke saying anything about that. You know how I am about forgetting things," said Matthews. "Besides, I'm sure it wasn't as important as the kids think it is." These were words designed to avoid the subject.

"Well, you are a professor," said Maureen, rising and kissing his cheek. She seemed to have surmised his reluctance to talk. "You're supposed to be forgetful, I guess."

"I don't forget that much," he said, a little over-defensively, and the image of a flowered, rose-colored shirt came to mind.

"Oh, yeah? I think you even forget my name sometimes." Maureen pouted at him. She pushed the potatoes off the cutting board into the skillet.

"You know that's not true. How can I forget the name of someone who's saved my life?"

"I think that's a slight exaggeration, don't you?"

"Not at all," Matthews said, and he meant it. Maureen had entered his life two years ago, at a time in which he had questioned the value of continuing living himself. The divorce from Elizabeth had been the tragedy of his life. His son had remained with Elizabeth after the separation. Matthews had wanted it that way, even when Elizabeth had decided to move back to Wisconsin, a move that meant his contact with Luke was certain to decrease. He thought his son needed a mother more than a father. His own move later, from Missouri where he had been stationed, back to Minnesota to attend the University, hadn't helped much. Even though Luke was only a few miles distant across the Minnesota-Wisconsin border, it was just enough to keep them disconnected. And their relationship had deteriorated; he and his son had grown farther and farther apart.

This bad situation was only compounded when Elizabeth remarried and moved with her new husband even farther away to a farm in southern Wisconsin. Luke's half sister, Annie, was born shortly thereafter. Luke now had a new "father," and Matthews could hardly bear to think about it. That Luke and his stepfather didn't get along, that the man drank, and that he'd even threatened Elizabeth, worried him.

Then, Elizabeth's husband had simply disappeared. One day there, the next day gone, and no one had seen nor heard from him since, nor had Matthews ever learned the reason he'd left. He really didn't care.

Life had become almost unbearable after that. Maureen was correct in her assumptions, though there was no reason to fear for her place in his life now. In the years following their divorce, he had never met anyone that could take Elizabeth's place. And then, Elizabeth, a woman he'd loved like no other to that time, was alone again, living without a husband on a farm with her two children. He had entertained the wild notion that he and Elizabeth might get back together, but her husband's disappearance didn't mean he was dead, or even gone for good. The two years following the husband's disappearance had been hell. Matthews's hopes had been raised only to be dashed again when he'd realized that there was no hope. Elizabeth had changed. She had become despondent, almost somnambulant, and had rebuffed his attempts to help. At that point his life had become nearly worthless. It was as though he was reliving the divorce all over again. Then, Maureen had shown up that opening day of class and life had begun anew.

It hadn't been so for Elizabeth. Her husband had never returned. Luke had moved out and come to live with Matthews to attend the university. Annie had gone east, to attend college. The photo of Elizabeth that Luke showed him when he arrived in Minnesota portrayed a woman whom he could hardly recognize, cheeks sunken, eyes haunted. His heart ached when he saw it and he'd grown angry that he was so unable to help in any way. It was the absence of her children and husband that had contributed to Elizabeth's death a scant two years later, Matthews was certain.

But even after Luke moved in, Matthews and his son had been unable to generate a close father-son relationship, at least so far. Luke's face floated before him, a face that reminded him so much of his own at a younger age. A knot formed in his stomach. Maybe someday ... .

"You're sweet to say that, dear," said Maureen.

"Hmm." Matthews tried to remember the train of conversation. He picked it up. "It's true," he said.

Maureen smiled sweetly at him and picked up the paper, looking at the picture of Lanslow and Christine Mallard. "She's pretty," she said.

"Yes, a good-looking woman," said Matthews.

"Did you know her?"

Matthews looked at Maureen quizzically, realizing her questioning was based on a little more than mere curiosity.

"I may have met her once, I can't remember," he said. "You know how forgetful I am."

Maureen looked at him quickly and saw he was teasing.

"Oh, you!" she said, and kissed him once again on the cheek.

The copies of the letters in Detective Lanslow's hands didn't smell like their originals, but he remembered the fragrance of Angelena's perfume, nevertheless. Her image rose in his consciousness again. He thought again how he would never have guessed at this side of his partner and how people truly knew very little about one another. Laura had called and he tried to apologize and explain and she hung up, angry. He wondered how long her patience would hold out.

He began to read. The letters at first spoke of the good times and good feelings but then began to speak of desperation. Near the end of the stack, Rosario pleaded often for Andrew to leave her alone. The relationship had been a mistake, she said. She had no feelings for him any longer. She was in love with Zeke Mallard, and they were to be married, she wrote. Of course, she wanted to remain friends, but that was all. He must quit hounding her, calling her, coming around. She was afraid it was going to lead to trouble. Rosario's fear and anxiety leapt from the pages.

All the letters were similar, except that in each succeeding letter the young woman's tone grew more frantic. Angelena had tried desperately to break it off with Andrew White, but he persisted, even after being roughed up by Zeke Mallard. It seemed the action only made him more persistent and angry. "You must never say those things!" Angelena had written in the next to last letter. "I have fallen in love with Zeke and we will be married. You must stop threatening me and him. It can only mean trouble for all of us. Please, please, Andrew! If you have any feelings for me whatsoever, please stop." Where she had signed her name, a big red X was marked over it.

The last letter was from a different person and had no envelope. It began with "Dear, dear, dear Andrew: I want to tell you what a great time I had with you last night. What a wonderful guy you are! I hope you feel the same about me." Lanslow smiled. The letter was obviously from someone quite young. The rest of the letter described the evening and the girl's enjoyment of every event, especially their time afterward in her apartment. She signed the letter, simply, "Sherry."

Lanslow glanced at the clock. Reluctantly, he placed the letters back in the evidence bag and placed the bag in his desk drawer. His mind still buzzing, he walked out into the cool, clear night. There was nothing more he could do, and Laura would probably be waiting up and he would have to explain again about being a detective.

13

The clock's buzzer sounded off. Matthews awakened and looked over at the luminous red dial: 5:30 A.M. He felt Maureen stir. He fumbled to shut the buzzer off. Maureen groaned, threw off the blanket and sat up mute, on the side of the bed.

"You're up?" he asked, barely able to make out her form in the morning light seeping around the corners of the curtains.

"Heaven will be when I get this damned degree and can get up at a decent time like some people I know," she said, rubbing her eyes.

"Hey, I went through it too."

"Maybe I should quit seeing you so I can get a decent night's sleep," she retorted.

He reached over and pulled her down beside him. He kissed her neck and cheek and forehead in succession.

"Why don't you just call old Professor Skinner and tell him you're sick?" he said. "I'll call in sick, too."

"Well, in the first place, his name isn't Skinner and he's not even a behaviorist, and in the second place I'd probably lose my assistantship and you'd probably lose your job. Think that's enough?"

"Not nearly enough," he said, and pulled her to him tighter. She kissed him fully on the mouth and his hand searched between her legs.

"Can't do this," she protested and rolled over. "Gotta get to the U."

"Do you really know what a 'behaviorist' is?" he asked, giving up having sex. He enjoyed testing her, just to get her going.

"A psychologist who fools around with rats and pigeons," she said and he heard the amusement in her voice. The distinctions between the schools of psychology weren't all that important to Maureen, he knew. She was "hands on," a doer, not a thinker, studying to become a clinical psychologist.

"You get an A," he said. "Grade inflation."

She popped a pillow down on his head. "No more of this." She left the room and he heard the bathroom door shut, the stool flush, then the shower come on. He folded his arms behind his head.

The sound of the hair dryer woke him. He had dozed off. He stared at the picture over his chest of drawers, now visible, of the Eiffel Tower and the Arc de Triomphe. He and Maureen had purchased it in a little store in Paris. As in the picture, it had been raining that day and they had wandered up and down the Champs Élysée under their umbrellas, Maureen peering out from under hers now and then to look and laugh at him. Maureen couldn't believe she was actually in Paris, and kept saying so over and over. "Can you believe this, Jack? Can you believe this?" They had visited the tower later and gone to the top. The "city of light" lay spread out before them. "I can't believe it!" she had exulted.

His thoughts turned to Luke and Annie. Luke was supposed to return, as far as he knew, later that night. He tried to imagine the kind of trouble Annie might be in. He could only hope that it didn't have anything to do with drugs, and that Annie's troubles didn't spell trouble for him and Luke.

Maureen entered the bedroom and began dressing. It was 6:00 o'clock. "You're awake?" she asked, as she pulled on her skirt. Matthews loved the little wiggle she made when she did this.

"Yeah, you're keeping me from my sleep."

"You can sleep later, can't you? What time is your first class?"

"At four. It's the late afternoon class. But I have to get in earlier."

"Why, for God's sake?"

"A little more writing, some papers to grade, and I want to do some stuff with Powerpoint on my lectures for next semester."

"All right, dear. I'll see you later."

"I won't be home until about seven-thirty. The class goes until seven."

"I'll give you a call at your office, then." She picked up her bag, gave him a peck on the forehead, and left. He heard her get her coat from the closet, heard the garage door open and close, then the house was silent.

Later, during his breakfast of cold cereal and orange juice, Matthews lifted the morning newspaper from the table and began to scan the news. The murder of the White Bear Lake police officer was still on the front page. The police had found a suspect, a young black man. The face of Andrew White, his eyes defiant, sat next to the text. There was also a picture of Lanslow, the caption identifying him as the slain officer's partner, and a picture of Brooks, identified as the lead detective on the case. Matthews was struck again by Lanslow's boyish features, especially so because he was a detective, a rank not usually reached at the tender age of thirty-one. Brooks, on the other hand, whom Matthews had met once or twice, looked like the veteran he was.

Matthews read the story through, searching especially for the motive. Strangely enough, it was not there. No mention whatsoever as to why the young man had murdered the detective. These detectives weren't fools. They probably had a motive in mind; they just weren't divulging it to the public. His curiosity aroused, Matthews made a mental note to ask his young colleague about that and the other details after his evening class.

∎

Andrew White pulled the curtains slightly apart and away from the window, just enough to peer out upon the street three stories below. Nothing seemed unusual. He studied the passers-by and the cars, especially those parked within sight of the apartment building where he was staying. This street was busy, even this late in the morning, mostly with students in heavy clothing, carrying backpacks, trekking to the lecture halls.

He looked at his watch. Nine o'clock. Sherry wouldn't be back from her classes until the afternoon. He turned again to the stories about him in the Tuesday morning editions of the *St. Paul Pioneer Press* and the *Minneapolis Star & Tribune,* which he'd picked up from the drugstore earlier. He was on page one in both papers. His picture, his name, a reporter's interview with Detectives Lanslow and Brooks of White Bear Lake. He recognized the younger policeman as the one he'd shot at and the man he'd seen when he tried to visit Angelena Rosario's house yesterday. What jumped out at him now, though, was that he was a suspect in the Mallard murder. He cursed.

White crossed the room, laid down on Sherry's unmade bed and tried to think. Why had he run? Of all the stupid things to do! Panic had gripped him, even though he'd had nothing to hide. Still, he thought, the mere fact he'd been around the crime scene was enough to get him into trouble with white police. That had been another stupid thing: thinking he could solve anything by confronting Mallard—at his own house, no less! The guy was huge. Bringing his gun was a recipe for trouble. He couldn't believe how stupid he'd been.

But how did they know who he was? He thought of Angelena Rosario. How would they know about her? No matter. It had to be her. She would have ratted on him, told them about his run-in with Mallard. That fucking broad had been more trouble than she was worth, right from the start. That she'd taken up with the white dude had made him angry and jealous. And a cop! Crazy! He had thought his troubled relationship with Angelena was solved when the cop was killed. Now, the bitch had ratted on him and he'd shot at a cop. It was all over between him and Angelena, for sure. That bitch! He should do something to her.

Reaching beneath the mattress of Sherry's bed, he felt for the cold steel of his gun, which he had hidden there. But no, he couldn't do anything now. Not right now, anyway. They'd be watching her house.

Why in hell had he shot? Again, panic. Now he was really in trouble. He'd been through it with white cops before. They would want to pin this thing on him, especially since Mallard was one of their own, and, if nothing else, just to get the press off their backs. But there was always the fact he was black, too, and that meant they would be after him even harder. They would question his mother, and his friends, and they would be watching his neighborhood.

They wouldn't be looking for him here, near the university campus, though. Sherry had come through for him. He didn't think she knew anything about the murder yet. He could only hope she wouldn't find out too soon.

She'd been late for class, lingering in bed a little too long with him. And he hadn't told her the kind of trouble he was in; maybe he would tell her when she got home this evening. He'd have to deal with it eventually. In the meantime, she was the only person he knew who might be able to hide him from the police. He couldn't think of anyone else who knew about Sherry, not even his mom, so they had no way to trace him here.

But what was he to do? He couldn't stay here in Sherry's room forever. He was in deep trouble, that was for sure. He cursed himself for panicking, most of all for the stupidity of taking a shot at the cop. What a dumb, crazy, fucking thing to do! Well, it was done. No crying over it now. Should he run? Get completely out of Minnesota? He avoided pursuing that possibility further and began to think back to the bizarre event he'd witnessed.

He still couldn't believe it: Mallard on the garage floor, blood all over him. He recalled the little white man walking briskly to the garage, then striding back across the yard to his car and driving away. What had he been wearing? A suit? Tie? No; no tie—he didn't think. Maybe not a suit. A sport jacket, maybe? Something light colored, maybe tan, maybe a top coat? He had to admit he didn't know for sure what the guy had been wearing. And who the hell was this guy, anyway? Why had he wanted to kill Zeke Mallard?

Andrew hadn't wanted to be seen, so he'd only gotten a quick look. He'd been trying to see, as cautiously as he could, when the little man had looked in his direction. He'd scooted down, but even then he thought the man might have seen him. He'd gotten only a brief glimpse of the man's face, just as the man had looked in his general direction. What age? In his late twenties, maybe late thirties? White men all looked alike to him and he'd always had trouble telling their age. Glasses? No. Dark brown hair? Yes, he'd had dark brown hair. Remembering that, Andrew was certain he would recognize him if he ever saw him again. That was unlikely, though. The bottom line was that even the image of the car was not clear. Dark color? Yes. Foreign? Probably. What color? Maybe black. No—more like a maroon. License plate number? No way. It was Minnesota, that's all he could say. A lot of fucking good that did!

The thought occurred to him that this little man, who'd been so "kind" as to take Mallard off his hands, was a key to beating the murder rap he was sure he was going to take, if the cops ever laid hands on him. Somehow, he had to get the cops on this guy's trail and off of his.

Rising from the bed, he pulled a jacket from Sherry's closet and tried it on. A little tight, but it would have to do. He pulled on one of her baseball caps, keeping the bill forward to help hide his face. When he had run from Lanslow, it was only with the clothes he now wore, shirt and pants, gun in belt (ready for whoever was at the door). He pulled his gun from beneath the mattress and slipped it in his pocket. His pants were so baggy the gun was easily hidden. He cautiously opened the door and looked down the hall both ways. It was better that he not be seen, if he could help it. He walked down the hall to the stairs, out the door, then quickly down the street. He'd have to find a pay phone. He had no way of knowing but what the police would have a caller ID or some other device that would trace the call if he phoned from Sherry's room. He checked his pockets for change. He'd walked about four blocks when he spotted a phone. Far enough from Sherry's room, he thought. He found the number in the phone book, and dialed. When the voice answered, he asked for Detective Lanslow.

∎

Christine's telephone call caught Lanslow before he was ready to talk to her. He had meant to call her as soon as he got into the office but some new reports had caught his attention and he had waited too long. He felt hypocritical in holding back what he'd learned about Zeke's affair with Angelena Rosario but he could see no reason to tell her for the time being. She would find out soon enough. She seemed skeptical of his explanation that the police simply didn't have any idea as to why a young black man named Andrew White had murdered her husband, but she hadn't pressed the matter.

Lanslow handed the letter from 'Sherry' across the desk to Brooks. "What do you make of this?" he asked.

Brooks read the letter. "Another girl? Have you found her.?"

"No. I was just about to start."

Lanslow was about to reach for the phone when it rang.

"Detective Lanslow speaking."

"Lanslow, this is Andrew White. I got something to tell you. Are you listening?"

Startled for the moment, Lanslow waited just a bit too long. He motioned to Detective Brooks at the other desk to pick up the phone.

"Lanslow, I'm not mother-fucking around here. Don't try to trace this. Are you with me?"

"I'm here, White. Where are you?"

"Listen, man, I didn't do it. I was there, but I didn't do it. I'll take the rap for shooting at you, man, but not for no murder."

"Go ahead, White. I'm listening."

"I was there, man, I saw it. It was this little white guy. He drove up, jumped out of the car and killed him."

"Who, White? Who was it?"

"Oh, fuck, I don't know. A little guy. I didn't want him to see me so I didn't get a real good look at him."

"You get a look at his car, the license?"

"No, like I tol' you ... "

"Why were you there, White?"

"Hey man, I wanted to talk to Mallard. He was after my girl, man, you know? I just wanted to talk to him. I was sittin' up the street in my car and I saw Mallard drive into his garage and this guy drives up behind him and runs in and, you know ..."

"White, we know you don't own a car, how did you ... "

"Aw, fuck, I stole it, man. It wasn't my car. Hey, Lanslow, you got to believe me. I ain't lyin' to you, man. I ain't lyin'."

"Where are you, White? You gotta come in here. If what you're saying is true, then you've got to turn yourself in ... "

"Oh, no! No way, man. I ain't fallin' for that shit. No way. I'm gone, man, before you trace this call, if you haven't already. Hey, man, I'm way ahead of you. You ain't going to find me from this call. You hear what I tell you?"

"Don't hang up, White. I'm telling you, it'll go better for you if you come on in."

"Oh, yeah, man. Fuck! I ain't crazy. You know 'bout this little guy now. You gotta start searchin' for the right man. I'm not the one."

There was a click, and White was gone.

"Did you get all that?" Lanslow asked Brooks.

"Got most of it." Brooks took the phone off his shoulder and turned off the recorder. "What do you think?"

"I'm thinking we got more than meets the eye here."

Lanslow punched the dispatcher's button. "Did we get that number that just called me, Roxy?" he asked.

"Sure thing," she said. "The phone is located over in Minneapolis. A pay phone on Third Street and Cedar Avenue. That's near the Augsburg and University campuses."

"Contact Minneapolis, have them send a squad to that phone booth. They're looking for a young black man, probably armed. Thanks, Roxy." Lanslow turned to Brooks. "He called from Minneapolis, near the Augsburg and University campuses. Minneapolis will check it out."

"He won't be there."

Brooks only nodded.

"Let's take a ride over to Minneapolis," said Lanslow to Brooks. "It's a long shot, but we might get lucky."

Brooks looked up and nodded again.

"Then," said Lanslow, "I think maybe we need to pay Mr. White's room one more visit, if we've got time. Might find something on this gal named 'Sherry.' I have a class to teach tonight."

"Absolutely," said Brooks.

14

On his way to his office during the break in his late afternoon class, Professor Matthews stopped at the open door to the office that Lanslow and three other adjunct faculty members shared. Lanslow was alone, hunched over some papers on his desk, apparently deep into preparation for his night class.

"Hi, Rich," said Matthews. "Getting ready for class?"

"Oh, hello, Jack," said Lanslow, looking up. "Actually, no. I'm jotting down some notes on the case."

"The Mallard case?"

"Yeah."

"Sorry, Rich. I know you and Zeke were close. Haven't had a chance 'til now to say so."

"Thanks."

"Got a minute?"

"Sure," said Lanslow.

Matthews seated himself in the chair next to Lanslow's desk. "I'm not asking you to jeopardize your case, Rich," he said, "but I'm curious, and I thought I might offer my help if I could."

Lanslow thought for a moment before he responded. He had appreciated Matthews's professional mentoring when he had first begun teaching. The professor had also gained his respect even before that as a consultant with the White Bear Lake police department. Even the small town of White Bear Lake had begun to have its problems with gangs, and Matthews was a recognized expert on gang behavior. They'd had long conversations about it.

"I'll tell you what I can," said Lanslow. "What do you want to know?"

"This Andrew White, is he the prime suspect?"

"He's all we've got right now," said Lanslow. This was already public information.

"Your partner was killed in his own garage, in a white neighborhood, by a young black man? It's very strange, don't you think, that this guy would even be there in that neighborhood, to begin with? The paper reported no motive. Why was he there, and why would he kill Zeke Mallard?"

Lanslow leaned back in his chair. Should he tell? Would Matthews talk? He didn't think so, and maybe the professor could help. "We have the motive, Jack. I can tell you only if you promise not to let anyone else know. Absolutely no one else is to know about it at this time."

"Sure," said Matthews.

"Jealousy. Zeke was having an affair with White's ex-girlfriend. No one knew about it, not even me."

"Not even Mallard's wife?"

"As best I can determine, no."

"You're shielding her?"

"Yes, in fact, we are. There's no need for Christine or the public to know right now."

"The girl, who is she?"

"I can't mention her name, but she's young, pretty and Hispanic."

"Uh huh. One other thing. The paper reported the murder weapon as a knife. That also struck me as odd, seeing as how he used a gun to shoot at you."

"We've thought of that. Maybe it's significant, maybe not." Lanslow paused for a moment, weighing whether he should tell Matthews more. "There's one other thing, too."

Matthews waited. Lanslow rose from his chair and stood, looking out the window at the parking lot, glancing at his watch. Cars were cruising slowly, their drivers looking for places to park. Students were making their way in the dim twilight toward the long, low building that housed the social-behavioral and the natural science divisions.

"I got a call this morning from Andrew White," Lanslow said, still peering out the window. "Claims he didn't do it but that he saw the guy who did."

"Wow! You know who it is, then?"

"Unfortunately, no. White couldn't name him, and he hung up before we could get much detail." Lanslow sat back down.

"You couldn't trace his call?"

"We got the number. He called right into the station. From a pay phone. That doesn't tell us much. He could be anywhere, maybe not even around where he called from. He steals cars whenever he wants to go somewhere."

Lanslow and Brooks had canvassed the area from whence Andrew White had called, showing White's picture, now enlarged, to various people in the shops and along the sidewalk, leaving their cards with their phone numbers, in case anyone might see him. The area near the Augsburg and University of Minnesota campuses was a busy one, mostly students coming and going. But no one had seen Andrew White.

"Do you believe him?" asked Matthews.

Lanslow rocked back in his chair. "White has the motive and means—and he admits he was there. He stole a car and drove to Zeke's house, intending to confront him about the girl. I checked the stolen car reports this morning. It checks out. It was reported a couple of days ago. The St. Paul police found it. It was the only stolen car reported in the Cities over that time, and it was found within a couple of blocks of White's house."

"You went over the car?"

"St. Paul says it's clean. Nothing. He must've wiped it down."

Lanslow paused, realizing he had perhaps revealed too much. But he trusted Matthews and admired his intelligence and his grasp of police matters. And, he thought again, Matthews might be of some help.

"He said he didn't know who the guy was that did it, huh?" Matthews's question was as much to himself as to Lanslow. "Did he say anything about him at all?"

Lanslow again hesitated. "He described him as a little white guy."

That revelation surprised Matthews. "Ummm." Matthews just sat for a moment, looking at the floor. Finally, he said, "What you tell me makes me think White may be telling the truth. Criminals don't always keep to the same MO, but statistically they do. The gun and knife don't necessarily match, especially with the murder of Detective Mallard. White was described in the paper as a small man. He'd be much more likely to have used the gun, just as he did on you. And the call ... highly unusual."

"You may be right," said Lanslow. "My gut feeling is that there's more to this case than we can see, too, but I'll be damned if I can figure out what it is."

"My hunch is that this kid is telling the truth about him not doing it," said Matthews. "He may have been at Mallard's house as a matter of pure jealousy, as you said, and he may have in fact witnessed the murder. How about family members? Was Mallard having any trouble there?"

Lanslow passed his hand over his face, as if trying to wipe away the fatigue. "Nothing there so far. I'm certain Christine didn't do it. All the other relatives live out of state and the brother-in-law has an alibi; both he and Christine's sister were still at work, and as far as I can tell, there were no family squabbles. Of course, I was as surprised as anyone that Zeke was having an affair, so there might be something else. But I doubt it."

"Well, if White didn't do it, and if you've eliminated the family members ... then ... could be a random thing, but probably not ... a 'little white guy' ..." Matthews was thinking out loud again. "Have you checked out any of the people Mallard arrested previously who might bear a grudge?"

"We're on it. Of course. But the crimes we deal with in our jurisdiction are mostly misdemeanors. It would be a little unlikely for a misdemeanor to bear that kind of malice. As I say, we're checking, though."

"Don't be too sure about a misdemeanor criminal not having anything to do with Zeke's murder. Sometimes the slightest things can set a person off. But, anyway, the only other thing I can come up with is that this may be a gang-related problem. Were you and Mallard applying any pressure to the gangs?"

"No. We haven't been having any real problem with them lately."

"Of course, it occurs to me, too, that, you know, it could be an initiation rite ... but, again, really, I don't think so."

"That occurred to me, too" said Lanslow, "but we haven't done anything with it yet. If nothing else turns out, we'll pursue that angle."

Matthews was silent for a moment longer. "You said 'malice,' before. This may sound silly, but is there something else other than the murder itself that points to maliciousness?"

Lanslow hesitated again. They had kept the gory details of Zeke's murder from the media. Should he tell? He'd gone this far. He shrugged. "I was just referring to the murder itself. But, since you ask, Zeke was stabbed in the neck, then his throat was cut, and then he was stabbed over and over in his left leg."

Matthews studied Lanslow's face. "That must have been real tough, finding Zeke that way," he said.

Lanslow squelched the sudden emotion that arose, remembering Zeke in the garage, slumped against the Town Car, his face frozen in death. "Yeah," he said, his voice catching in his throat. "It was rough."

"Well, the repeated stabbing puts a whole different light on it," said Matthews. "Sounds like a real bloody affair. Whoever did it would have blood all over him, though I've read of bloody cases where the perpetrator didn't."

"It would seem that way. We find him, we'll probably find bloody clothing, if he hasn't done away with it."

"A crime of passion," Matthews said. "Jealousy could certainly account for it; or extreme hatred and anger, or ... any number of emotions. It becomes very difficult."

Lanslow saw that Matthews was again talking to himself as much as to him. "Why are you so interested, Jack?" he asked.

"Oh. Well," said Matthews, as if brought back to the present, "professional curiosity, mostly. And, of course, you're a colleague."

Glancing down at his watch, Lanslow said, "Got to get to class."

"Oh, yes. Me, too."

"Remember, Jack. Not a word about this."

"Don't worry. Nothing passes my lips on this. Well, thanks for sharing, Rich."

Lanslow nodded. "No problem, Jack. We can use some help right now."

As he walked to his class, Lanslow thought about what had just transpired. He was beginning to regret letting Matthews know the gruesome details of the case, lest it become known to Chief Bradbury or Brooks or Johnson. This was information only the killer and the police would know and it could be used later to positively identify a suspect. But he had come to the conclusion that Andrew White hadn't killed Detective Mallard, and he was at a standstill. White could very well leave the state and just disappear, so any additional help he could get, if only another point of view, might be the break they needed. Brooks and the others didn't need to know anything about his and Matthews's conversation, anyway. It was none of their business ... for the moment at least.

After his class, Professor Matthews returned to his office, spent. He closed the door and sat at his desk thinking for a few minutes, staring distastefully at a stack of students' papers waiting to be graded. He needed to return them to his students tomorrow. On the other hand, he wanted to go to the University of Minnesota library to do some research on his new book. There was Time, again, "rearing its ugly head." Time, Father Time, not enough of it and running out. Maybe he could stop at the university on his way home and then grade the papers later. He hoped Maureen would not be over tonight. She had not called and told him otherwise. He decided not to call her and raise the issue. He needed to work.

He was about to put the student papers in his briefcase when his phone rang. It was Luke, on his cell phone, from the airport.

"Do you need a ride home?" asked Matthews.

"No. Joan will meet me outside baggage claim."

Joan was Luke's girlfriend. Matthews had never met her face to face. He had seen her only once from a distance when she sat outside in Luke's car one day, waiting for him. Luke had made some excuse for her not coming into the house, but Matthews had been disappointed. He regarded any of Luke's girlfriends as potential spouses and he would like to have gotten some impression of her, at least.

"How is Annie?"

"Annie is depressed again, Dad" Luke said. "She wants to come to the Twin Cities. I don't blame her. Going to that church college must be boring."

Matthews tried to squelch his concern at this. "What's she depressed about this time?" he asked, thinking that from what he'd heard about Annie she had always seemed to be depressed. This he didn't need.

"I think she just wants to get away from that place, and this guy she's going out with. Craig is too possessive. He tries to control her too much."

Not a bad thing, Matthews thought to himself, from what he knew of Annie. "Let me guess: Annie wants to stay with us when she comes here?"

"For a while, anyway."

"Listen, Luke. I know Annie is your sister and all, but ... I don't know ... I'm going to have to think about this. When does she want to come?"

"She's ready. She wants to do it as soon as she can. I told her I'd have to talk to you about it."

That's nice, thought Matthews, sarcastically. "Look, son, I can't say right now. This is a big change. Give me some time on this."

Matthews received a long silence over the phone as a result of this last statement. He suspected he wouldn't be seeing his son tonight. It was just as well.

He gathered the student papers and stuck them in his briefcase, put on his coat and locked his office.

Despite Luke's call, the drive to the university was pleasant and his thoughts turned to his research. His second book was taking shape. It was an attempt to distill the latest findings on the relationship between the family experiences of youths and their membership in gangs. There was little doubt what the majority of the research was saying. Almost always, negative family relations led to gang membership and delinquency. He would bet his house that when they found the murderer of Zeke Mallard they would find a man with a bad family background.

At the library's computer he found the articles he wanted, and copied them on the copying machines then sat down at an isolated desk to do some reading and take some notes. When he finally looked at the clock on the wall, it was nearly ten-thirty. Time had slipped past him once again.

Matthews rose, stuffed the articles into his briefcase and walked to the elevator to take him to the first floor. As the elevator descended, he leaned back against the wall and closed his eyes.

15

Dorian had only meant to take the girl's carrying bag and be off with it. But Linda talked him into forcing the girl back into the woods that lined the parking lot. He had grabbed her from behind, squeezing her throat with his arm so she couldn't scream.

When they were in the darkened woods, Dorian pulled the girl downward on her back from behind, then, kneeling over her from the side, held a knife to the girl's throat, his hand over her mouth. He began pulling the girl's outer clothing and panties down around her legs. The girl looked up at Dorian, extreme fright in her eyes. He cuffed her across the forehead.

"Don't look at me, bitch!" he said with a growl. She whimpered and began to cry. Dorian took the girl's ski cap and pulled it down over her face until it covered her eyes, nose, and chin. "Don't try to remove this to see," he said, then he let Linda take over.

Linda tried to be gentle, not mean, compared to Dorian. Dorian watched, still holding the knife to the girl's throat. The girl whimpered but did not try to resist. "If you try anything," Linda told her, "I will allow Dorian to do whatever he likes." The girl whimpered again, her breathing coming in short desperate gasps.

"Dammit! Don't mention our names," Dorian spat. "Now, for sure, we'll have to kill her." He pressed the knife a little harder to the girl's throat. The girl now became very agitated and Dorian placed his hand harder over the girl's mouth to keep her silent.

"Did you hear that?" said Linda. "He will kill you. You can't tell. You keep this to yourself. Do you understand?" The girl whimpered and tried to nod her head beneath the heavy pressure of Dorian's hand.

"You see, Dorian? We don't have to worry. She won't tell. If she does, you can kill her, and her family, too."

"Yes, I'll kill you if you tell anyone," said Dorian. "I'll find you and your family. Do you understand?"

The girl nodded and whimpered again.

When Linda was through with the girl, Dorian searched through the small travel bag the girl had been carrying, taking her wallet from her purse. Then he threw the bag by the girl's side. "Remember, if you tell, you will die. I promise. Wait here for ten minutes before you go to your car. If you don't, I'll know and I will find you."

Linda pushed Dorian aside, bent over the girl, and raised the ski cap just enough to kiss her on the mouth. For a moment she stroked the girl's hair that fell from beneath the ski cap, then she wheeled and was gone.

▌

Glenda Morrison heard the footsteps running through the leaves of the forest. Her fear overcame even the cold. She dared not move until she heard them fade away. She tried to count the minutes and seconds. After what she thought was surely more than ten minutes, she struggled to her feet, shivering.

She felt wetness between her legs. She reached down, feeling with her fingers. They came away wet. It was a woman, she thought. I heard her. But where had she come from? Had she been hiding in the woods, waiting? Was she a lesbian? Did she use something to penetrate her? But where, then, had the semen come from? What in hell had just happened to her? She scrambled to her feet.

Morrison took off her ski cap and used it to wipe herself clean. She pulled up her panties and outer clothing and brushed off the dead oak leaves clinging to her shoulders and backside. Retrieving her bag, she staggered out to the edge of the woods and looked across the parking lot. All was silent. The Minnesota night sky was dark as pitch, a heavy layer of clouds hiding the moon and stars. She would have to cross the lot again, as she had been doing when the man attacked her, to get to the bus stop.

Leaning against a tree, she dropped her bag at her feet and cupped her head in her hands and wept. She sobbed deep and long and her body shook uncontrollably from the fear she still felt. After a while, regaining some composure, she looked inside her bag to check for sure whether the man had taken her wallet as she thought he had. It was gone, and with it her credit card, her driver's license, her university ID, and the two-hundred dollars she'd just received from her mother that morning. Her mother had warned with anguish that it was the last they had. They could help Glenda out no further.

Glenda Morrison continued leaning against the tree and cried some more, trying to work through the desperateness of her situation. The two hundred dollars had offered some hope for a time. Now, this. This rape, this robbery. Why her? Life was hard enough as it was. She thought of her mother and of her invalid father, confined to a wheel chair, who could barely afford their medicine, much less money to help her with college.

Morrison stepped away from the tree and the dark shadows. She would cross the vast expanse of that parking lot. She would get on the bus. She would get another credit card and another student loan if she had to. And she would get her education, become a teacher, and take care of her mother and invalid father. She would fulfill her dream if it took every ounce of willpower in her body.

She began the journey across the parking lot once again. She broke into a run. All Glenda Morrison could think about was to get to her room and get clean.

∎

It was later than he'd wanted it to be when Matthews finally got home from the university. The house was dark, and he hoped from this that Maureen had decided not to stay over. He had student papers to grade that were way overdue. With some dismay, he saw his son's car, parked to the right of the house in its customary spot on the circle driveway. That didn't necessarily mean he was there, Matthews reasoned. Luke had left the car there when Joan had taken him to the airport and he could still be with her. When Matthews pressed the remote control to his garage door, Maureen's car was not there and he sighed with relief. He was just not in the mood for Maureen or Luke right now. He felt that it would be mutually beneficial for him and Luke to have a little space and time intervene before their next meeting.

He turned on the kitchen lights and was pouring himself a glass of orange juice when he heard a sound coming from Luke's bedroom. Matthews turned on the hall light and walked quietly to the door. The door was open slightly. The room was dark. He pushed the door open a little farther so that a shaft of light from the hall illuminated part of the interior. The sound he had heard was of very faint music. He could see Luke's body in the bed, the comforter partially over his head, as usual. According to his mother, Luke had always slept with his head covered, only his forehead projecting, and the radio turned on softly to music. He had depended on his wife for such descriptions, a form of "distance learning," he thought, ironically. Her descriptions had been accurate.

Matthews looked around the room and could just make out Luke's backpack, thrown carelessly on the floor by the closet. He located the direction of the music. He walked quietly to the side of Luke's bed and turned off the radio. He stood by his son's bed for a moment, listening to the low, regular breathing. His misgivings about Luke's news of Annie gave way. For an instant he felt the impulse to bend down and kiss Luke on the forehead, even to wake him, to say hello, and to talk. But he decided not to wake him, after all. It would wait until morning. If he could catch him in time, they could maybe have breakfast together. In the meantime, he had papers to be graded.

Matthews closed his son's bedroom door, returned to the kitchen, finished his glass of juice, then picked up his briefcase. He was very tired. He tried to remember what he'd been thinking about when he'd left the university, something he'd told himself that needed to be done. Something to do with his new book. Something very important. Now, try as he might, he drew a blank.

Irritated at his forgetfulness, he carried the briefcase to his bedroom, removed the papers and placed them on his bedside table. He decided to go to bed and grade the papers there before going to sleep. He would shower in the morning. He looked at the clock. It was nearing midnight. He settled back against the headboard and stared into space for a moment before picking up one of the papers. Then he made the mistake of closing his eyes.

▌

Dorian and Linda had put them all in danger once more. Conrad called the group together again. It was late, and they were all tired, but one by one, then ten in number, they emerged from the shadows into the lamplight, all except the little man. No one expected the little man to join them; he had refused to join their sessions before. Conrad, as usual, had been trying, but he'd once again been ignored.

"We're in trouble, here," Conrad began. "Dorian, you can't keep doing these things, you and Linda. We have enough trouble without you two bringing on more. We've just been lucky, so far."

"That's true," said Gary, trying to show Conrad he was on his side. "We all have to pull together here. We just can't continue to go off on our own like this. It just exacerbates things." Gary hadn't seen Dorian or Linda since he and Conrad had talked about their situation several days ago. Once again, he was fearful he'd overstepped his bounds and he looked in Dorian's direction quickly, to see his reaction.

"*Exacerbate?*" said Dorian, emerging from the shadows. "Shit! You're beginning to sound just like the little man ... and why doesn't that little asshole ever show up here, anyway? I did what I needed to do for him. Just once I wish he could take care of himself. And as for this last thing, it was Linda, as usual, who fucked up." He tittered at his own pun, even though he hadn't meant the statement to be one.

"Listen, Dorian," said Conrad, menacingly. "You're the one who messed up this time. Both you and Linda. The little man had nothing to do with this."

Linda withdrew from the lamplight, deeper into the shadows, crowding in among the others, but she didn't leave—a good sign. Still, Conrad knew he had pushed a little too far. He had to go very slowly and gingerly. He saw Dorian stiffening, growing defensive. Dorian, Conrad knew, was dangerous and he would leave at the slightest provocation, as would Linda.

"We have to fight together to get through this situation," said Gary. "Not only for the little man but for Larry and Brian, too. We have to protect the children."

Larry, a boy of about eleven, looked up from his place beside the sofa and smiled. He liked it that they were talking about him. Brian, the seven-year old, was fast asleep for the time being.

"Things will only get worse if we don't," said Conrad. "I, for one, need you all to understand that. This splitting off and going our own way is driving me crazy. Sometimes I just can't keep things under control. And it's getting worse."

"Well, that's really your problem, pal," said Dorian, "We all got problems here. I got a problem. Linda's got her you-know-what problem. Gary is so fucking screwed up it's pitiful!" Dorian was glaring at Gary, just hoping he would say something. Gary looked down, deciding not to push it. "And the little man's got a problem—him and his fucking mother and 'daddy.' He can't seem to think of anything else. They were his parents, not mine, and I don't really give a damn one way or the other, but I'm the one who has to bail him out. And, last but not least, you got a problem, Conrad; you gotta keep us all together. I do what I can for this bunch, the only way I know how, and you gotta do the same."

With that, he disappeared into the shadows and was gone. One by one the others left, too, except for Conrad and Gary. They just sat there, looking at one another helplessly.

■

Sherry still didn't know the truth as to why Andrew was holed up in her room. She hadn't asked any questions. Sherry wasn't worldly. She never read anything other than her textbooks, and she only got news inadvertently through TV, or when she heard strangers talking about it, because, from what Andrew could tell, she didn't have any friends.

"I'm getting bugged, here" White said to Sherry, as she put leftover pizza in the microwave.

"Why don't you go out, then?" she asked, perplexed. "Are you in trouble with your mother, or something?"

Deciding to forestall as long as he could, Andrew said, "I tol' you. My mom's mad at me. She threw me out."

Sherry, a tall, freckle-faced redhead, looked at Andrew sternly. "You didn't tell me that. What's she mad at you about?"

"I tol' you that. This morning. Don't you ever pay no attention to me?" Andrew whined.

"Come on, Andrew. You know you didn't tell me. What's she mad at you about?"

"You," he said, secretly amused at his lie.

"Me? Your mom knows about me?" Sherry asked, surprised.

"You bet, baby. I couldn't keep from talkin' 'bout you, you know?"

Though Sherry wasn't worldly, she wasn't dumb. She realized Andrew was teasing her.

"Oh, you shit!" she said. "You and your shit! How can I ever know when you're serious?"

"I'm serious, baby," said Andrew, as he pulled Sherry to him. "Real serious."

After they made love, they warmed up the pizza again and ate, while they watched some TV. Andrew, the remote control in his possession, made sure they didn't watch the news, not that Sherry would have wanted to anyway. He'd changed his mind about confessing to his predicament.

Later, when they had gone back to bed, Andrew couldn't get to sleep. He knew his situation would only get worse if the police couldn't catch the little man who'd killed Mallard.

Thoughts of Mallard still rankled. He'd run into this type of officer before: a bulldozer physique, power-arrogant, taking advantage of their authority, racially prejudiced agents of an oppressive racist society, brutalizing and holding down black people like him. Mallard was dead now, though. Good riddance.

White grinned in the darkness. Still, he was at a loss as to what to do, and sooner or later, he was going to have to get out of Sherry's room or go crazy.

16

Matthews woke early Thursday morning, still tired and with a migraine headache. He stumbled to the bathroom in a cold sweat, feeling nauseous. He struggled with the lid of the prescription medicine bottle but finally managed to shake a couple of pills into his palm and gulp them down with a cup of water. As he returned to lay down and let the pills do their work, he spied the stack of student papers on the table. He thumbed through several of the top ones, then he thumbed through several of the bottom ones. There wasn't a single one with a red mark or grade on it.

"Aww, crap!" he said to himself. He looked at the clock: six-fifteen. He tried to think about how he would explain not getting the papers back to his students today since he'd already had to make up an excuse earlier in the week for not doing so. He tried to think back to why he hadn't graded them last night. He couldn't remember. Father Time, again. He must have fallen asleep.

He looked at the clock again. Six-thirty-five. He would lie back down for now and try to get rid of the headache. Then he would call in sick to the college. He couldn't help it. He just couldn't make it to class today. He set the alarm for seven-fifteen.

∎

Midmorning Thursday, at his desk, Lanslow rubbed his eyes and massaged his forehead and temples. He and Brooks had gone through

Andrew White's room Wednesday evening. Over Brooks's mild objection, they hadn't notified the St. Paul police, since the original warrant for search was still valid. Mrs. White let them in. Lanslow had been looking specifically for anything that might tell them who "Sherry" was. But they had found nothing to identify her and nothing else that might lead them to White. Roberta White claimed she didn't "know no Sherry." Their attempts to obtain information from White's friends, whose names Lanslow had gotten from Mrs. White, had met with the same fate—all of those they were able to locate had resisted giving them any information. Lanslow, however, wasn't particularly exercised about this. He was growing less and less concerned with Andrew White.

It was true that they had a strong circumstantial case against White. He had motive, means and opportunity and they had his admission on tape putting him at the scene of the crime. He had avoided arrest and shot at a police officer. The tests on the rubber from the black marks on the pavement had revealed a match with the car that White had admitted over the phone he had stolen and driven to Mallard's house. So they would arrest him if they could find him. But Lanslow's intuition told him that White didn't do it. He had to admit it: they were stumped. Besides, he had his doubts they would ever find Andrew White, unless he wanted to be found.

▮

Vortices. Vortices of pain and fear, of repulsiveness, of dirtiness, ugliness. Who could love anyone like him? Screams. Screams inside, that no one else could hear.

The little boy hears the laughter somewhere above him. He hears his "daddy" tramping around in the hayloft above. Dust from the hay fills the air, hanging in the shafts of sunlight streaming through the cracks in the barn. Every now and then his "new daddy" peers over the edge of the loft in a leer.

"Still there, little man? Don't you go away now, little man. Daddy'll be finished here pretty soon, now."

The little boy has wet his pants, several times. He is desperate to put on dry clothes before "daddy" finds out. But he has been told to stay where he is and now he hears "daddy" coming.

His "daddy" stands before him, but, somehow, he finds himself floating upward and away and in a different place. The place is full of people, arranged in a semicircle in a bowl-like room, in semidarkness. They are all peering down at a man with an aura of light around his body. He's standing with a long white stick in his hand, pointing to different parts of a white, glowing screen. The man is talking and pointing, and pointing and talking. The little boy floats downward and sits on the man's shoulder.

A video jumps on the screen. A single male lion, huge, with a magnificent black mane, is moving toward a lioness who crouches, baring her fangs. The male gets closer and she lashes out viciously, but the big cat merely brushes her thrusts aside and bowls her over. She backs off and crouches in the brush, snarling but helpless.

The male continues on through the brush with absolute purpose in his yellow eyes. And there, just in front of him, one of the lioness's cubs growls and paws at the air bravely. The lion pauses, frozen in still frame, for just an instant. Then, with one quick pounce the cub is caught in the male's jaws, bitten nearly in two, squirming and writhing as the male holds it down, shaking it, biting it again and again, until it's small body is limp and lifeless. Two more cubs meet the same fate.

There are gasps from the audience. The man is talking, pointing, talking, pointing. "Having taken over the pride from the previous males, the new males will thus have disposed of the previous male's offspring. The females will now come into heat," he is saying, "and the new males will have insured the passing of their own genes to their own offspring. We perhaps think it's brutal, but the male lion is merely ensuring the survival of his own genes. He is driven to this act by his genes' commands. And take note: as Homo Sapiens we are not free of this command. It works in us, just as it does among the lions, though often hidden by our social norms."

The room goes dark. The boy leaves the man's shoulder, swims upward though a dark void, opens his eyes. His "daddy" stands above him, a leather belt in his hand, a thin smile across his lips.

"You've pissed your pants again, I see, you prissy little bastard."

"Daddy" raises the belt to strike. The boy moans, then looks up. Remembering the lion cub, he looks straight into his "daddy's" eyes. The man sees it and breaks into a fury.

"Don't you look at me like that, you little bastard. Don't you look at me like that!" The belt starts to descend. The little boy leaves his body again and floats away, into the sky.

The little man awoke from the dream with a start. He continued to lie on his bed for a while, eyes open, peering into the darkness of the curtained room. He felt his forehead. It was cool, clammy. He wanted to get back to sleep, knowing if he didn't he'd be dragging all day. He shut his eyes, then realized he was squeezing them shut, and the rest of his body was being held, too, in a tense grip. Despite himself, his mind was now whirring.

The dream again. He'd had similar versions of the dream several times recently, as well as others. His dreams were pathways back in time, to his early childhood, a time marked by the scars of beatings, beratings, humiliations, mortifications, rebukes, debasements of every nature and kind; too painful to dwell upon for very long except as detached intellectual exercises from which emotion had been exorcised. And that's what he did now.

Dreams, he thought, are merely memories, without the moorings of time and space; images, sounds, odors, feelings, all jumbled up, traipsing around freely in the brain. Yet, perhaps, as Freud had said, they carried some meaning. He began to sort through the dream's details.

His "daddy's" voice came back to him, but not so much from the dream now as from the real past: "You tell anybody, little man, and I'll kill you. I'll just tell everyone you ran away. You hear? And I'll kill your mother, too, and your sister. Best for you and everbody else to keep your pretty little mouth shut, you hear?"

And the little boy had kept his mouth shut, the terror and loathing bottled inside.

Lying there, the little man suddenly recognized in the memory of his "daddy's" voice the low growl of the male lion in his dream, on its mission to kill the deposed male's cubs. The whole thing became clear to him, as if a spotlight had been shone upon a dark closet of his mind. It was true, then. Dreams did have meaning. They were even the stuff of revelation. He was his mother's cub. His new daddy was the male lion, come to kill him.

And this revelation brought another: his "daddy" was a man, not an animal, and mankind had morals, and rules, and conscience. So, what did that mean? If mankind was a moral being, actually knew good from evil, then it made any act of brutality and sadism even worse. Had he discovered the meaning of evil? His "daddy" knew that what he was doing was horrendously wrong but did it anyway and even enjoyed it. His new "daddy" was evil personified, and had perpetrated evil acts upon him. At the time, though, he hadn't understood, and he simply thought he himself was no good, unlovable, an object to be hated and punished. He knew now, intellectually, that it was untrue, that he had been duped. The emotions flooded back, of grief, of despair, and then of hatred and writhing, poisonous anger.

◾

"He knows now," said Dorian.

"Yes, maybe it's a breakthrough," said Conrad. "Maybe I can talk to him."

But Dorian spoke again. Maybe it was a breakthrough, he said, but not the kind they'd hoped for. The difference in the little man's case and the lion's case, he said, was that "daddy" had not finished the job. Now, the little man was no longer a cub. And "daddy" wasn't dead. He was out there, somewhere.

Conrad and Gary knew exactly what Dorian meant. There was nothing they could do now except let him take care of the problem once again.

■

Luke Matthews rose at ten o'clock. He listened to see if he could hear his father. The house was quiet. He came out of the bedroom and peered down the hallway at his father's bedroom. The door was shut. He listened: no sound.

Luke returned to his room, washed his face, dressed—except for his shoes—picked up his backpack and again came out into the hallway. He glanced at his watch. He walked, in his stocking feet, to his father's room and listened. Gently, he opened the door an inch or two and was surprised to see Matthews asleep. Luke had seen the open bottle of painkiller on the sink in the bathroom and guessed his father was suffering another one of his headaches. That was probably why his father wasn't in class.

Luke closed the door quietly. He slipped into the kitchen and pulled out a can of soup from a cabinet, and a spoon from a drawer, and stuffed them into his backpack. It would be his lunch after classes. He let himself out of the house, closing the door silently behind him.

As he drove to the college, Luke thought of last night when his father had stood over his bed for a while. Why had he pretended to be asleep? Somehow, he couldn't talk to his father, even when he wanted to, except about intellectual things. As for their intellectual discussions, he had found his father to be of great help in his studies, and he could remember several times when they had discussed some issues for hours. These discussions were titillating, refreshing, and they both loved them. He and his father merely chided one another over their differences. Luke knew that his father was especially proud of him for following in what he had called "the life of the mind," even though Luke always made it a point to remind his father that he might or might not go on for his doctorate.

When things got personal, however, when his father began moving in a little too close to his inner feelings and emotions, Luke retreated. Luke wanted it to be different. But there were things he just couldn't talk to his dad about, now. Yet, remembering his dad standing over him, he wished now he would have gotten up and hugged him right there and they could have sat down and talked.

God only knew, he needed to talk to someone.

17

Lanslow woke at four-thirty and couldn't get back to sleep. As he lay there, Laura asleep beside him, visions of Zeke Mallard, slumped against his Lincoln Town Car in his own garage, kept returning.

It was still dark. He closed his eyes. He needed sleep but the visions persisted. He gave up after awhile. He flipped the blanket off his body, swung his legs over the side of the bed and got up. He dressed quietly and left the apartment at five, leaving Laura still asleep. She would, no doubt, know where he had gone, but he wrote a short note, as apologetic as he could make it, and left it on the kitchen counter. On his way to the station he stopped by the all-night cafe and had some breakfast. He finished off his last refill of coffee, waved good-bye to Harry, the proprietor, and pulled on his coat at six.

Breakfast had offered a respite from his terrible visions, but as he drove to the station his thoughts returned to the case. Somehow, his intuition told him, the girl named "Sherry" might be a key in finding Andrew White—not that he believed any longer that White was the murderer. But not knowing who the girl was and how she was linked to White was just a loose string that needed to be gathered and tied, and finding White might produce other leads.

Suddenly, he remembered a name. Albert. Albert. Where had he heard it? When he reached the station and parked, Lanslow pulled out his notebook and began to flip through the pages. Near the middle he saw the scribbled name "Albert," and next to it, more scribbling "ride share with White." He remembered now: Angelena Rosario had said that Albert was the man who had given Andrew White a ride to work every morning. He had meant to talk to this man earlier. The intention had simply slipped his mind. He decided he would find this Albert now. Maybe Albert would know something about Sherry and perhaps something more about White himself.

The man the little man's mother had called his new "daddy" hadn't been as hard to find as Dorian had expected. A computer search had yielded what he needed to know. It was amazing, the information one could access on the internet. The greater surprise was that "daddy" was living in the Twin Cities.

Concrete steps led down to a single door at the bottom of the stairwell. There was no bell, so Dorian knocked. A short time passed and he was about ready to knock again when the knob turned and the door opened slightly, then a bit wider, and a man in a faded blue shirt and jeans peered out.

"Daddy" had lost a lot of weight, though he was still bulky, and his hair was thinning considerably and turning gray. The skin of his face was heavily creased and dark, as if weathered from the sun, especially around the rheumy, pale blue eyes. The stubble of his beard looked to be at least a week old. The hands were still large and powerful looking, hands that had folded the belt to improve the beating. Seeing the hands, Dorian almost went for "daddy's" throat then and there.

"Yeah? Whadaya want?" asked the man, his eyes riveted on Dorian's face.

"Do you remember me?" said Dorian. "We knew each other once."

The man looked Dorian up and down, then studied his face closely. "'Fraid not," he said, finally. "When ... where'd we know each other?"

"A while ago," said Dorian. "Look a little closer." Dorian took off his cap. "Do you remember me now?"

"Well ... can't say as I do, I ... " The rheumy eyes squinted in the pale autumn sunlight and the man moved a little closer. "Naw, don't think so ... say, are you trying to pull somethin' here? I wouldn't try nuthin' if I was you. I kin take care of myself." He brandished an almost empty wine bottle in his hand that he'd kept hidden behind his back.

"I'm a friend of the little man," said Dorian. "He wanted me to look you up. You sure you don't remember?"

"Little man? What the hell are you talkin' about?" The man stepped a little closer. He peered at Dorian's face again. The man's jaw dropped. His face blanched. "You! Well, I'll be goddamned!" he exclaimed. "How ... how did you find me? "

"Not so hard. The computer, a few bucks." The alcohol from the man's breath set Dorian's blood to boil.

"How's your mother?" asked the man."

"His mother's dead," said Dorian, coldly.

The man looked at Dorian quizzically, squinting. He shrugged. "Oh, well, ... sorry to hear it," said the man, somberly. He paused, as if digesting the news. "I truly am. I called her awhile ago. Her and me, we were ... close ... for a while, until ..." He glanced at Dorian's face, attempting to read his thoughts. The man paused, then shrugged his shoulders. "Well, anyway, whadaya want with me?"

"He just wants me to talk to you, clear some things up," said Dorian.

"He? He wants to clear things up?" The man struggled to understand. "What things?"

"May I come in?" asked Dorian.

"May I?" repeated the man sarcastically. "Goddamn! You got yourself educated?"

"Some," said Dorian.

"Prissy-assed as usual, I see," sneered the man, staggering backward slightly. "Oh, sure. Come right on in to my *domicile.*" He laughed a hoarse laugh, then coughed, a deep racking cough, the cough of a life time smoker. "I don't know what the hell I can do for you, though. I done all I could for all of you. It wasn't enough." He turned, wiping the spittle from his lips with the back of his hand, and disappeared into the room.

Dorian followed him in. "Yeah, I know what you 'done,'" he said.

▌

Andrew White had walked farther than he had intended but the October day was somewhat warmer than usual for Minnesota and, against his better judgment, he decided to walk on. The fall colors were brilliant. It was sunny here, but back to the northwest a gray mass of clouds was creeping in.

Sherry's room had finally gotten to him. He had again pulled on one of her jackets, a baseball cap and gloves, and had walked down to the east campus of the University of Minnesota. From there he had strolled through the main campus to the walkway above the Washington Bridge which crossed the Mississippi River and thence to the west campus. Despite the warm weather, he decided to take the covered part of the walkway, its walls plastered with hand-painted and hand-lettered signs advertising every event, club and happening on the campus. He paused before a kiosk with a poster of a Rolling Stone cover featuring an article by Keith Richards on "Life and How to Live it." Richards looked like his life had been a living hell. Farther along, a sign read, "Acid is groovy, kill the pigs," and another sign advertised the University Pagan Society.

"These cats are strange, man," said White to himself. As he walked, he imagined himself a student. What degree would he be pursuing? He laughed. What a crock of shit! He could make more money in one hour on the street than any of these crazy privileged assholes would make in a month.

With that thought, he contented himself with watching the female students, though they were disappointingly covered in heavy jackets and jeans. But even that activity couldn't keep him from returning to his problem for long.

He couldn't keep this up. They'd get him sometime. Killing a cop was something you didn't get away with, especially if you were black. Never mind that he didn't do it. Even this walk was dangerous. His name and face had been splashed in the papers and on TV for days now. He knew it was these kinds of lapses in discretion that could get him caught. But he had to get out of Sherry's room, if only for a half hour or so. He pulled the baseball cap down low over his forehead. He needed his sunglasses, left in his room when he'd run from Lanslow, and he swore again at his predicament.

The walk was a long one. He passed the Hard Times Cafe and snickered, thinking "that's the truth." Farther up the street he found himself in a run-down area off campus, consisting of jerry-built apartments, themselves occupied mostly by Somali immigrants. Trash littered the sidewalk, clinging to the base of trees and caught in the tall grass and weeds. He passed the Riverside Islamic Center, and continued on.

Turning to look back from where he had come, he saw the figure of a man emerge from a stairwell a couple of hundred feet or so behind him and it stopped him cold. A small man. Not a Somali. White. Andrew stopped and watched him, a feeling of déjà vu holding him to the spot.

The man halted at the top of the stairwell and peered in both directions, pausing for a moment to stare at Andrew, then turned and walked hurriedly to the corner of the block where he joined a small group of people waiting for the light to change. White watched in a trance as the man appeared to be talking to another individual. Then the light changed and the man walked across the street away from Andrew. Andrew stood frozen for several more moments, watching the small figure move away from him with the other pedestrians before he realized who he'd seen. It was him. The man at Mallard's house.

Andrew began to jog back toward the disappearing figure. The man rounded the corner of a building and disappeared from sight. Andrew began to run. He got to the corner of the building and peered around it. He saw a car pull out from the curb and drive away. He saw several people, but the man was nowhere in sight. Andrew ran as fast as he dared, taking the risk of drawing attention to himself, to see if he might be able to catch the car at a stoplight, or at least get the license plate number.

It was no use. The car, what appeared to be a dark-colored Japanese make, was too far ahead and pulling away faster. He stopped, cursing to himself.

The enormity of what had happened began to dawn in Andrew's consciousness. By an absolutely improbable coincidence he was sure that he and Mallard's murderer had crossed paths again, with practically the same result. He was gone. The only thing Andrew could remember about him was the color of his coat and his car, but, again, he'd also caught a glimpse of the face, though from a distance, beneath a hat. A moment or two earlier, Andrew could have come face-to-face with him, could have followed him and gotten his license number. Hell, he might have even been able to mug the little bastard, or hijack his car, and turn him over to the police right there, or gotten his driver's license, credit cards, or anything else that could have led to his identification and arrest.

"Shit, shit, shit!" Even old Lady Luck is biased against black men, he thought.

Andrew's anger at his bad fortune began to subside. He began to think a little more about the situation. Why was the man here? What was he doing here? He'd come out of that stairwell, some yards back. Was that where he lived? Had he perhaps found the little bastard after all? Andrew turned around again and began to trace his steps back to the stairwell where he'd seen the little man emerge a few minutes ago.

█

It was 11:30 A.M. when Lanslow parked the unmarked squad car as near to the store as he could. As he exited, he noted a car parked in the handicapped space without a handicap sticker. He called dispatch on his cell phone and alerted them to the violation. Some dude attempting to save the few seconds it would have taken him to walk only a few yards farther would soon wish he hadn't.

Inside the store, Lanslow stopped the first salesperson and asked for the manager. He was directed to the rear of the store where he found a middle-aged man hunched over a desk, absorbed in a pile of papers, his computer screen glowing luminescent greens, reds and blues, showing a grid with a lot of numbers. The sign on the door read "Greg Wolden, Manager."

"Mr. Wolden?"

The man looked up from his stack of papers, through lenses so thick his eyes looked like they were about to pop out of their sockets. "Yes sir, what can I do for you?"

Lanslow held his badge up as he spoke. "Mr. Wolden, I'm Detective Lanslow, White Bear Police. I'm looking for a man by the name of Albert. We don't know his last name, but we know he works here, or at least he did."

Wolden's look turned to concern. He frowned. His eyes became a little smaller. "Yes. We have a man by that name. Albert Carter. He's in the back."

"Could I speak to him?"

"Of course. Can you wait here? I'll go get him."

"If you don't mind, Mr. Wolden, I'd like to go with you and talk to him directly," said Lanslow.

"Oh ... yes," said Wolden, "of course. He's back in the stockroom."

Wolden rose and proceeded across the store, Lanslow walking close behind.

"What has Albert done, Detective?" asked Wolden, over his shoulder, as they passed the sporting goods section. "Is he in any kind of trouble?"

"No, nothing," said Lanslow. "He may know someone we're looking for. Did you ever see him with a Mr. Andrew White?"

"I can't say. I don't know an Andrew White." He stopped suddenly and turned to face Lanslow, his concern deepening. "Isn't Andrew White the man suspected of murdering that policeman?"

"Yes, he's the one," said Lanslow.

"Oh, my. Albert knows him? I've never seen Albert with the young man shown in the papers." He looked quickly at Lanslow. "Of course, my relation with Albert is only as a store manager." He turned and continued walking toward a large double door that read "Employees Only."

"I believe Mr. Carter provided a ride for Andrew White when he worked at Val Mart," said Lanslow.

Wolden pushed the double doors open and held them as Lanslow passed through. At the same time a huge black man, in his late thirties approached, coming down the aisle pushing a cart loaded with merchandise. They walked toward him.

"Albert, this is Detective Lanslow of the White Bear police department. He says he'd like to talk to you."

Lanslow extended his hand and nodded to Albert Carter. Carter wore a goatee and the man stood nearly a full foot taller than Wolden and had a good three inches or more on Lanslow. He looked like a Minnesota Vikings lineman. His hand completely enclosed Lanslow's and Lanslow could feel its crushing strength despite the limpid grasp. Although he had extended a hand, Albert Carter's look was not friendly.

"What do you want to talk to me about, Detective? Andrew? I was wonderin' when you'd get 'round to me."

"Yes, Mr. Carter, it's about Andrew. Just a few questions. I understand you two were friends?"

"Well, I wouldn't say Andrew and me was friends, exactly. We from the same neighborhood, and he ast me if I would give him a ride to work since we work in this same shopping mall. I'm always willin' to help out the young dudes, if I can, but that's all I did for Andrew. Nothin' else. I done my time. Mr. Wolden knows that, and I'm stayin' straight."

Lanslow glanced at Wolden.

"That's true, Detective. Mr. Carter is one of our best employees."

"Mr. Carter, I'm not here to check up on you," said Lanslow. Then, turning to Wolden, he said "Mr. Wolden, I would appreciate it if I could talk to Mr. Carter alone, if you don't mind. Mr. Carter is not in any trouble. I'd just like to ask him some questions about Andrew White."

"Oh, ... yes. Of course," said Wolden. "I'll talk to you later, Albert," he said as he turned and left.

Carter looked down at Lanslow, waiting.

"Are you still on parole, Carter?" asked Lanslow.

"You guessed it, Mr. Detective," said Carter. "I'm gonna be real nice to you."

"Okay, Carter, that's good, 'cause your little friend may have killed my best friend and a cop to boot. So I'd appreciate anything you can tell me."

Carter shrugged his huge shoulders, then smiled sardonically. "I'm all yours, Detective."

"I'm trying," said Lanslow, "to find out if Andrew had a girlfriend by the name of Sherry, and if you might know anything about her ... whether you might have heard Andrew mention her in any way."

Carter thought for only a moment. "Oh, yeah. She was his latest, I think. He talked a little 'bout her 'fore he quit Val Mart. After he quit we didn't have much to do with each other, so that's all I know."

"No last name? Nothing about where she lives?"

"Nope ... no, don't think so. I know she was a student at the university, though. I think he mentioned that."

"The University of Minnesota?"

"Yeah, I think that's the one. Yeah, that's it, 'cause he ast me to give him a ride over to her house one night, when we got off work. I ast him where it was and he said over on the east side of the campus, near University Avenue. When he said that I said no, I couldn't give him no ride way over there. Had to get home."

"He didn't give an address?"

"No ... well, maybe, but I don't remember it, if he did."

Lanslow had the feeling that Carter wasn't being totally forthright. "Carter, if you know anything else about this dude, you'd better tell me, 'cause, as I say, this little asshole may have killed my partner and if I find out you've held back something I'm not going to feel real kindly about it." Lanslow stared hard into Carter's face even though he knew that Carter could flatten him like a bug.

The glare Carter returned was more than malevolent. Lanslow could see the sheer hatred in the man's eyes, could see that Carter was doing everything he could to suppress his desire to strangle Lanslow at that very moment.

"Her last name was Carter," said the big man at last, expelling his breath slowly. "I remember, 'cause it was the same as mine."

18

The door at the bottom of the stairwell was slightly open. Andrew looked both ways before he descended. He tapped lightly. There was no answer. He pushed the door open just a little more and peered in. The interior was dark. He couldn't make out anything except some heavily wrapped pipes running along the back ceiling. He tapped lightly again.

"Hello? Anybody home?"

There was still no answer. He pushed the door open a little wider and tapped again. "Hello? Hello?" No answer.

He pushed the door open just enough to allow him to pass. A peculiar odor hung in the air. He entered fully and looked around. The apartment appeared empty. Andrew closed the door behind him, but it wouldn't close completely until he pushed hard. He heard the latch click. He felt about the wall until he found a light switch. He flipped it on and a dim light filled the room.

Andrew surveyed his surroundings. To his right was a small kitchen with an apartment-sized refrigerator, a stove and a small folding table. The sink was full of dirty dishes, mixed with wine bottles. The table was covered with dirty dishes, too. He was standing in a small area that served as a living room as well as a bedroom. A small television sat on an end table next to a lumpy, blanket-covered couch. The occupant apparently used the couch as a bed. To his left was a curtained off area. The curtains had been strung from the myriad pipes running across the ceiling. From behind the curtain he thought he heard water dripping on a tin surface. Plink ... plink ... plink ...

◾

A cursory check of the phone book had yielded no information on Sherry Carter. Dispatch, too, had failed to turn up her address. Lanslow then had to get the registrar at Bremer College to give the registrar at the University of Minnesota a call. Student records were closed without sub-poena or a judge's order and he didn't have the time for either. Lanslow knew, though, that a call from another college registrar, presumably in-terested in obtaining information on a prospective student, would prob-ably yield all the information he needed. He had become friends with the woman registrar at Bremer when he first started teaching there. Now, she agreed to help him out. But the whole process of getting her on the phone, explaining his situation, her calling the University's registrar then calling him back had taken almost an hour.

"Got it," said Lanslow, as he hung up the receiver. "Albert Carter's story checks out. We have a Miss Sherry Carter with a Southeast Fourth Street address. Let's pay a little visit to Miss Carter."

"Absolutely," said Brooks.

◾

Andrew White pulled back the plastic curtain and shrank back in hor-ror. A man sat on the floor, his back propped against the metal shower stall. The man's head was slumped upon his chest, his eyes staring at the floor, unseeing. He sat in a pool of his own blood, and blood oozed from several wounds in his legs. The shards of a broken wine bottle were scat-tered across the floor. From inside the stall he heard water dripping.

Andrew's breath caught in his throat as he reeled backward from the scene. He pulled the curtain back to hide the sight. He stepped slowly backward, away from it.

"Holy shit! Holy shit!" he said, as he turned, opened the door and, as covertly as possible, made his way up the steps of the stairwell. He looked back and forth. Only one man was in sight and he was walking away, his back turned. Andrew began to walk down the sidewalk quickly, watching for other people—and dark colored cars.

"Man! Got to get out of here. Got to get out of here. That little mother fucker is crazy!" he said aloud to himself.

He walked with long, rapid strides back across the Washington Street Bridge and across the main university campus, toward Sherry's room.

19

Lanslow pulled the unmarked car alongside the curb only a few parking spaces down from the building where Sherry Carter lived. The Minneapolis police van pulled up to the curb and the SWAT team emerged. Some of the heavily armored men jogged to the rear of the building while the remaining men made their way into the building, their guns ready. Several other squads had pulled up, blocking off the street. It had all been laid out.

"We should've done this ourselves," said Lanslow, as he got out of the car.

"No way," said Brooks. "If White is here, and he starts shooting again, it's better the SWAT takes him than us."

"You and I both know that White isn't our guy. We just need to question him."

"You think that, but I'm not convinced, and the chief would raise holy hell if anything went wrong," said Brooks. "This is the proper procedure."

They walked to the front of the building where Minneapolis Detectives Manfredy and Morgan stood behind a squad car, watching the proceedings. The landlord of the building, a Mr. Astor, stood nervously alongside them. A search warrant had been served. The SWAT team had disappeared into the building and would now be in the process of securing the building before they entered Sherry's room.

"This will be over real quick," said Manfredy to Lanslow and Brooks as the two detectives approached.

"Hope so," said Brooks.

Only five minutes later the SWAT leader called on the voice-activated microphone. "The building is under control. We didn't force the door to the room yet. There's no answer. I'm coming down." A moment later the commander stepped out from the front door and motioned for the men to come in.

"We're going up," said Manfredy, turning to Astor.

"Will they break the door down?" Astor asked.

"Not if they don't have to. You have the key?"

"Thank God," said Astor, "yes, right here." He pointed to a set of keys hanging from his belt.

"Let's take a look, then" said Manfredy.

Manfredy and Morgan, followed by Lanslow and Brooks, with Astor just behind, went up the steps. When they went inside, Lanslow saw that members of the SWAT team had stationed themselves along the hallways at intervals. Astor and the detectives followed the SWAT commander up a set of stairs to the third floor. A hallway led directly away from them toward the back of the building. Lanslow could see the doors to several rooms.

"Down here," said the SWAT commander, pointing down the hallway.

They made their way down the dimly lit hallway to room 306 where two other SWAT members stood, one with a battering ram in his hands, the other with a 12-gauge shotgun.

Somewhere, the muted sounds of rap music from a radio that had been left on drifted through the air.

"At least they play it quiet, here," said Brooks, grinning at Lanslow.

∎

Andrew White had been spooked by his chance sighting again of the man who had killed Zeke Mallard, and the discovery of another of his grisly murders. He had become super cautious.

It was a good thing. He approached Sherry's building, watchfully, from the south, avoiding the streets and sidewalks and moving through alleys. He cut through the apartment building across the street from Sherry's room and stood in a stairwell window on the third floor observing the building for a few moments. With mounting alarm he saw the police van and several squad cars pull up, and watched the SWAT team enter the building, then he watched the two men coming down the sidewalk to join another group of men. He recognized one of them as Detective Richard Lanslow.

Maybe Lady Luck was on his side after all, White thought. They would have had him. Still, he wondered how they had discovered his hiding place. He had to give them credit.

He watched them from behind the glass, remaining in the shadows so they would not see him if they happened to look his way. He watched as a SWAT team member came out of the building, and continued watching as Lanslow and the others entered.

He fished in the pockets of his pants and pulled out the unlisted phone number Sherry had written on a piece of paper. He rushed out the back door of the building and hurried back the way he had come. He figured he had about five or ten minutes.

■

Matthews woke up groggy and tired. He checked the time on his watch: 4:15 p.m., Thursday. My God! Had he really slept that long? He remembered getting up and getting dressed, intending to go work after all, despite the headache, hoping he could get through the day on acetaminophen and codeine. The headache had returned with a vengeance, though, and he'd taken some more medicine, phoned in sick, then laid back down, still in his clothes. He felt the spot over his left eye and pressed on it. He dropped back down on the bed. His headache was still there and getting worse.

Matthews looked at his watch again. It now read four-thirty. The day was shot. His head was still pounding. Time. Time. Time. Where did it go? Would they give him an appointment with his doctor at the HMO this late in the day? Probably not. He was too sick to go through the hassle anyway.

Matthews went to the bathroom and rummaged around in a drawer. He found the small cloth bag with tie-strings that Maureen had gotten for him at a medical supply outlet, returned to the kitchen and filled the bag with ice cubes. Wearily, he returned to the bathroom and took another pill.

On his way out of the bathroom the phone rang, splitting his head. He grimaced. Maureen's voice said, "Just checking on you. Are you okay?"

"I have one hell of a headache. Didn't go to the college."

"I tried to reach you at your office yesterday and earlier this morning. You need anything? "

"No, no. Thanks. All I need now is some sleep. I took something."

"Oh, okay. I won't come by, then. If you need anything, let me know."

"I will. Thanks."

He placed the phone in its cradle, sat on the bed and removed his clothing down to his boxer shorts. When he laid back down on the bed, he tied the bag to his forehead so that the ice pressed against the spot over his left eye. His head was pounding and even when he closed his eyes he continued to see small white sparks of light. Thirty minutes later, the pounding had begun to subside. The last thing he saw before falling asleep once again was the clock on his bedstand reading five-thirty and, just beside it, the stack of student papers, waiting to be graded. Later, he began to dream of blurred, shadowy men walking toward him, their figures growing larger and larger until their blackness overwhelmed him.

"We didn't go in, yet" said the SWAT commander. "Figured you wanted to be here since we got no reply."

"I have the key," said Mr. Astor, looking fearfully at the man with the battering ram. The commander nodded. The landlord inserted the key, unlocked Sherry Carter's door and stood back. The man with the shotgun entered the room, swiveling the weapon in all directions. The room, indeed, appeared to be uninhabited for the moment, as they had surmised.

"Room clear," he said.

Light in the room was dim, almost dark. Someone turned on the overhead light and the detectives entered the room.

It was a typical student's room, clothing hanging on the chairs and strewn over the bed. A desk, doubling as a study area and a place to store a DVD player, sat off in a corner. A phone sat on the desk alongside a calendar and Lanslow wondered why he had been unable to find Sherry's number in the phone book. A small microwave oven sat in an alcove off to the other side. Two paper plates of partially eaten pizza sat on the table beside the microwave. Sherry Carter had company recently.

Curiously enough, however, there were no additional signs of another person living there, certainly not a male. All the clothing in the closet was for a woman. There was not a single item of male clothing. The unmade bed gave no telltale signs. The small study desk yielded no clues as to the presence of another. Several doors down the hall a door opened and a young girl stuck her head out. She looked up and down the hall at the men stationed there and at the group at Sherry Carter's door. She spied Astor. "Hey! What going on?" she asked.

"It's okay, Maddie," said Astor. "The police just want to talk to Miss Carter."

"Sherry's not in. She's probably in class," said the girl, eyeing the detectives and SWAT members suspiciously.

"Oh, Miss?" said Brooks, suddenly, catching the eyes of Manfredy and Morgan. The men nodded an unspoken assent.

"Yes?" said Maddie.

Brooks walked down the hall toward the girl. "Could I talk to you for a moment?"

The girl looked Brooks over, then looked at the other men down the hall behind him. Lanslow had remained in Sherry's room. Brooks took out his badge and showed it to her.

"You're real cops?" she asked.

"Yes, ma'am. We're here to ask Sherry Carter some questions. Maybe you can help us?"

A male voice from inside the room said, "What is it Maddie? Who's there?"

"It's okay, Jim. It's some policemen, looking for Sherry."

Jim stuck his head out behind Maddie's. His eyes widened at the number of men in the hall. "What's Sherry done?" he asked.

"Just some routine questioning," said Brooks.

"Doesn't look all that routine to me," said Jim.

"Do either of you know if Sherry Carter has a roommate?" asked Brooks.

The girl shook her head. "No, Sherry has the room by herself, as far as I know."

"Has she had any visitors lately? A black man? Goes by the name of Andrew White."

"We have lots of black guys here," said Maddie. "None by that name, though."

"This guy wouldn't be a student, ma'am," said Brooks. "He would just be visiting for a while."

"Sorry, I don't know Sherry that well. But I haven't seen anyone."

"Me neither," said Jim.

Lanslow, still in Sherry Carter's room, was beginning to doubt they had found Andrew White's hiding place when Sherry's phone rang.

Lanslow hesitated, looking questioningly at Morgan, who was standing just outside the door. Morgan nodded toward the phone. Lanslow let the phone ring again before he picked it up gingerly with his latex-gloved hand.

"That you, Lanslow?" the familiar voice of Andrew White asked.

Somehow, Lanslow wasn't surprised. "It's me, White. You're a pretty lucky fellow."

"Luck ain't got nothing to do with it, Lanslow. You ain't never goin' to get me, man, if I don't want you to. And you fuckers ain't goin' to find anything in that room, you take my word for it."

"Okay, White. Why are we talking here? You ready to come in?" Lanslow looked at the other detectives, holding his hand over the phone's speaker, softly mouthing "White, White, it's White," but the other men only looked at him dumbly.

Andrew laughed. "Shit no, man. I got no chance with a bunch of fucking white cops. I know it and you know it. Hey, Lanslow, I got somethin' for you; I just saw the little white guy again."

For the second time since Zeke Mallard had been murdered, Lanslow couldn't believe what he was hearing. "Where'd you see him, White?"

"Over on the west campus. And guess what, Lanslow? You got another dead guy on your hands."

20

Lanslow dropped the phone back in its cradle. He looked at the other men. "That was White," he said. "We've got another murder."

"What the hell do you mean?" said Manfredy. "That was the guy we're looking for? Here?"

Lanslow nodded. "White says he found a body. Over past the west campus."

"Another body? What the hell is going on here?" exclaimed Manfredy. "How did White know we were here?"

"He must have seen us. Called from somewhere around here."

"For Christ sake!" said Manfredy, looking at Morgan. The detective was suddenly galvanized. "I'll have our guys canvass this area for the suspect," he said, pulling out his cell phone.

"Right," said Morgan. "And this room is a crime scene. We need to get CSI over here ASAP." He barked more orders into a cell phone.

Manfredy turned to the White Bear Lake detectives. "Now, where is this body?"

"White said it's on South Sixth Street, up the street from the Riverside Islamic Center," replied Lanslow. "That's all he said."

"All right. We'll get some squads over there to check it out. We'll take the lead," he said. "You can follow. I'll report to dispatch."

As they jumped in the car, Brooks, his face incredulous, said, "You sure that was White? He called you while you were in Carter's room?"

"You got it. He says he saw the guy who killed Zeke again, and he says he's killed someone else."

"Damn! How'd he know we were here?"

"Didn't say. He must have seen us. Manfredy has his people looking."

"Bullshit! I can't believe it. Maybe he's just pulling one on us," said Brooks.

"I don't think so, Dean. Just hit it." Manfredy's and Morgan's squad car was pulling away.

∎.

A Minneapolis police squad was already at the scene when Brooks and Lanslow arrived, following Manfredy and Morgan. A uniformed officer stood at the head of the stairwell. Brooks shut the blue light off and he and Lanslow followed Manfredy and Morgan to the officer, showing their badges. The officer's name plate read "Grossman."

"You found it," said Manfredy.

"We saw the door open here, figured this was it," said Grossman.

"Lou, this is Detective Lanslow and Sergeant Detective Brooks, from the White Bear Lake police department," said Manfredy.

Grossman nodded to the detectives.

"What've we got?" said Morgan.

"One body, stabbed in the neck and legs. Definitely a homicide, Detective. Harvey's inside."

"Okay, Lou," said Manfredy. "You've called the ME?"

Lou nodded. "They're on their way, Lieutenant."

"String that tape out pretty far; we don't want anyone too close, including the press. They'll be on us anytime." Manfredy motioned toward a crowd of people forming beyond the perimeter, many of them females dressed in black, wearing the traditional Muslim chador. "Keep them back. I'll send Harvey back out here and he can begin getting some statements, if there are any."

"Don't think we have any witnesses, Lieutenant. I've checked," said Grossman.

"Well, Harvey can check again," Manfredy said. Nodding toward Lanslow and Brooks, he said, "I'll allow these men in, seeing as how there may be a connection to a murder they're working on. I'll see that they're logged in."

Grossman nodded. Manfredy turned to Lanslow and Brooks, as he walked down the stairwell. "We'll be sharing our evidence with you here later. I've read about your case and I was at Officer Mallard's funeral. But you can fill me in a little more on the walk through." Morgan followed behind.

"What do you think?" asked Brooks, as he got into the car and slid behind the wheel of the Crown Victoria.

"Same guy," said Lanslow. "Almost the same MO, except for the throat. I'll send the ME's reports on Zeke to Hennepin County to verify it, but I'm certain it's the same guy."

"Seems incredible that White would run into this guy again, don't you think?"

"Yes, incredible," said Lanslow. Both men sat staring out the car window as the man's body was hauled out and placed in the ambulance. It was fully dark now and a slow, cold rain had begun to fall.

"Maybe a little too incredible," said Brooks.

"Maybe," said Lanslow. He was still sifting through the day's events.

"You think this White is a whacko? Maybe he's playing around with us."

"Maybe ... but I doubt it. As weird as it seems, I think he actually ran into the guy again."

"I dunno," said Brooks, as he twisted the key in the ignition and turned on the windshield wipers. "Just too damned weird."

The wipers slapped back and forth softly, and Lanslow felt the fatigue returning as the adrenalin waned. From some papers they'd found in a drawer, they had determined that the dead man's name was Barrows. Now who the hell was this Barrows, he wondered. What did Barrows's and Mallard's murders have in common other than the fact that apparently the same person had murdered them both? "Did you see those wounds?" he said to Brooks. "Same as Zeke's."

"Yeah. It's the same guy, no doubt," said Brooks, watching the ambulance pull away.

"So what the hell is the motive? This guy is one angry son of a bitch. What's the connection between Zeke and Barrows?"

"Hell if I know," said Brooks. "I still can't help but believe White has something to do with this. Like I said, he may be jerking our chain, getting a kick out of it."

Again, Lanslow grudgingly considered the possibility that White actually was the murderer. The circumstantial evidence was overwhelming. But as much as this was true, he still couldn't buy it. It just didn't fit. Their only hope now, he thought, was that some new lead might turn up from the forensic evidence, if there was any.

∎

Andrew White had fought the impulse to be around where he could watch the police at the crime scene. After the call to Lanslow, he had boarded a bus and headed back to St. Paul. He'd been lucky this day and he didn't want to push it. Had he been spotted, he would've had little chance of getting away on foot, given all the cops around.

"Fuck!" he said under his breath, as he rode across Interstate 94, the main link between Minneapolis and St. Paul. His life had been going pretty good until that mother fucker cop had shown up. How the hell had they found him? They were getting too close. Things weren't looking good for his future.

In a funk, Andrew rested his head on the cold glass of the bus window and watched the buildings go by through the drizzle. He was cold, in Sherry's light jacket. He pulled the pair of gloves from his pocket and put them on, jammed his hands in his pockets, settled deeper inside the jacket and leaned his head once again on the glass. He had to think.

His situation was bad and getting worse. It was for sure he couldn't see Sherry again, at least not for a while. He had no place to stay. He had only the clothes he was wearing. Most of his money and his stash had been left in his room at his mother's house when he had fled. He feared going there and trying to retrieve his things. And he couldn't risk calling her. What the hell was he to do?

Andrew's thoughts turned to the little man whose life had become so intertwined with his own. His only hope was that the cops would find the little killer. But Andrew doubted those stupid cops would ever catch that little mother fucker. In a way he admired the guy. Anyone who could run circles around the damned cops deserved his admiration. But until the cops were able to catch the little man, Andrew's life was for crap.

The more he thought about it the more he became convinced his life in the Twin Cities was for crap anyway. At least for now. He'd lost Angelena. The cops wanted him. They wanted him even if they knew he hadn't killed Mallard. Just on principle. You didn't shoot at a cop and get away with it.

It was raining a little harder now, as he got off the bus, a steady, heavy drizzle. He went into a cafe at the corner of the street. He found a booth and ordered a cup of coffee, cradling the warm cup in his hands, and brooded. He thought about Angelena Rosario. She was the one girl he'd felt deeply about. Then that damned cop had showed up. And she'd ratted on him. She wouldn't be of any help.

On impulse, White rose and went to the pay phone in the corner of the restaurant. He pulled the few remaining coins he had from his pocket. He dialed Sherry Carter's number. To his surprise Sherry answered the phone.

"Hey, baby, you're there. It's me."

"My God, Andrew," exclaimed Sherry, "What have you done? The police are looking for you. They were here."

"Anyone there now?"

"No, no one. They say you murdered someone, Andrew. They said you killed someone."

"Okay, okay, baby. Just calm down. You know I couldn't do that. I ain't no killer."

"Why would they say that, Andrew? There were a lot of them. They tore up my room. They think you killed a policeman!"

"No way, Sherry. I didn't do it. I saw the guy who did it, though, and they're trying to pin it on me."

"You saw him? The murderer?" Sherry said, obviously aghast. "Why were you even there?"

"It's a long story, baby, but listen, I need your help."

"Andrew, I can't help you. You must not involve me in this. I'm frightened, Andrew. You must not contact me again. I'm leaving, tomorrow. I can't stay here. I'm afraid. Good-bye, Andrew."

The phone clicked dead. Andrew swore. He dialed Sherry's number again, but she didn't answer. He slammed the phone into the cradle.

In an unmarked police van parked just down the street from Sherry's building, every word of their conversation had been recorded. But the duration had been too short, and the police had failed to trace the call.

Andrew knew the cops had probably tapped Sherry's phone. They couldn't catch him. Still, he knew he was pushing his luck.He sipped his coffee and looked out the window of the restaurant, at the people and cars, hurrying to wherever they were going. Normal people. With normal lives. Sometimes he wondered what that would be like. The rain had turned to snow.

He decided there was only one thing to do.

Later that night, Andrew stole a car and headed south on I-35. The car wouldn't be missed in all probability until tomorrow. He would drive all night to East St. Louis, Illinois. He had an old girlfriend there. Maybe she hadn't hooked up with anyone else, or maybe she had, but she'd help him out for a while. He'd bum some money, maybe, till he could get on his feet again.

21

Matthews didn't wake until Friday morning. The clock read 5:00 A.M. He lay on his back, arms folded behind his head, staring into the darkness of his bedroom, trying to recount the events of Thursday. The headache had been a bad one. He tried to remember the last time he'd looked at the clock. He thought it had been around five-thirty yesterday. Yes, that was the last time. He had slept most of the day and all night. This was nothing new. He had done it before, sometimes even for two or three days and had missed his classes. His dean never took it well at the college, of course, but it couldn't be helped.

He remembered that Luke had returned. He lay in bed, listening. Nothing.

He began to think about Luke and his situation. They still had to settle the question of Annie. He groaned. He swung his legs over the side of the bed, sitting there for a moment, feeling the cooler air on his legs. The stack of student papers still sat on the table.

Matthews rose and walked to Luke's bedroom. He peered in the open door. The bed was empty, unmade, clothes hanging helter-skelter here and there. He shook his head reprovingly. One thing his stint in the military had taught him was neatness. It had become a near obsession. Even after all these years he still hung his clothes with the collars of his shirts buttoned, the hangers evenly spaced across the bar, the trousers folded across the hangers all the same. Everything had its place and was promptly put there when he finished using it.

A pity Luke hadn't had the benefit of military training, thought Matthews. After Luke had come to stay with him, he had suggested to his son that he should join the military after college.

"Why?" Luke had asked.

"It will be part of your career progression and, besides, it'll make a man of you," Matthews had said. He didn't add that it would teach him neatness, too.

At the suggestion, though, Luke had looked like he'd been mortally wounded, and only then did Matthews realize he'd said something he shouldn't have.

"They'll make me cut my hair," Luke had said, and had just walked away.

Matthews rubbed his eyes free of sleep. He had immediately regretted saying it. Luke had always been sensitive about his physical stature. And Matthews knew Luke had taken his comment as a put-down, though he hadn't meant it to be that at all. The look Luke had given him!

Matthews frowned at the mess in Luke's room. Luke would never straighten it, he knew. Maybe he would come back to Luke's room later and tidy things up a little. Right now, he had to have some breakfast, then he would have to grade papers.

Matthews took out a skillet from one of the cupboards, poured a small quantity of oil in it, cracked an egg and let the egg slide in. He turned on the burner. He dropped two slices of wheat bread into the toaster.

Returning to his bedroom, he picked up the stack of student papers. He heard the toast pop up and hurried back to the kitchen. He set the stack of papers down on the kitchen table, flipped the egg over, then buttered the toast. In a few moments, he sat down with his egg sandwich, orange juice, and a cup of instant coffee. He opened the first student paper and began to read.

By the time he was through grading the papers, it was 7:30 A.M. He rose from the table, glancing out the kitchen window. The gray of the early morning had turned into a pinkish rose that promised a brighter day, but in Minnesota such promises were easily unkept. The yard and driveway were still wet, and the leaves, piled in the low places from the wind, were frosted lightly with new snow here and there. He had to take the leaves up soon or it would be too late. "Too little time," he said to himself.

He stuffed the papers in his briefcase. He would have to get to his office early enough to enter the grades into the digital grade sheet on his computer. He checked his watch once again. Just enough time to shower, dress, and perhaps straighten Luke's room.

At eight o'clock, Matthews stepped into his son's room and began to make the bed. He pulled back the curtains to the windows and the light flooded in. He picked up some Playboy magazines and stacked them on Luke's desk. Books were scattered on the floor at the base of the book-case and he picked those up, too, and reshelved them. He picked up two pairs of Luke's sneakers and opened the closet door to place them there. As he dropped the shoes to the floor, he spied a small brown package placed far back in the corner of the closet. Curious, he bent and picked it up. He removed the rubber band. Inside the brown paper sack was a wallet with a checkbook and a number of plastic cards. He read the names. They were all of a girl, named Glenda Morrison. The last card was a University of Minnesota ID card. The picture of a young woman, in her late teens or early twenties, smiled back at him. A dark-haired girl, pretty.

Matthews was puzzled. Why would Luke have a girl's wallet with her checkbook, credit card and ID? Unless things had changed even more drastically than even he had imagined, young people didn't usually share their credit cards, much less their ID or wallet. Still, Matthews thought, he was a middle-aged man and there was a generation gap. What did he know?

He rewrapped the rubber band around the package and placed it back where he had found it. It was eight-twenty. He would have to hurry to get the grades recorded before his nine o-clock class. He made a mental note to query Luke about the wallet. The image of the package with the wallet inside, the credit card, and a packet of checks, bothered him. Who was this Glenda Morrison and what had happened to Joan, Luke's present girlfriend?

As he exited his driveway, Matthews noted that the morning newspaper had not been delivered. He had no time to read it now, anyway. He'd have to clear up the problem when he got home that evening—something else to do, so little time to get it all done.

■

In the afternoon, Friday, the records clerk brought a sheaf of faxes to Lanslow's desk. Brooks had left his own desk to talk to Lieutenant Johnson. The faxes were the reports from the Minneapolis police.

The dead man's name was reported as Henry Barrows, a fact they had already determined on their walk-through with Detectives Manfredy and Morgan. A quick background check had shown that Barrows was divorced. His former wife was a Mrs. Geneveve Cartwright, deceased. No children of the couple was reported. Barrows had held no official job or position for the last seventeen years. He apparently lived on his Social Security check from month to month. There was no record of where Barrows had lived before he came to the Twin Cities area, at least as of yet. He had no police record. He had no current driver's license.

Lanslow leaned back in his chair. The information was meager, at best. Nothing in that information connected Barrows to Mallard nor pointed to anything further as to who killed him or why. The complete autopsy and forensic reports would be coming in later and Minneapolis would continue their investigation of Barrows, but Lanslow didn't expect them to turn up much. Like Zeke's murder, this one also appeared on the surface to be random, except that Lanslow knew it wasn't.

Lanslow dug deeper into the faxes. He examined the photos of Barrows's body over and over.

"Those from Minneapolis?" asked Brooks.

Lanslow jumped. "For Christ sake, Brooks! Don't do that."

"Sorry," Brooks said, picking up the faxes Lanslow had set aside. He flopped into his chair, the faxes in hand. He pushed a layer of papers away, clearing a spot on the desk, and laid the faxes down.

"Anything?" he said.

"Nothing," said Lanslow. "Barrows is another dead end—no pun intended. The man didn't have a job, he doesn't have a prior, he doesn't drive, and he lived on Social Security and cheap wine in that rat hole where he was murdered."

"Says here he was divorced from a woman named ... Jergens. What about her? Anything on her?"

"She's dead," said Lanslow. "I didn't notice the date. Her maiden name was Cartwright. She remarried after her divorce from Barrows."

"Ummm ... says here ... hey, early this month. She's not been dead that long."

"So?"

"How did she die?"

"I don't think the cause of death is in the report."

Brooks searched the report again. "Yeah, you're right. Well, that's interesting."

"Yeah, why is that?" asked Lanslow.

"Just thinking that maybe she might have been murdered by Barrows, and someone, maybe our perp, murdered him in revenge."

Lanslow looked at Brooks quizzically. "Man, you're stretching, now. You mean someone like Mrs. Jergen's husband?"

"Possibly. What about him? Is he still alive?"

"He's still alive. Minneapolis contacted him when they learned she'd been Barrow's former wife. His name is Carl Jergens. He's confined to a wheelchair, in Somerset, Wisconsin."

"Uh huh," said Brooks, sheepishly, astonished at Lanslow's recall of the details of the case. "They have any children?"

"Two, a son and daughter. The daughter lives in Somerset with her husband. The son lives in California." Lanslow was still trying to figure out why Brooks was continuing to pursue what appeared to be an obvious dead end. "Why are you pushing this, Dean?"

"I'm getting a little desperate, just a shot in the dark—obviously," said Brooks, with some chagrin. "I think out loud a lot. Always gets me in trouble."

"Yeah, you told me," Lanslow said, with a smile. "Doesn't hurt, though. Someone killed Barrows for some reason, the same guy who killed Zeke. But it wasn't Carl Jergens or his kids. And I doubt highly that Barrows had anything to do with Mrs. Jergens's death."

"Well, I suppose I'd better read these reports, you think?"

"Absolutely," said Lanslow.

Brooks gave Lanslow a quick searching stare, looking for some hint of slight. Seeing none, he grinned. For the first time since his partner's death, Lanslow grinned back.

"Hey, partner. We're gonna get this guy," said Brooks, giving the thumbs up sign. Lanslow smiled and nodded. Brooks began reading the reports and Lanslow continued reading the remaining ones, waiting for Brooks to start thinking out loud.

"The ME's preliminary report says the weapon that killed Barrows is consistent with the type of weapon that killed Zeke," said Lanslow, beating Brooks to the punch. He had faxed the Ramsey County medical examiner's reports about Zeke Mallard's murder to the Hennepin County medical examiner late Thursday. The report merely confirmed what they'd already learned at the scene. Lanslow scanned the photos of the body again. The two murders weren't exactly alike but were similar enough. Again, a crime of horrendous anger and rage. "This is our guy. But for the life of me I can't figure out the connection."

"I'm telling you, our best suspect is Andrew White," said Brooks. "That little bastard is playing with us."

"Maybe," said Lanslow. "If he is, why would he pick such a victim as Barrows—a down-and-out drunkard?"

"Easy to kill?" said Brooks.

"Zeke wasn't easy," said Lanslow.

"That's for damned sure," said Brooks, "but we know White's motive for killing Zeke. Maybe he's just pushing the envelope now."

Lanslow shook his head. "Maybe. I'll be damned if I really know at this point."

Lanslow entered through the rear door to the social and behavioral science department just as Matthews was leaving, on his way home.

"Hi, Rich. I haven't read the papers yet. Any new developments in the case?"

"Several," said Lanslow. "Got a minute?"

"Sure," said Matthews, as Lanslow unlocked the door to his office.

Matthews settled into the guest chair beside Lanslow's desk. "A breakthrough?" he asked.

"No, we've had another murder. Same perp."

"Really? Who was the victim?"

"Can't say till they finish checking out his next of kin. A wino, living over near the university."

"A wino? What's the connection to Zeke's case?"

Lanslow ran through the events of Thursday. When he finished he said, "So, that's it. I can't see any connection except that White discovered the body, and the MO is almost exactly the same."

"Multiple stab wounds?"

"Yes."

"To the legs, same as before?"

"Yes."

"You still don't believe White is the perp?" asked Matthews.

"Well, Detective Brooks seems to think so, but I just can't buy it. Unless White is stringing us along, getting his kicks, there's no other reason I can think of that he would be the killer of this last guy; and it's real hard to believe he just happened to run into Zeke's killer again that way—but I've seen stranger things. White called his girlfriend afterward. Minneapolis has him on tape denying the whole thing to her. Not that that counts for much."

"Hmm. The thing that strikes me, as I said before, is the stab wounds to the legs. The stab wounds are acts of strong passion, maybe even vengeance."

"Uh-huh," said Lanslow, momentarily thinking that Matthews was perhaps belaboring the obvious. From their conversations in the past, however, Lanslow knew that the professor was merely laying some sort of groundwork.

"If White did it," continued Matthews, "he killed Detective Mallard not only out of jealousy, but probably something more. As a black man, especially, he could hate the police, so you may have a combination of jealousy as well as hate. But the wino? Why the stab wounds to him? Simply because he's white? It's possible, but I don't think so. And, then, why would he call the police and alert them to this man's murder? Has his possible hatred of the police led him to a vendetta, a game of cat and mouse?"

"Sounds possible to me," said Lanslow, "but too farfetched. I don't buy it."

"And neither do I," said the professor. "Racially motivated killings are almost totally by whites against blacks, selected somewhat randomly. And in either case, white or black, they are usually performed with guns, from a distance, not with knives, close-up, in the victim's home. And I don't know of any cases of such racially motivated killings being connected to a game of cat and mouse with the police. Cat and mouse types of crimes are usually carried out by psychotics for psychotic reasons. They take pleasure in eluding the police and proving their superiority. Any reason to believe White is psychotic?"

"St. Paul did a background check on White and there was nothing to suggest he is."

Matthews sat for a moment in thought.

"You're thinking that White didn't do it now, for sure," said Lanslow, anticipating Matthews's conclusion.

"I would say he probably didn't. White's connection to Detective Mallard's case was not accidental. He had a reason to be there. But his connection to the second case probably is—purely accidental, as improbable as it may seem. How unusual!"

"Well," said Lanslow, "I appreciate your ideas but, as I said, I've already figured myself that White didn't do it, even if Brooks believes he did. Anything else?"

"I'd say the only connection between the two murders is that they were done by the same person, and that's it. And whoever the murderer is, he did it because he was angry, vengeful. The type of anger and vengeance manifested in both cases are products of an injury or an affront to the individual. Both your victims may have simply slighted this guy in some way so as to threaten his concept of self, or his ego—in popular parlance. It didn't even have to be a physical threat, just some gesture he perceived as a put down ... that lowered his self-esteem. For that, he made them pay. It would be a matter of vengeance and retribution."

"Pardon me, Jack, we all get our egos slammed from time to time, but we usually don't commit murder because of it."

"True enough, but as I say, these are crimes of passion, of vengeance—of extreme vengeance, it seems to me. How many times did he stab Zeke Mallard in the leg? Half a dozen? A dozen? This killer is not your everyday, normal Joe ... not that any killer is 'normal,' of course, but you know what I mean. You may be dealing with a paranoid psychotic here, or some other psychosis, which means that these feelings and motives are the product of a lengthy developmental process. The result is that, over time, any perceived offense, no matter how small, is built up out of all proportion. The fact that the two victims don't seem to have any connection to one another leads me to believe they may have just run into this guy, set him off somehow, and he reacted."

Part Two

Winter

22

November is generally the month in which autumn turns definitely to winter in Minnesota. By December, temperatures fall more or less regularly into the twenties and low thirties during the day, into the teens at night, and a thin layer of ice has formed on the lakes. There is snow on the ground and on the bare limbs of the trees. Winter brings with it a black, gray and white motif.

The White Bear police department had settled back into normal routines. Though it remained open, Zeke Mallard's murder case was beginning to slide into the background. Lanslow was finding it difficult to spend time on the case. To make matters worse, budget cuts had been imposed by the city and the chief was forced to order a reduction in overtime for both him and Brooks. He continued to fret and chafe at his inability to find the murderer of his former partner. Lanslow found himself working the case frequently on his own time. And this, as usual, wasn't sitting well with Laura.

"Why do you have to go down now, Richard?" she asked, as he slipped on his coat. "You know we need to get our Christmas shopping started, and the weekend is about the only time I have to do it." She was talking to him as she placed the breakfast dishes into the dishwasher.

"Laura, you know I have to do this."

"This thing is driving you—and me— crazy, Richard. I'm beginning to think you're having an affair, or something."

"Laura, as soon as this is over ... ."

"Oh, blast! I've heard that before. I'm getting tired of being here alone all the time, never knowing where you are, or when you'll get back."

Lanslow stared at his bride-to-be and wondered if their pretest was failing. He shrugged. "Listen, hon, I promise—I'll be back early and we'll go shopping. We can have dinner out, and then shop some more if we have to."

This appeared to mollify Laura somewhat, and her frown softened. She walked around the counter that separated their kitchen from the living room. "You're sure? You've promised before ..."

"I'll be back by one, hon." He gave her a hug, looked into her face, kissed her.

She leaned back, studied his face for a moment. "Okay. You're a rascal, though. You'd better come home."

Lanslow smiled and kissed her again. "I'll be here," he said. "You just be ready, okay?"

"Ha! I'll keep my end of the bargain if you'll keep yours."

As he entered the elevator and descended to the basement garage, Lanslow was already dreading the crowds and lamenting the time he'd lose in pursuing a cop killer. But he had made a promise, and he knew that if he wanted to marry this girl he'd best keep it.

❚

Lanslow dumped a now overly full binder on his desk once again, for what seemed to him the thousandth time. This was his own copy of Zeke Mallards's case file, which he kept on a shelf on the wall beside his desk so that he could take it down when he had a few minutes. Wearily, he thumbed through the records until he found the list of all of Zeke Mallard's prior collars that Brooks had compiled earlier. He pulled out the large thick envelope that contained reports on each of the individuals they had interviewed. He began to look over each of them one more time, subconsciously resigned to not finding anything new. But he didn't know what else to do.

By the time he had gotten through the fifth report, he realized he hadn't been paying attention to what he was reading. As usual, his mind had wandered. It was of no use to go through them again. Each individual had been thoroughly tracked and only two on the entire list even remotely offered such a possibility. Lanslow had interviewed each of these men himself and had come away convinced they had nothing to do with it. As far as the rest of the file was concerned, he'd been through it so many times he practically had it memorized. There was nothing there.

Lanslow leaned back in his chair, folding his hands behind his head. Try as he might to think of new possibilities, he kept returning to a conclusion he'd drawn from his last conversation with Jack Matthews. The professor's insistence that Zeke's and the wino's murders were done purely out of passion or vengeance, and that the connection between the two might be purely coincidental, had begun some time ago to be the only thing that made any sense. Matthews's reasoning, if correct, meant that they would have to search for someone in Zeke's background who might have felt resentment and anger toward him, someone he had somehow "slighted," as Matthews had put it. That thought had given him a sense of helplessness. It was like trying to replay Zeke Mallard's entire life to find anyone and everyone he might have affronted or offended. He'd done his best. He knew more about Zeke's life, probably, than Christine. Nothing in particular had shown up, however.

He pushed the binder away from him, placed his elbows on his desk and massaged his temples. Closing his eyes, he tried a different tack, going over the events of the past couple of months, putting them in chronological order without looking at the timeline he and Brooks had already constructed. He wanted to break out of the routine. He wanted something to just pop up in his memory. He'd found this technique useful sometimes in revealing an angle he hadn't thought of, or in making him rethink a particular angle through again. At the very least it tended to impose some order to thoughts that otherwise zipped randomly in and out of his consciousness.

Lanslow sat back in his chair and propped his feet on the desk, folded his arms behind his head and stared out the window. A shaft of sunlight streamed golden through the window. The snow was melting now, dripping from the tree limbs and the roofs of the buildings. It was supposed to snow again during the night, though. The department was unusually quiet, even for a Sunday. He watched the water drip steadily from a small icicle that was still clinging to a downspout. He just sat there and watched it drip, one drop after another.

In an almost hypnotic state, Lanslow's shock of brown hair, neglected for the moment, crept down over the side of his forehead. His narrow mouth and blue eyes bespoke his English-German background. The mouth, usually set in a self-confident quarter-smile, had now lost some of this appearance. He simply stared, straight-faced, at the dripping water. He kept staring for nearly five minutes.

Unbidden, from somewhere deep in his unconscious, the image of the broken wine bottle near Zeke's body emerged, and then, the image of another broken wine bottle at the scene of Henry Barrows's murder; and then he began to think about the wino, Henry Barrows. Because the case had fallen under the Minneapolis PD's jurisdiction, he hadn't gone through those files as thoroughly. Maybe he would find something there, anything that might give the investigation a new boost. He dropped his legs to the floor and pulled the manila folder containing the files from the file cabinet drawer and once again began to go through the Minneapolis police department's reports on the murder of Henry Barrows. He pulled the officer's follow-up report of Barrows's background check once again, skipping over parts of it, reading fast:

Unemployed at time of death ... Divorced ... no record of victim ever being remarried ... No children ... Victim lived alone at time of death, no living relatives, no close friends ... lived at his last address since 1997 ... Sold farm to a Dave and Pauline Landon ... retired (no work record since sale) ... various other addresses after sale of farm until his death ... Income source at time of death: Social Security ... No bank accounts ... No record of other financial accounts ... No insurance policies appear to be in existence ... Previous wife, Geneveve (maiden name Cartwright) Jergens, remarried to Carl Jergens ... deceased ... Carl Jergens, confined to a wheelchair ... two living children, Charles Jergens (2014 Palm Lane, Center City, CA) and Rebecca Hodges (3400 Decatur Ave., Somerset, WI) ... stated in interviews that, to their knowledge, Mrs. Jergens hadn't had contact with Barrows since their divorce ... Victim's landlord ... reported victim was seldom delinquent on his rent (which included utilities) and was "no trouble at all." None of the co-residents of bldg. reported knowing him or anything about him. Victim frequented liquor store about two blocks from residence as reported by owner. Victim frequented grocery store, same area. Patrol officers Cunningham, Dixon and others report sighting the victim at various times as he walked to and from his apartment. Victim has no priors of any kind. Victim's Wisconsin driver's license had expired ... license not renewed. Interviews with neighbors in the area revealed nothing out of the ordinary. Telephone interviews with Mr. and Mrs. Dave Landon, Box 4427, Somerset, WI, who purchased victim's farm ... indicated they had not heard anything more from victim since the sale.

Lanslow scratched his head, and rubbed his eyes. His hopefulness waned. Nothing. Absolutely nothing. He read the report again, this time in detail. He tried to put a time-line on Barrows's life. He began to check the dates.

Suddenly it occurred to Lanslow that there was a gap in Barrows's life that had been left unfilled in the reports. What had Barrows done in the time interval between his divorce and the sale of his farm? Had he merely continued, without incident, to work his farm? Why hadn't he remarried? Had he had other jobs as well as farming? Other activities? Had something happened? Did something happen during that time that gave someone, the same person who'd murdered his partner, a reason to kill him, as Dean Brooks had suggested offhandedly some time ago?

Apparently the officer who had done the background check and filled out the report hadn't bothered to find out. This death was that of just another wino, after all. And until now, Lanslow hadn't thought about it either. In all probability, nothing during that time period had happened, at least nothing that would shed any light on the murder of his partner. But, like Brooks, Lanslow was growing desperate.

The detective glanced at his watch. It was nearly eleven-thirty. In his pursuit of this new angle, time had flown. Reluctantly, he put the reports back into the folder and returned them to the file. He would try to find out what had happened to Barrows in those intervening years, but not until Monday. Now, reluctantly or not, he had to go Christmas shopping or risk losing the girl he was sure he loved and wanted to be his wife.

23

By the evening, the warm spell had dissipated and a layer of gray clouds had inserted itself between the sun and most of the state of Minnesota. Temperatures had fallen into the teens. Lanslow had succeeded in fighting the almost overpowering impulse to remain at the station to work more on the Mallard case. Instead, he found himself on the streets of White Bear Lake, struggling with Christmas packages as Laura peered into a storefront window hoping to find the perfect gift for her mother. Sarah would be coming to Minnesota for Christmas. Lanslow suspected Sarah's trip was as much to check on his and Laura's relationship as to celebrate the holidays.

Despite the jostling and pressing of people on all sides, the hubbub of voices and street traffic, the piped-in holiday music issuing from every store, Lanslow couldn't stop thinking about the new possibility he'd worked out that morning.

He followed Laura into a store, struggling with the slipping, sliding packages they'd already purchased.

"What do you think, Richard? Do you think Mother would like it?" Laura held up what looked like a replica of a Greek vase.

"I have no idea, hon," Lanslow said, drolly. "I like it, so Sarah might not."

Laura frowned. "Richard, don't be like that. Help me out here. Christmas will be here in a couple of weeks and we're not going to have our shopping done and packages sent. But you're probably right." She moved to the next window. Lanslow chastised himself for not encouraging her to buy it. He had learned his lesson.

He followed Laura into a clothing store and sank gratefully into a chair. Laura took a leather jacket from the rack that had a sign on top proclaiming that everything was now fifty percent off. She tried it on. Lanslow knew the jacket would cost more than they could afford.

"Mother's gained some weight. We used to wear the same size, but now ..."

Lanslow appraised his fiancé's figure for the ten-thousandth time and still felt the same pleasure he'd felt when they had first met. Laura was not short, but not tall, either. She had a great butt. Auburn hair normally fell about her shoulders, framing her oval face, with its pouting underlip and soft, creamy complexion. This evening she had her hair tied in a ponytail that protruded from a Minnesota Twins baseball cap he had purchased for her shortly after they had met. She was wearing a red ski jacket. She looked quite young, and her usually perky character only added to the perception.

"Sarah's gained weight?" Lanslow asked, in secret delight. "How do you know?"

"I showed you her latest picture, didn't I? She looked heavier."

"I'm sure it would fit," said Lanslow, remembering his lesson, willing to shell out the bucks to ease his aching arms.

"I don't think she'd like the color anyway," said Laura, with pursed lips. She hung the coat back on the rack, to Lanslow's dismay.

They returned to the street. The outside air seemed to be warmer, now. Lanslow had read somewhere that Minnesota had the most variable weather in the world, except for Siberia. Snow had begun to fall, the huge, soft, wet flakes drifting down lazily out of the darkness, coming into view finally under the streetlights. Already, it had coated the parked cars in a downy white. In the street, the snow had turned to slush from the traffic. Laura lifted her face to the night sky, letting the flakes land on her cheeks, turning red now from the colder air, and she laughed, a wonderful laugh, denoting her cheer and ecstasy in all of it. Lanslow's dislike of shopping evaporated at the sight of her.

Down the street, on the corner under the streetlight, the fake Santa Claus, far too made-up, rang his bell and proffered his red bucket to the shoppers. He shook the bell so hard it flew out of his hand and rolled across the sidewalk into the gutter. Laboriously, he managed to bend down, adjusting his false stomach, and pick it up, while cars splashed snow on his red and white cap. Just the smallest of little curses escaped his painted lips before he regained his composure, repositioned himself, and began to ring the bell even harder.

■

Lanslow heard a snowplow go by. He rolled out of bed, trying not to disturb Laura. Pulling the bedroom curtains aside, he saw snow flurries. The overnight fall had deposited several new inches. He was anxious to pursue the new line of inquiry into Zeke Mallard's murder.

When he got to the station at seven-thirty, Lanslow's first act was to call the sheriff of St. Croix County in Wisconsin to see if he could fill in some of the gaps in Barrows's background. The sheriff, George Barton, was in—apparently an early worker as well. He had an authoritative sounding voice, the result, no doubt, of a long tenure and lots of experience, enhanced perhaps by the early hour.

"I gave a lot of this info to Minneapolis already, Detective. What does White Bear Lake want with it?"

"You heard about my partner, Detective Zeke Mallard, Sheriff Barton?"

"Sure. Went to the funeral. You got nothin' yet?"

"We think the guy who killed Zeke also killed Barrows, and I'm just trying to get some new leads. Maybe something in Barrows's background can point to this guy."

"Uh huh. Well, I knew *of* Henry Barrows," he said. "We had a couple of calls over to his place. As I remember, Barrows's neighbor accused him of threatening his boy and shooting his dog. Barrows claimed the dog had killed one of his calves. We investigated it but couldn't verify anything. The calf was dead, and we found the dog shot dead on Barrows's property next to the carcass. Barrows claimed he didn't threaten the boy and Barrows had his property posted, so, bottom line, it was Parson's word against Barrows's and the neighbor was at fault for letting the dog stray. That's all that ever came of it."

"What about this neighbor, any possibilities there?"

"I wouldn't say so. I think Minneapolis questioned the neighbor, too. You don't have the report?"

"The only report I have doesn't mention the incident or the interview." said Lanslow. "What's the neighbor's name?"

"Parsons, I believe it's Dave, Dave Parsons. As I say, nothin' ever came of the incident, and I don't recall anything further after that."

"Anything else you can tell me about Barrows?"

"There was a young woman living with him. I can't remember her name, now. She came after the dog incident, so I never met her. Wait a minute, I'll pull that file. Hang on." Lanslow heard the phone's receiver thump on the desk. A short time later, Barton returned. "Okay, I got the file. I was a deputy at the time and took the call. All that's in here is my report, and what I told you before is about all that's in it. Oh, yeah, the woman's name was Geraldine Matson."

Lanslow scribbled the woman's name in his notebook. "You said there were a couple of calls?"

"Oh, yeah. The woman's son, he got into some trouble. The boy allegedly assaulted a girl sexually. That's in another file. Hang on ... " Lanslow heard the phone thump again as Barton laid it on his desk. He heard voices in the background this time, people arriving to work, perhaps. A short time later Barton picked up the phone.

"Yeah, here it is. His name was John ... John Paul Matson. The boy was accused of molesting a girl at the Oakwood school. The girl's parents filed a complaint. We did some questioning, then referred the case to the county juvenile authorities. I'm not sure of the disposition from then on, though. We have no further record. He was a juvenile, and his record was closed. Oh, there was a younger sister, too. Name of Lee Ann."

Lanslow wrote rapidly in his notebook. "Either one of the kids still around there?"

"Don't think so. Haven't heard anything about them. We can check."

"We can do that, Sheriff. What about the woman ... the Matson woman? She still live around there?"

"Seems to me she died not too long ago."

"We can check that, too. I'd like to come over there and interview the new owners of Barrows's farm, though, and maybe some neighbors. Maybe they can be of further help."

"No problem," said the sheriff. "Come right ahead. Let me know if you need any more help."

"I appreciate that, Sheriff. Thanks."

∎

As Jack Matthews trudged up the cleared sidewalk from the parking lot, he thought about how many times he had done this for the past fourteen-plus years: taken this path to the door of the building, walked the short distance to the elevator that had a sign warning it was for custodial use only, ridden upward to the third floor where he then made his way to the social and behavioral science department, past the secretary's desk, to his corner office.

It was a rhetorical thought. He wasn't interested in the actual number of times he'd made the trip. So much of such detritus composed so much of one's life, after all. It was a given. What was important was that he had ended up here, at this little backwater college, where so many of his dreams had withered.

The elevator door opened and Matthews walked down the hall to the social and behavioral science department. Marjorie, the department secretary, biding her time until she could retire at the end of the year, quickly punched a key on her keyboard, eclipsing the game of solitaire she'd been playing. Matthews had seen it though.

"Good morning, Jack," Marjorie said, with too much enthusiasm, removing a piece of paper showily from the in-box. A huge banana plant sat in the corner of the office, partially shielding Marjorie from the view of passers-by through the hallway window. Matthews believed Marjorie had put it there for that very purpose. On the wall next to it hung a sign-out board, the brainchild of the former chair of the department, which had never been used by any of the faculty as far as Matthews could recall.

"Good morning, Marjorie," said Matthews, walking directly to check his mailbox, as he had done a thousand times before. As always, there were the complimentary textbooks, the notes from students who would not be in class because their grandmothers had died, and the usual administrative injunctions and admonishments.

Standing at the window of his small office, looking over the parking lot, Matthews watched the students wending their way through the snow to class. Some of them were his students, no doubt, unenthusiastically finding their way to the lecture hall where he would reiterate for the ten-thousandth time the meaning of concepts, the subtle differences between the various theories, the importance of the scientific method, etc.

Over and over through the years he had repeated these things to an ever-changing audience, the members of which, he knew, mostly didn't give a damn. The important thing for them was that his introductory course filled a general education requirement, or that it fell at a convenient time in their schedules, or that they didn't want to load up on any really hard courses while they took their math. For this he had forfeited any chance of working in a graduate school with doctoral students and with research-oriented colleagues. And now, any chance of these things had slipped past, in the steady stream of time. Though he had written a book on gangs which had been relatively well received, and was working on another, he knew he was fast approaching an age when, realistically, he couldn't expect to contribute significantly to his discipline.

How had he ended up here? It was the usual case, as it is for most lives: chance events, situations. The decisive event for him, no doubt, had been his divorce from Elizabeth. After the divorce, freed from family responsibilities, he had eventually wound up back in college at the University of Minnesota, on the GI Bill. After receiving his Ph.D., he'd taken a position at Bremer College, temporarily, or so he'd thought. That had been fifteen years ago. For one reason or another, mostly laziness, he had stayed.

The divorce from Elizabeth hadn't been a nasty one, all things considered. There were incidents, of course, in which they had yelled, had tried to hurt each other in more subtle ways, too. Such incidents were infrequent, however. After returning from a year and a half assignment in Japan, during which Luke had been born, things had gone bad between them almost from the start. Less than a year later Elizabeth just announced she was leaving. She took Luke and returned to Wisconsin, to live with her parents.

Why had the marriage failed? Elizabeth had complained about his mood changes, even before they were married, and was adamantly against him making the Air Force a career. She harped about his near fetish for neatness, his bouts with depression, and what she called his "lack of drive." The memories brought back the pain.

He was too young then to know, as he did now, that the breakup of his marriage had probably hurt Luke, not quite two years old at the time, just as much or more than it had hurt either him or Elizabeth. The divorce probably explained much of the string of troubles Luke had later gone through, some involving the police. And now, Annie, Luke's half sister, was showing symptoms of her own traumas. He knew he would, of course, consent to Annie's moving in with them, but he worried about how to deal with her and how her presence might affect his and Maureen's relationship. That relationship was the most valuable thing he had, now.

When Elizabeth moved back to Wisconsin after the divorce and he matriculated at the University of Minnesota, the distance between them had effectively eliminated Matthews's ability to help Luke. When she remarried and moved even further away, he only heard about Luke's troubles by letter or phone. He and Luke were together once again, though, and that was a first step. He could only hope, as he did fervently, that they could someday overcome their early separation.

But, now, he was worried about Luke.

"I don't know where it came from," Luke had said when Matthews had inquired about the wallet and credit card he'd found in the closet. "I've never seen it before, and, anyway, what were you doing in my closet?"

Luke's puzzlement had seemed genuine. There was no other explanation, however. The wallet couldn't have gotten there by itself.

The thought occurred to Matthews that maybe Luke had merely found the wallet and hadn't returned it. Though he hadn't said so, Luke had read his thought.

"Come on, Dad. I have no idea how that wallet got there. I don't know the girl. Never heard of her."

My son doth protest too much, Matthews had thought. "Luke, you know if you need money, you only have to ask me," he said. Luke had looked at him curiously and then it apparently had dawned on Luke what his father was suggesting.

"You think I stole it? You think I would do that?"

"Luke, I'm just saying, if you need the money, or anything else, I'm here for you. This is serious business."

Luke had handed him the wallet with a disgusted look and simply left, with no further explanation.

Matthews placed the wallet in his desk drawer in the study. He would decide what to do with it later. It was still there, in the drawer, nearly two months since he'd found it. He didn't want to involve the police, given Luke's prior troubles, and he kept putting off trying to call or locate the woman whose name was on the cards. He feared that when he did so, it might be another turning point in his and Luke's relationship.

∎

It was nearing eight o'clock when Lanslow received the call from Brooks.

"Alma's come down with something," Brooks said over the phone. "I'm gonna take her in to the doctor. I'll be in a little later."

Lanslow said he understood, hoped it wasn't serious, then hung up the phone and shrugged. It was just as well. He was anxious to get to Wisconsin. He quickly thumbed through the remaining pile of mail and other assorted messages and paperwork on his desk to check for anything demanding his immediate attention. There was a note that he'd received a call from Professor Jack Matthews, but when he tried to reach him he got a voice mail message. It took him nearly an hour to clear his desk and return other phone calls.

The drive to Somerset from White Bear Lake took the detective east on State Highway 96, through suburban country, dotted with mostly middle-class homes set back from the road, partially hidden in Scottish pine, oak, maple, aspen and birch trees, somewhat visible now only because the deciduous trees had lost most of their leaves. He passed the Dellwood Country Club with its tennis courts and posh championship golf course, and proceeded to State Highway 35 which ran south through Stillwater. A sign at the city limits boasted of Stillwater being the birthplace of Minnesota.

In downtown Stillwater the Christmas shopping crowd was thin at this early hour. The streetlights were decorated with red, blue and green lights. Blue spruce wreaths with bows of red ribbon hung from each lightpost on Main Street. Stillwater was known especially for its antique and gift shops and other unusual stores. Lanslow made a mental note to suggest he and Laura return to Stillwater to complete their unfinished Christmas shopping here, later during the week, with maybe dinner at the Cattle Baron Hotel. That might make the shopping a little more tolerable and help inch him back into Laura's good graces.

He turned eastward again to cross the old drawbridge over the St. Croix River into Wisconsin. The rest of the trip to Somerset took about twenty minutes. Driving past the River's Edge Restaurant, he remembered the time he and Laura and Zeke and Christine had spent a lazy afternoon tubing down the Apple River, with dinner afterwards at the restaurant. His earlier sense of loss at Zeke's death returned, and he worried that the lead he was now following was simply a waste of time.

Lanslow had verified with Sheriff Barton the last name and phone number of the people who now owned the Barrows's farmstead. He had called the Landons, gotten directions, and set up a time to visit. It was almost ten o'clock when he pulled onto the snowy dirt road that would supposedly take him to the Landon's farmhouse. He passed a yellow warning sign with the image of a leaping deer. Someone had painted a red nose on the deer.

He spotted the Landon's name on a mailbox and pulled into the drive leading to a two-story house—a wood-frame structure, with an off-white stucco exterior, fronted by a wooden deck that wrapped partially around the northeast corner. The main door of the house was on the north side facing the road, but curiously there were no steps by which to gain access, nor was there any pathway leading to it from the driveway. This entrance-way seemed to have been abandoned. One had to climb the stairs to the deck to enter the house via what appeared to be a back door.

Lanslow knocked on the door, turning to survey the farm's layout as he waited for an answer. A long row of large, round bales of hay partially screened a barn to the south. Several white-faced Hereford cows leaned heavily against the railing that protected the hay, their necks stretched as far as they could, attempting to pick up a stray morsel or two. They had already trampeled the snow to a black mush.

The door opened and the detective was greeted cordially by a medium-height, heavyset man in his early to middle fifties.

"Good morning, Sir," said the man.

"Good morning. Mr. Landon? I'm Detective Lanslow. I called earlier?" Lanslow showed the farmer his badge and extended his hand.

"Yes, yes, come on in," said Landon. "We can talk at the table."

The door from the deck led directly into the Landon's kitchen, through a small vestibule that served as a "mud room." Two pairs of black rubber galoshes sat just inside the door, and coats, scarves and caps were hung on wooden pegs fastened to the wall. A shelf just above the pegs held more caps and gloves. The room smelled of wet, musty clothing and just a tinge of manure, but Lanslow got a whiff of fresh-brewed coffee coming from the kitchen, too.

"Let me take your coat," said Landon, and Lanslow removed it and handed it to the farmer. Landon hung the coat over another coat on a peg. "In here," he said, and motioned toward the other room.

When they were in the kitchen, Dave Landon motioned toward his wife. Mrs. Landon, wearing an apron, was a small, wiry woman, with tightly curled hair, rimless glasses and a warm smile. She wiped her hands on the apron and shook hands with Lanslow.

"This is my wife, Pauline," said Landon. Dave Landon's grip had been like a vise, and Pauline's was firm. Both grips the result of hard farm labor, Lanslow thought.

He was offered a seat at the kitchen table. Dave Landon sat down across from him and Mrs. Landon served them hot, steaming cups of coffee. The farmer dumped one spoon of sugar into his coffee cup and poured a generous amount of cream into it as well. Lanslow drank his black. Mrs. Landon went back to the sink where she had been drying dishes.

"Well, sir," began Landon, "you said this had something to do with the former owner, Henry Barrows?"

"That's right, Mr. Landon," said Lanslow, taking out his notebook. "We're trying to put some more background material together on Henry Barrows to help us get a bigger picture. Anything you can tell me would be helpful."

"What has Barrows done?"

"You haven't heard about Barrows's death? He was murdered a couple of months ago."

"You don't say? Well, that's too bad. I never knew Barrows that well, you understand, other than what little I got to know about him when we bought the farm," said Landon.

"Anything you can remember might be of some help."

"Well, what do you want to know about Barrows, exactly? It was quite a while ago ... when we bought the farm ... but I remember the man. I guess he was goin' through a terrible time. We thought he was goin' through a divorce, but we learned later that the woman was not actually his wife ... that was after the sale. Some neighbors told us later they weren't married, that she just stayed with'im. Took up with Barrows, I guess, just livin' with'im, then left."

"Do you remember the woman's name?" asked Lanslow, attempting to cross-check what Sheriff Barton had told him.

Landon frowned and shook his head, turning to his wife. "No, I don't. You remember, Pauline?"

Pauline paused from drying dishes, and thought for a moment. "Seems like the Parsons said the last name was 'Martin' or 'Mason,' or something like that. I can't say for sure. They said she had a little boy and girl."

"They weren't here when Barrows showed us the farm," Dave interjected. "We looked at it several times, and no one else was here except Barrows."

"Would you know the names of the boy and girl?" asked Lanslow, cross checking his information.

"I remember hearing the boy's name," said Pauline. "It was like mine. 'Paul,' it was. I don't remember the girl's name at all."

"We learned a little more about Barrows and the woman later from the Parsons," Dave said. "I think the Parsons said she'd left him by then. I think he was pretty stressed about it. I think that's why he was sellin' the place."

"The Parsons?" Lanslow asked, feigning naiveté.

"Neighbors, just down the road, on the next farm. They're the ones you should talk to. They lived here while Barrows was here. Bill Parsons told me he'd had some trouble with Barrows."

"You know what kind of trouble?" asked Lanslow, still cross checking the info he'd received from Sheriff Barton.

"I think Barrows threatened him, or something. Can't say for sure."

"If you don't mind, could you tell me if your purchase of the farm went through okay? Any trouble there?"

"Oh, no," said Dave. "We took out a mortgage through the bank. Barrows got his money. We never saw him again after the closing."

Dave Landon's directions led Lanslow to the Parsons's farmstead, about a mile and a half down the road. Unlike the Landon house, the Parsons lived in a three-story, wood-frame structure with gables and wood siding, painted white. The driveway to the farmhouse was lined with white wooden fencing on either side. There were several other outbuildings, also painted white. Huge oaks surrounded the house, their partially snow-covered limbs creating veins of black against the gray sky.

When Lanslow pulled up in his unmarked squad, a brown mongrel dog ran out of the barn, barking, and a man followed and stood, staring, jacket open despite the cold, dusting off his coveralls. Lanslow exited the car and trudged toward him through the snow. The man bellowed at the dog and it stopped barking and ran to Lanslow, wagging its tail and sniffing at his legs and shoes. Lanslow bent down and patted the dog on the head.

"Are you Mr. Parsons?" Lanslow asked, as the man approached. He extended his hand.

"Yes," said the man, extending his hand in return, removing the heavy leather glove. "What can I do for you?" Parsons appeared to be in his late sixties. Lanslow was aware of movement from another person inside the barn. Someone, perhaps a young man, appeared to be looking out at him. He had a pitchfork in his hand. The figure disappeared back into the barn.

Lanslow pulled his badge holder from his pocket, showing the badge to Parsons. "Mr. Parsons, I'm Detective Richard Lanslow, from the White Bear Lake police department. I'd like to ask you a few questions if I could."

From across the way, three horses stood with their necks extended over the fence, their ears pricked up in the two men's direction, steam issuing from their nostrils.

"A little out of your jurisdiction, aren't you?" said Parsons, smiling.

"That I am, sir," said Lanslow, "That I am."

"What can I do for you?" Parsons repeated.

"I understand you knew Henry Barrows, the former owner of the Landon farm down the road?"

Parsons's expression darkened. "I knew him," he said. "What about him?"

"Mr. Barrows was murdered last October. You may have heard about it?"

"I didn't know about Barrows. But it's good riddance, if you ask me."

"You and he didn't get along?"

"I guess you might say that," said Parsons, sarcastically. "He threatened my son, Benny, and killed my dog. Said my dog killed his calf. I don't know what killed Barrows's damned calf, but my dog didn't do it. Old Dago was just attracted to the kill; but Barrows shot him." Parsons appeared to utter these words with the same emotion he'd felt at the time.

"Threatened your son? How so?"

"Told him he'd shoot him, too, like he shot Dago. Benny went to search for Dago when he didn't show up. Benny saw Dago and he went over to check. That's when Barrows threatened him. Benny told me."

Lanslow saw a movement in the barn again. He saw a dwarfish figure with a pitchfork in his hand emerge from the doorway and stand watching him.

Parsons, noticing Lanslow's stare, turned and looked toward the barn. "That's Benny," he said. "Benny was a Down's syndrome baby. He wouldn't hurt a flea. Dago's death really upset him, and that son of a bitch Barrows scared him real bad."

"You had a quarrel with him?"

"No quarrel. I called Barrows up, told him if he ever did that again he'd have to answer to me."

"What happened then?"

"Barrows called the sheriff. Claimed Dago killed his calf and Benny was trespassing. Sheriff told me Barrows was legally within his rights. I didn't push it."

Lanslow noticed Benny ambling toward them from the barn, his shoulders swaying from side to side.

"How long did you know Barrows, Mr. Parsons?"

Since we bought our farm. Barrows was here on his own farm then. He'd inherited it from his parents, I think. His family had farmed here since back in the twenties, maybe before that."

When Benny reached them he drove the pitchfork in the ground then knelt and patted the dog, grabbing its head in his hands and ruffling its ears.

"Benny, this is Officer Lanslow, from the police department," said Parsons to his son.

"Hello, Officer Land Low," he said. "This is Bouncer." he ruffled Bouncer's ears again, holding his face close and the dog tried to lick him but he jerked back, laughing. Benny rose and extended his hand.

"Hello, Benny," Lanslow said. "Nice dog you got there."

"Sure is," said Benny, stroking the dog's head. Lanslow noted that Benny was not a young boy, but appeared to be a mature adult.

"Other than the problem with your son—were there other problems?" Lanslow asked Parsons.

"That man had a mean streak, but he kept mostly to himself, which was good for everybody else. I didn't want nothin' more to do with 'im. Everybody pretty much left him alone."

"You know if he had any run-ins with anyone else besides yourself?"

Parsons looked at Lanslow quizzically. "I hope you don't think I had anythin' to do with Barrows dyin'," he said. "Like I said, I lost track of 'im after he sold the property to the Landons. We had that one run-in. That's it. I had as little to do with 'im as possible after that."

"Mr. Parsons, you're not under suspicion. There may have been someone else, though."

"No. I don't know of nobody. There might have been. But I don't know of nobody."

"I understand that there was a woman who lived with him for a time, with a couple of kids. You know anything about them?"

"They moved in with him. A real pretty woman, quite a bit younger than Barrows. I think Barrows was about my age at the time, maybe a little older. Geraldine must have been no more'n twenty or twenty-five, already had two little kids. The boy's name was John. They called him by his middle name, Paul. The little girl's name was Lee Ann."

"What was the woman's last name?" Lanslow asked, feigning ignorance.

"Matson. I never could understand what a woman like her saw in that SOB. But there it was. How do you explain it? Barrows had some money, probably inherited from his folks. Maybe that was it. She was hard up. She put up with that bastard's abuse a long time 'fore she left. Of course, I heard she had the 'wanderin' eye,' if you know what I mean, so maybe she asked for it. I think she was just using Barrows. I heard he caught her with someone once."

Benny turned and ran after the dog. Bouncer had taken off toward the horses, barking. The horses paid the dog no attention at all. Benny held one of the horse's head in his arms and stroked its nose.

"Abuse? He abused her?" asked Lanslow.

"Not her, far as I know. Barrows beat the little boy bad, though. That little boy came over to our place one night, trying to hide. He had bruises on his legs and back. There was some talk that Barrows molested the boy. I don't know if that was true, but Barrows was a son of a bitch, I can tell you. I'd had that run-in with him once. I sent the boy home. I was sorry for him, me and the missus, but I didn't want nothin' to do with Barrows—him and that rifle."

Next to the name "John Paul Matson," on his notepad, Lanslow wrote: "Grudge/revenge" and placed a question mark by it.

"Was that why Miss Matson left Barrows?" Lanslow asked.

"I suspect that was part of it, but there were rumors she cheated on him, too" said Parsons.

"Any names?"

Parsons looked quizzical. "Names? Of people she cheated with? I never heard any."

"Do you have any idea where Miss Matson is now?" Lanslow asked, just to further verify what Sheriff Barton had already told him.

"She's dead. Died not too long ago; fairly young. I read the funeral notice in the paper. She had a hard life, I think."

"What happened to the boy—Paul?"

"He left for the service, some time after Geraldine moved out of Barrows's house. I heard he had some kind of trouble with the law, maybe before that, in school. I never heard anythin' else about 'im. I don't think he came back here. I'd have heard about it."

"Which branch of service, do you know?"

"I think it was the Air Force. Not sure about that, though."

"Do you know about when he joined up?"

"Umm. Well, let's see ... no, not really. Not sure about that, either."

"How about the sister? Is she still around?"

"I think she left somewhere later, too. Haven't heard anythin' 'bout her."

Lanslow looked up from his scribbling. "Well, Mr. Parsons. You've been a big help. Thanks."

"You're welcome, Sir. I hope you catch the guy."

"Thanks, Mr. Parsons. I intend to." He handed Parsons his card. "If you think of anything else, please call."

When he exited the Parson's driveway and had gone some distance down the road, Lanslow guided the car carefully off to the side, pulled out his notebook and reviewed what he had written. Next to Parsons's name he had also written the name 'Benny,' but next to both he had put only a question mark. Next to this entry, he wrote to himself, 'improbable.'

The part of the interview with Parsons that stood out for the young detective, however, was what he had said about the boy, Paul, being abused. And the boy had been in trouble in school, too. Could Paul Matson have borne a grudge against Barrows for the abuse all these years, tracked Barrows down and murdered him? Would he have seen Barrows at his mother's funeral? And did Paul Matson connect with Zeke Mallard somehow? Was Matson a psycho, as Jack Matthews had suggested? He didn't remember the name as one of Zeke's collars but he'd have to go over the list again to be sure.

Lanslow searched backward in his notes of the conversation with Sheriff Barton. Barton had referred to the boy as John Paul, not just Paul. In his notes he wrote the name "John" next to the name of "Paul," so that he could be clear on the boy's full name.

John Paul Matson. Lanslow could hardly contain his excitement as he started the engine, steered the car onto the gravel road, and headed back to White Bear Lake. There was much more to do, but now he felt he had a possible lead, at last.

24

The wallet he'd removed from the package sat on Matthews's desk. The cone of light from the single desk lamp—providing the only light in the otherwise darkened study—illuminated it ominously. He had taken it out of the drawer, removed the plastic cards and laid them there. He stared at them for sometime before he picked them up. He pulled out the ID. Glenda Morrison's image stared back at him, smiling.

He tried again to answer his questions: How had Luke come into possession of this wallet—complete with checkbook, credit card and ID? Had the girl lent him the wallet because Luke needed money, or gas, and he didn't want to admit it? Was he thus simply embarrassed that he had Glenda Morrison's wallet, with a set of checks, and her credit card? But, if she was lending him money, then why the whole wallet, with blank checks, credit card and even her ID? Why would she give up her own access to money, or to gas for a car and access to the University library as well? It was just too unbelievable.

The most probable explanation would be that the girl had lost it, Luke had found it, taken the money and not returned it. That was bad enough, and he could understand Luke being embarrassed about it. But he couldn't understand Luke compounding the situation by keeping the wallet and then lying about it, especially since the wallet could not have gotten into Luke's room without someone putting it there.

Perhaps Luke didn't want him to know about Glenda Morrison, and that's why he had lied about it. Did Luke's lie, if it was a lie, imply something worse, maybe? Again he asked himself, who was this Glenda Morrison and what was her relationship to Luke? Why would Luke wish to conceal the relationship (if, indeed, he did)?

There was the other possibility that he had already considered, that Luke had already denied: maybe Luke had stolen the wallet. Such a possibility would certainly better explain Luke's denial. He had asked for money to fly back east. Luke had said he'd take care of any remaining airfare, and, then, Luke had come back agitated. Maybe Luke was in trouble again.

There was little doubt left in Matthew's mind: he was going to have to try to contact Glenda Morrison.

∎

"Daddy" is coming. He hears the heavy shoes plodding up the steps. The door opens. "Daddy" grunts, takes another drink, sets the bottle on a table, removes his belt, folds it in half, then raises it to strike ... He scurries away from the descending belt. He is with a pack of wolves. He becomes half-boy, half-wolf. He is the runt of the pack and has to fight for scraps of food after all the others have eaten. He lives on the margins of the pack, bullied constantly, barely surviving. Suddenly, he is back home, he is Bobo, the puppy and is constantly bullied by the cocker spaniel, Lady. He turns back into a full-grown wolf and harasses and bullies Lady savagely until she creeps off and dies. He is with some young boys, in a school yard. They're shooting guns, killing several classmates and wounding several others. He is one of the shooters, understanding completely how the boys feel and why they'd shot everybody, especially the jocks. But then the boys turn the guns on themselves and he thinks, Wow! I guess you can take only so much, then you have to do something, even if it means dying yourself.

∎

Lanslow returned to the station that afternoon and Brooks was there, submerged in piles of paper.

"How's Alma?" Lanslow asked. He'd met Alma a couple of times, a petite, pretty woman, probably once quite a looker. With age, her body had grown a little plump and lumpy, as he remembered.

Dean Brooks looked up and leaned back in his chair. "She's better, now. Maybe come down with the flu. That stuff is going around."

"Hope not. Listen, I got a lead, Dean. I think we got a break here."

"On Zeke?" Brooks asked.

"Yeah, on Zeke. I got to thinking. You suggested once that someone might have murdered Barrows in revenge. Well, I think you were right. I've been doing some checking on Barrows's background, over in Wisconsin."

"That so? What have you got?"

"Barrows was a real low-life apparently. Before he sold his farm, a woman by name of Geraldine Matson and her two kids were living with him, a boy and a girl. A neighbor reported that he had abused the boy. The kid's name was John—John Paul Matson."

Brooks seemed to mull this over for a bit, then he said, "You think this kid killed him?"

"I think it's the strongest thing we got going right now."

"That's not saying much. What does this have to do with Zeke?"

"I had a talk with Jack Matthews. Like you, he thinks revenge might have been the motive for killing Zeke."

"Matthews? The professor? Haven't seen him around for a while."

"He thinks Zeke's killer is a psycho of some sort. This psycho maybe just happened to run into Zeke and, for some reason, killed him. No other connection than that. He killed Barrows later, maybe out of revenge."

"That's the only connection between the two?"

"I'd almost bet on it."

"What kind of psycho are we talking here?"

"Matthews mentioned paranoia."

Brooks looked skeptical. "It sounds like a long shot. You gone any further with this? You know where this Matson character is?"

"That's next. I gotta talk to Johnson. We gotta have more time on this."

"Johnson can't authorize it. You'll have to see the Chief, but he's at some kind of conference in St. Cloud."

"Well, I'll catch him tomorrow, then."

Brooks looked at his watch. "Hey, you can call me at home, later, huh? Alma's got me Christmas shopping tonight and tomorrow, if she's not too sick. You're remembering I got a day off tomorrow?"

"Oh, yeah. I'd forgotten," said Lanslow.

"Just give me a call tomorrow and let me know."

"Sure," said Lanslow. "No problem."

▌

Dorian's act of killing Henry Barrows had generated a state of fear and anxiety among the members of the group that they'd never experienced before—even when he'd killed the policeman—and they had broken down into a state of quarreling and carping at one another. As the weeks went by and the police didn't seem any closer to knowing who had killed the men, however, the fear had diminished and the quarreling and carping had subsided. One thing kept them on their guard and wary, however: the little man's continuing bad dreams and his nights of sweating anguish and festering hatred. It seemed that killing Barrows had not been the solution to the little man's troubles, after all, and the dreams and sweats were getting worse. Each of them knew that the dreams could only mean more serious trouble for them in the future.

Fearing the dreams meant he would kill again, the group gathered around Conrad one day, trying to figure out what to do, waiting for him to make a pronouncement.

"Well, what the hell do we do about these dreams?" asked Dorian, after Conrad had waited a little too long to respond to their queries.

Conrad winced, as always, at Dorian's rudeness.

"It's like before," said Gary, abruptly. "He's building up to something again."

"Maybe," said Conrad, "maybe not."

"Oh, that's a lot of help! Maybe he is, maybe he isn't," said Dorian. "We all know it just means more trouble."

"Why is he always dreaming about animals?" asked Linda.

"We're animals, too," said Gary. "He sees the similarities between us and them. Really, there's not much difference, when you think about it."

"Cut that philosophy crap," said Dorian. "But you're right. He's boiling up again. I can see it, too. And I'm going to have to bail him out, whatever he decides to do."

"Well," said Conrad, resignedly, "we all have to do our part. We have to take care of him. That's what we're here for, that's all we can do, that's ... ."

Dorian looked at Conrad with contempt and Conrad closed his mouth and didn't say anything else.

25

Glenda Morrison's phone number was listed on her checks. Matthews had expected the number would no longer be in service, but to his surprise he got a ring. After the sixth ring he was about to hang up when a female voice answered.

"Hello?"

"Is this Glenda Morrison?" asked Matthews.

"Yes, who's this?"

"Miss Morrison, I am Luke Matthews's father."

There was a long pause. "Okay. So, what about it?"

"You know Luke, of course."

"Luke? What was his last name?"

"Luke Matthews, my son."

"I never heard of him. You must have the wrong person."

Sensing that the woman was about to hang up the phone, Matthews said, "Miss Morrison, don't hang up. Did you, by any chance, lose your wallet some time ago?"

A longer pause. "Who are you?" said the woman, with a note of what Matthews thought was not only caution but fear in her voice.

"My name is Jack Matthews. Luke Matthews is my son. He found your wallet, Miss Morrison."

"Where did he find it?"

"Well, actually, I'm not sure. I found it ... in his room. He says he doesn't know how it got there. I just wanted to return it to you and clear up any misunderstanding."

"Oh sure, you do, mister. Sure you do. Listen! If you so much as even call me again, I'll have the cops on you. You understand?"

There was a click. Glenda Morrison had hung up.

Bill Bradbury hadn't even had time to hang up his hat when Lanslow knocked on the door of his office, requesting more overtime. The chief had a jaw befitting his position, square, authoritative, jutting out like Dick Tracy's. It was set hard now, and the gray eyes bore in on Richard Lanslow.

"You're going to have to show me something pretty special to justify cutting your and Brooks's time on your other cases, Rich, especially with these budget cuts. It's not likely we'll replace Zeke anytime soon. What have you got?"

"I've got a name, a new suspect. I need to find him, and it's going to take more time."

"Who've you got?"

"A boy ... a man, now ... name of John Matson. He was the son of a woman who was living with Henry Barrows, the wino who was murdered in Minneapolis. A neighbor reported that Barrows beat on the boy and possibly sexually abused him. Matson may have murdered Barrows out of revenge."

"What does that have to do with Zeke?"

"Andrew White claims he saw the same man at the scene of Barrows's murder as he saw at Zeke's, and the way in which Zeke and Barrows were murdered is very similar. I think there's little doubt that both men were murdered by the same person. Matson may be that person."

"I can see the motive for murdering Barrows, but why would Matson want to murder Zeke? What's the link, there?"

"I don't know yet, but I'm thinking we have some kind of psycho on our hands. I'm thinking this psycho just happened to run into Zeke. Something happened. He followed him home and killed him."

"For God's sake! A psycho? What kind of psycho?"

"I'm not sure," said Lanslow, unwilling to divulge his talk with Professor Matthews just yet to the chief. "But if Matson did kill Barrows and if we can find him, maybe we'll find out about Zeke."

"Well, hell, and maybe I'll be president some day," said Bradbury.

"I know, Chief. I know. But it's a lead. What else have we got?"

"That's supposed to be my question, Rich, not yours. What about White?"

"It just doesn't make any sense that White would call us unless, like Dean says, he gets a kick out of playing around with the police, and I just don't buy that. It just doesn't fit."

"Where is Brooks, by the way?"

"His day off today."

"Oh, yeah, well … that figures. You come in asking for more overtime and Brooks takes a day off." Bradbury picked up his hat from the top of his desk and set it atop a file cabinet. He dropped heavily into his chair. He opened the case file Lanslow had placed in front of him. Bradbury scanned the files closely, noting that the official reports, other than Lanslow's latest, were now nearly two months old. There had been no word on Andrew White since he had called Lanslow about Barrows's murder.

Bradbury pushed his salt-and-pepper hair back from his forehead, studying the interior of the file. As if talking to the file itself, he said, "I know you've been pursuing Zeke's case on your own time, Rich. I know that, and I don't feel real good about it." Bradbury laid the file down and looked up at Lanslow. "So, all right, Rich. White still seems to be our prime suspect, but maybe you've got something here. You and Brooks take more time on this. I'll clear it with Johnson. Take whatever overtime you need but keep me informed. I'll need to see some progress here, something more than hunches, and pretty damned fast. You've got two weeks."

∎

As she dropped the receiver into its cradle, Glenda Morrison was shaking. The call caused the whole event that night some months before to replay. She had tried to forget the images. Now it all came back. She could still feel the strength in the man's arms, jerking her, dragging her to the cover of the woods; could still hear the man's voice, see the face, feel the ski cap being pulled over her face, her clothes being removed, then the woman's voice, the penetration, the threats, the footsteps in the leaves, silence, waiting, fear, wiping herself with the ski cap, recovering her bag, the ride back to her apartment on the empty, late night bus, the deep racking sobs in the long shower.

Many such showers had failed to remove the man's odor from her memory. She could still smell him, a peculiar cologne, maybe, or aftershave lotion. And the woman, the same smell for both of them ... that had been curious when she thought about it later. The woman had appeared from nowhere. The woman had penetrated her with something—not something artificial, something that had felt quite normal. Glenda Morrison puzzled over that, too, again and again. Raped by a lesbian who was helped by a man to hold her down? And the wetness, obviously semen! Had the man or the woman raped her? Or had both? The whole thing was bizarre, and she was at a loss to explain exactly what had happened to her. In the pain and shame of it she had finally tried to put it behind her and regain some normalcy to her life.

But now, the man on the phone.

She began shaking again. She wanted to flee. She stifled the impulse, began to think. Was it a ruse? The voice was not the same. Had he said he'd found her wallet in his son's room? Yes, he had, and he'd given a name ... Luke ... Luke Matthews, and the father's name was ... Jack. But the voice was different, older. And the woman who had raped her had used the name Dorian. Was the name of the man on the phone a fake? Was the caller Dorian? Was he back? Hunting her again?

Fear rose again. Why had she been so stupid as to not get a different phone number and to move, despite the cost and trouble? What had she been thinking?

Control, get control, she thought. She tried to think it out: Why would he call her? It would be like a warning, and wouldn't make any sense if he was hunting her. If he had her wallet and her phone number he would have her address, so why would he call? Maybe what the man on the phone had said was true. It made sense. Maybe he had found her wallet in his son's room. What did that mean? If the man's message was true, that his son had taken her wallet, then the son could have been the male collaborator in her rape … maybe it was the son who was Dorian. No, he had said his son's name was Luke. Maybe the son had just found her wallet and not returned it.

Her thoughts were racing again. Fear rose again. She was losing control. She had to get control. She squelched the fear once more. She sat down. What was the bottom line? Everything considered, everything all told, there was one possibility that overrode everything else: the man on the phone could be the rapist himself … .

There was only one thing to do.

Glenda Morrison lifted the phone's receiver to dial 9-1-1.

Matthews thought about calling the woman back, but the whole exchange and the obvious fear in her voice had shaken him. Why was she so afraid? She'd said she had never heard of Luke. He glanced at his watch. He had a class at nine. It was already eight-thirty.

Hurriedly, he went to the closet and pulled on his overcoat, got in his car and backed out of the garage. He guided the car around the circle driveway and pulled into the road. It was all done mechanically, by habit, while his mind raced.

He turned the car in the westerly direction, taking him to the perimeter road circling the lake that lay to the east, a block and a half from his house. The lake was frozen over, now, and ice-fishing houses, sitting in separate clusters, huddled on the snow-covered ice like little villages. The day was overcast and gray. Winter rain was in the forecast. This drive around the lake and then on to the college was usually a respite for Matthews, a time in which he could let his thoughts roam freely or perhaps listen to the radio to get an update on the news. Not this morning.

If Glenda Morrison didn't know Luke, then the question still persisted: how in hell had Luke come by the wallet? The conclusion was one Matthews didn't want to draw. He wanted the thought to go away. But it kept coming back: Luke must have stolen the wallet. It all came down to one thing: his son was a thief, perhaps worse. And the thought occurred to him that he didn't need this now. He'd hoped and begun to believe that Luke had turned his life around. Now, it seemed, his own life was headed toward one of those valleys again, plunging downward from what had been at least a higher elevation only a week or so before.

▌

Glenda Morrison hung up the phone before anyone answered. She had suddenly remembered the rapist's words, imprinted in her memory: "He will kill you," the woman had said.

"Yes, I'll kill you if you tell of this," the man called Dorian had promised. He'd said he would search out her family and kill them, too.

The image of her mother standing by her on one side, her father in a wheelchair on the other, flashed into consciousness. She was the only one of her extended family ever to go to college. They'd had a neighbor take their picture. Glenda's mother kept it on a table in the family's small living room, beside the picture of her older brother, who hadn't been heard from since he had left the detox unit at the correctional facility over a year ago.

Morrison sat at the small table that functioned both as a place to study and eat. She stared at the books on chemistry and English, the heavy volume of American history, lying there. She liked the smell of them, the weight of them, the marching print. A whole new world was in those books, a world beyond any she could have imagined.

She hesitated. The voice on the phone wasn't the rapist's voice. She would have recognized it. But he could have changed his voice. No matter, the rapist was out there. If she called the police and they didn't catch him, she could endanger not only herself but her mother, as well, perhaps even her father and brother.

She continued sitting. It was nearing time for her first class to begin. Still, she just sat there, unable to move.

26

At his desk after talking with Bradbury, Lanslow called Brooks at his home, doubting the detective would be there, but the sergeant answered on the third ring. "Sorry to bother you," said Lanslow. "You done Christmas shopping already?"

"No. Alma slept late. She's feeling better. We're on our way out now. What did the chief say?"

"We got some overtime. I'm going to get on this new lead now."

"That's good!" said Brooks. "Hey, I'm with you on this, but Alma is expecting me to go shopping. I've been putting her off as long as I can."

"Don't sweat it, Dean. Believe me, I can sympathize. I just wanted to let you know where we are."

"We'll get back on this together tomorrow. Okay?"

"No problem," said Lanslow, smiling at Brooks's guilt and his obvious attempt at redemption. "I'm going to spend the day trying to track Matson down from my desk here. Might save some legwork. I'll see you tomorrow. Enjoy your shopping."

"Oh, yeah. Sure thing," said Brooks, dolorously.

Lanslow stood up and stretched, did a few toe touches, then sat down at his desk. He pushed the cases of petty theft and vandalism out of the way and put Zeke's heavy case file in the cleared spot. He let the file sit there for a while. He just wanted to think things through one more time.

Impulsively, he pulled out the St. Paul phone book and turned to the M's. To his surprise only about twelve names showed up under Matson. Scanning down to the J's, he found no listing of a name starting with J.

Okay, next step. He reached for the phone and dialed 411.

"Qwest local, national and 800 directory assistance, researched by telephone number or name. For what city?" asked a disembodied voice.

"Somerset," said Lanslow.

"Please say the city," said the disembodied voice.

"Somerset," Lanslow repeated.

There was a pause. The phone rang.

"This is Jerry, for what listing, please?" said a real voice.

"I'm trying to find the phone number of a John P. Matson, residing in Somerset, Wisconsin."

"Thank you. One moment please ... I'm sorry, we have no listing for that name in Somerset, Wisconsin."

"How about Wisconsin in general," asked Lanslow.

Another pause. "I'm sorry, I can't find a listing by that name."

"Okay, thanks anyway," said Lanslow.

He repeated the whole procedure for Minnesota, Iowa, North Dakota and Michigan with the same result.

So much for that, thought Lanslow. He had expected as much. Next step.

Lanslow turned on his computer, and got on line. A good place to begin to find out what Matson looked like would be the Minnesota State Bureau of Vehicle Records. If the man drove a car, he would have to be licensed, and the license would provide a physical description and possibly even a photo. He already knew something about the killer's appearance. He knew he was a small man, and a Caucasian. From the information he'd gathered in his interviews, Lanslow estimated John Paul Matson to be in his late thirties to early forties. If they were going to find him, though, the information provided by the driver's license—height, weight, color of eyes, hair, whether he wore glasses, and especially the photo—would prove invaluable.

When the search page came up, he typed in John Paul Matson's name. The screen showed no record. He picked up his phone and asked the dispatcher to contact the Bureau of Vehicle Records for Wisconsin. He got the same information from the clerk. There was no vehicle registered under the name of John Paul Matson. Lanslow lamented to himself, as he had done before, that he'd had no time to talk further to Andrew White. He wanted to ask white several questions including whether the man had driven a car, and, if so, its description. An opportunity lost. White was gone. He could be anywhere.

Lanslow got off-line. He pulled up the records department's screen and typed in his password and identification number. Another screen appeared listing the records to which he had access: the master index file, the report files, the crime file, serial number file, stolen object file, etc. Since Zeke's murder had occurred in White Bear Lake, it was possible that Matson was familiar with the area or maybe even lived nearby. And there was a chance he had run afoul of the law. If so, his name would be on one or more of these files. Lanslow clicked on the crime file and entered Matson's name. A message on the screen read, "No record found." It was the same for all the other records. Lanslow was not surprised.

In what he suspected would be a futile effort, Lanslow went on line again and called up the Federal Bureau of Investigation National Crime Information Center's home page. He entered the necessary identifying information and gained access. Typing in John Paul Matson's name, he waited. Again, no record.

Lanslow smiled wanly to himself. The search for John Paul Matson wasn't going to be that easy. He took his pen from his pocket and began to write the names of the other records he would have to search. John Paul Matson was out there, somewhere, and he was going to find him.

■

Professor Matthews didn't want to be at work three days before the end of the fall semester, grading the essay questions on the final exams. But here he was, and his mind was running on dual tracks—actually, several tracks. He was thinking about Maureen and their Christmas plans, wondering about Annie coming to live with them, worrying about Luke, mulling Zeke Mallard's case, and trying to grade papers.

The call to Glenda Morrison was also on his mind even as he opened a bluebook and began to read. "Societal change takes three basic patterns," the student had written in his essay, and Matthews read it out loud to himself, trying to focus, while at the same time thinking about Glenda Morrison and Luke, and how he was going to handle this very bad situation. "The most basic of the three patterns is what is called a 'dialectic' pattern, after Karl Marx ..."

The student had underlined the words "basic" and "dialectic" and "Marx," as if, somehow, he thought they deserved special attention. Matthews circled the passage in red ink, took mental note of his own action, and at the same time tried to envision the way in which he might confront Luke that evening—if Luke came home.

On the page of the bluebook the student had drawn two diametrically opposed arrows, then had drawn a third arrow pointing downward, dissecting the point at which the diametrically opposed arrows met. At the origin of the left arrow he had written the word "thesis" and at the origin of the right arrow he wrote the word "antithesis" and beneath the downward pointing arrow he wrote "synthesis."

"Marx referred to this basic pattern as the 'materialist dialectic,' the student had written, and Matthews found himself for the moment wondering if the young man understood the importance of Hegel's and Marx's concepts of the dialectic. While most of his students were merely regurgitating his lectures on the dialectic, even the best ones, Matthews watched the process working before him everyday. Amusingly enough, he thought, conflict was the best description of his present dilemma.

There was the slight chance that there was another explanation for Luke's possession of the wallet, but Matthews recognized the thought as merely a hope, accompanied by the ever growing dread of what the actual explanation might be.

He closed the blue book, marking a B+ in red on the outside cover, and placed it on the growing stack to his right. Blue books on the left awaited grading; blue books on the right were finished. The stack to the left was larger than the one on the right. Matthews sighed. It was lunch time.

He returned from the cafeteria with a bowl of soup and a half of a sandwich. He pulled his copy of the White Bear Press, the local community newspaper, from his briefcase and scanned the headlines as he ate, his feet propped on the corner of his desk. There was a small story about Zeke Mallard's murder and an interview with Detectives Brooks and Lanslow on the front page. There had been no progress on finding the killer. Matthews doubted that anything would be reported even if the police had found any evidence or learned anything further.

He thought back to his last conversation with Lanslow, during which he had advised the young detective that there might be no connection between the murders of Mallard and the wino, that the murderer was probably a psychotic. He'd called Lanslow once and Lanslow had called back and left a message, but he hadn't been able to contact him again. He pulled his organizer from his coat pocket and wrote another note to call Lanslow again, perhaps that evening, to see what was new. Directly beneath that entry, he made another note to try again to talk to his son, Luke, and under that he reminded himself of his dinner engagement with Maureen.

∎

Bradbury's voice woke Lanslow. The detective jerked upright.

The chief looked at Lanslow's tired face. "For God's sake, Lanslow! How long have you been here? Go home. Get some rest. "

Lanslow rubbed his eyes. "Sorry, Chief. Don't worry. I'm on my own time. Just checking some things before going home."

"I thought I gave you enough overtime. What things?"

"Records, any records I can think of that might tell me where this John Matson is."

"Find anything yet?"

"I've checked the NCIC and our own records. Nothing there. I'll have to check with Wisconsin, next. I've checked with the IRS and Social Security—nothing. I've checked state vehicle records, and health department records. Nothing yet there, either. The man hasn't committed any crimes, pays no taxes, doesn't even have a Social Security number, doesn't own a car, and has never been in the hospital as far as I can tell. It's hard to believe that a man can just disappear like that, leave no trace whatever."

"He can't, Rich. There will be something, somewhere. In the meantime, you go home. You and Brooks can get on this thing hard tomorrow morning. Just figured you might still be here."

Lanslow glanced at his watch. He had slept, his head and arms resting on his desk, for almost half an hour. It was nearly five o'clock. His shift had officially ended at four. "Good grief!," he said. "Just didn't realize what time it was." He wondered why someone hadn't awakened him sooner.

"Go home, Rich. We'll see you tomorrow."

As Lanslow left, Bradbury watched, shaking his head.

∎

Headed home, Lanslow glanced again at his watch. Laura would be home already, waiting. He was tired, bone tired, but he couldn't help himself. Maybe the recruiter's office wouldn't yet be closed.

He pulled out his cell phone and punched 411.

"For what city, please?" said the disembodied voice again.

Lanslow went through the process as he had done several times already. He was given a number, and tried it.

"Air Force recruiting, Sergeant Mayfield, may I help you?"

"Sergeant Mayfield, this is Detective Richard Lanslow, White Bear Lake police department. We're trying to locate an individual we suspect is involved in a murder who may have enlisted in the Air Force through your office some time ago, not real sure when. I'm wondering if you might be able to help us out."

"Certainly, Detective. We have the records here that I can check. I'll need your badge number first, though, if you don't mind."

Lanslow gave it to him, then was put on hold.

"Okay, Sir. What's the name?" Sergeant Mayfield asked after a few minutes.

"Matson, John Paul."

"Can you hold, Sir?"

"No problem."

Lanslow heard the phone click. He waited. He was just about to hang up and call again when Sergeant Mayfield said, "Detective Lanslow?"

"Yes?"

"I'm sorry to keep you waiting. I've checked all of the records for that name. Nothing shows up. When do you think he enlisted?"

"Late sixties, early seventies probably."

Oh, well, we wouldn't have those records here, then, Detective," said the sergeant.

Are you sure?" said Lanslow, his disappointment obvious.

"I'm certain, Sir. Those old records would be in the microfiche files in St. Louis by now."

"St. Louis? Missouri?"

"Yes, Sir."

"All right," said Lanslow. "Thanks anyway."

"You're welcome, sir. Sorry we couldn't be of more help."

Lanslow turned off the cell phone. He pulled over and stopped his car. Taking out his notebook, he thumbed back to where he had interviewed the Parsons, to recheck his memory. There it was. Parsons had said John Paul Matson had joined the Air Force, but he had also said he might be wrong. Maybe Matson had joined another branch of the service. Or maybe he hadn't joined the service at all. He picked up the phone again and hit the re-dial button.

"Air Force Recruiting, Sergeant Mayfield. May I help you?"

"Sergeant Mayfield, this is Detective Lanslow. Sorry to bother you again but I was wondering, are there recruiting stations in or around Somerset for the other branches of service?"

"No, Sir, Detective. Just us. The other services are in Maplewood, Minnesota. We'll be moving there, too, eventually. I can give you their numbers."

"Yes, that would be helpful." Lanslow wrote the numbers in his notebook. "Okay, Sergeant. Thanks again."

He would check out the other services, and then if that didn't pan out he'd have to see if John Paul Matson's records were in St. Louis and how he could get them. He glanced at his watch again. He thought about going back to the station to try to get the process started. Then he thought of Laura, waiting. They'd planned to eat out and they still had more shopping to do. He'd have to wait until tomorrow.

∎

Luke Matthews sat in his car for a moment, going over and over what had just happened only a half-hour before.

"Luke," she had said softly, staring out the window, "I think I want to call it off."

They were in his car. A cold but gentle rain, trying to turn to snow, was falling, melting on the heated windshield. Rivulets of water trickled in zigzag patterns over the glass. He had been expecting those words for some time, dreading them.

"I don't understand," he said. "What have I done? What can I do?"

"Luke, don't start. Please!"

"I just don't understand," he said, miserably.

"Luke, you've been so sweet. We've had a good time. Really, you've been wonderful, and it's been fun."

"Is there someone else?" he asked, staring straight ahead.

"Yes. Maybe. Whether or not there is, though, I just want to move on."

Her words sounded so callous to him. Didn't she know how he was ripping apart inside?

He turned to her, reached out, cupped her face in his hands, kissed her gently on the lips, with all the passion he could muster. She didn't struggle to get away. Surprisingly, she returned his kiss, and in it he felt the sorrow and sadness of his life wash over him because he knew it would be the last time. He lingered, clung to her a little too long. She pushed him away, sat silent, as the rain thrummed a little harder.

"I love you, Joan" he said, simply.

"Luke, you don't, you don't. We're both so young. We've had a good time. There will be someone else, for both of us."

"I don't want anyone else," he said, fighting to hold back the tears. "I don't want anyone else."

But in the end she had left, unwilling to draw it out any longer no matter how much he wanted her to stay, to talk to him, to reason with her. She had opened the car door, exited into the rain. He had watched her go, her figure so familiar to him now.

He remembered her face as he had kissed her, remembered the feel and taste of her lips. She had been perfect. But not him. He was not perfect. Anything but. He had been unable to keep her, as he had not been able to keep any of the others. It had happened to him again.

He cursed himself. Alone in his car, he wept. Emotions flooded through him, a vast sadness—sorrow, anger, resentment at the lot he had drawn in life, despair.

He cried until he could cry no more. As usual, though, the crying helped.

He looked out into the night from inside his car, at his father's house. The rain was now mixed with snow; it was supposed to turn fully to snow by tomorrow. Some kind of animal running across the driveway tripped the porch light on. Strange, he thought, that there would be an animal out this late at night, in the wintertime. So far, the winter had been relatively mild. Even some of the geese and ducks had stuck around. The snow ringing the driveway, where the snow blower had thrown it, wasn't as high as usual, at least as he remembered it these last two years that he'd been in Minnesota. In the yard the snow was shallower, only a half foot or so. He stared at the light, glinting through the cold rain-and-snow mix on the windshield. Even in his misery he marveled at the mystery of the darkness beyond the light, at the sounds of the night, the dripping of the rain and snow from the brown oak leaves still stubbornly clinging to the limbs. These remaining leaves wouldn't fall until spring when the new leaves would insist they give up their places.

The world and life were wonders to him. He loved the world, this universe—was awed by its beauty. During one of his frequent self-analyses he'd guessed that his wonder and awe of the world were the more poignant because of his feeling of separation from it. He smiled at his self-pity; he was beginning to remind himself more and more of his dad.

His emotions subsided after a while, replaced by reason. He had to go in, get some sleep. He hoped his father wasn't at home. He knew his dad would just want to talk about Annie and it was the last thing he felt like doing now. His father, he knew, also, had his own problems, and he didn't want to add to them, especially since Annie had called, wanting to come to Minnesota. He understood his father's reluctance. He had mixed feelings about her coming to Minnesota himself.

Luke opened the door of his car, grabbed the backpack from the floorboard and made his way through the rain, to the front door. He inserted the key and opened the door quietly, listening for any telltale signs of his father. The house appeared to be dark throughout. He removed his shoes and walked to his father's bedroom. The door was open, the room empty. He walked to his father's study. The door was closed. He listened, but heard nothing. He opened the door slightly, surprised to find the desk lamp still on. But his father wasn't there. As usual, his father's desktop was clean and uncluttered, except for a wallet and a small packet of plastic cards, lying on top of his dad's organizer and calendar. Luke walked to the desk and picked the packet up.

The photo of Glenda Morrison smiled up at him. Luke shuffled through the plastic cards, all with Morrison's name on them. He pulled his father's organizer across the desk surface, turning it so he could read the scribbles. He knew his father always filled out his "action list" and then, as the jobs were accomplished, would check them off. The open page read "Tuesday, December 16th" and underneath, in his father's unrefined writing style, he read that day's list:

√ 1. Call Glenda Morrison,
2. Finish grades.
3. Call Detective Lanslow.
4. Talk to Luke this evening
√ 5. Dinner with Maureen

27

The group gathered again Wednesday morning, at Conrad's insistence. He had awakened early, the result of an all night struggle to resolve their problem. He had put the problem to them once again, and they all looked worried.

"She probably knows his name. She can go to the police. Perhaps she already has," he said. "It could destroy us."

"Destroy? You mean we could die?" asked Linda.

"Very possibly," said Gary.

Each was silent for a while.

"This Glenda Morrison bitch can't be allowed to live," said Dorian, finally.

Conrad and Gary stared at him, their faces ashen. Linda stepped back, scrutinizing Dorian's face.

"Dorian, this has to stop," said Conrad. "I've said this time and again. We've been lucky. These killings and rapes are only going to bring us trouble. They will destroy us."

"If she goes to the police, that will destroy us for sure," said Dorian, angrily. "What else can we do?"

"He may be right," said Gary. "Much as I hate to admit it ..."

"There has to be another way," said Conrad. "We just can't continue to handle things this way."

But once again he knew it was true: Glenda Morrison, like the others, had to be taken care of.

∎

At one o'clock Lanslow and Brooks headed to Wisconsin. They had already been at the station, returning calls, clearing paperwork. Lanslow had initiated a request for John Paul Matson's service records from St. Louis, Missouri. It would take some time, they told him, but they would fax him any information they found. Working on the assumption that Matson might be a local resident— since that would be the most likely explanation of how he and Mallard had had contact— they had slogged through various other records searching for John Paul Matson's name, to no avail. They decided to head back to Somerset, to where Matson had apparently grown up. Lanslow called the Oakwood school principal and made an appointment for that afternoon. They would pursue other avenues after that, provided they had the time.

An overnight snow had left the countryside white and gleaming in the sun, almost blinding. The boughs of the pines dipped low, some just beginning to release their loads slowly, despite the cold, as the sun climbed toward its zenith. Lanslow loved the snow, especially as it lay in the deep shadows of the pines and birches. Images from the days of his boyhood formed in his consciousness, days of sledding and skiing, of building tunnels in the deep drifts, of ice hockey on the pond behind their house, of hoary frost covering the tree limbs in their front yard, back-lit by the early morning sun.

As a teenager he had worn his hair long, tied in a ponytail. He remembered lacing on his skates by the side of the pond, the first rush down the ice, the sliding stop, the spray of ice, the spirited game between the neighborhood boys. Hip-checking had been one of his favorite things to do during the game, knocking another player into the deep snow ringing the pond. After the game, he would trudge into the house with ice crystals packed in his hair and eyebrows and he would get a kick out of his image in the mirror.

"Ever play ice hockey, Dean?" said Lanslow, glancing sideways at his partner.

"Never got around to it," Brooks said. "I preferred basketball. Couldn't do both at the same time."

Lanslow tried to imagine the short, stocky Brooks in a basketball uniform. "What position?" he asked.

"Well, it sure wasn't center," said Brooks, laughing. "You probably won't believe it, but I was the starting point guard. The play maker."

"I believe it. Sure. You must've been a lot lighter back then, eh?" Lanslow glanced at Brooks, grinning.

"Would you believe a hundred forty-five?"

"No shit? Naw!"

"Yep, 'fraid so. Put on about another fifty since then. Alma feeds me too well."

Lanslow smiled to himself. More like another sixty or seventy, he guessed to himself. "Get your shopping done?" he asked.

"Nah. Alma wants to go out again tonight. I hope to God this is the last of it. Legs and back can't take that crap anymore."

They were silent for a while, both entranced by the winter wonderland before them.

"You still have doubts about this being Andrew White's doing?" asked Brooks, after awhile.

To Lanslow, Brook's question implied that his mild skepticism hadn't abated since Lanslow had broached his new theory of the murder. The young detective could sympathize: it was just his own hunch, after all, that was taking them to Wisconsin. As usual, however, Brooks had taken the suggestion with aplomb. With age, and retirement looming, it seemed Brooks was becoming more tolerant.

"I don't know anything else to do at this point. I know he went to school in Somerset. I'm thinking we might come up with a photo of Matson, or some other stuff. I'm just hoping something might turn up."

"Sure," said Brooks, as he settled deeper into the seat. "This will be a good start."

Lanslow noticed Brooks looking at the passing landscape. "A little different from Los Angeles, huh?"

"California isn't that great," said Brooks. "I missed the seasons more than I thought I would."

"What're you going to do when you retire, Dean? What do you have now, a couple of years to go?"

"A couple, maybe. Alma wants me to do it this year. It's tempting."

"Guess you're not gonna buy a condo and live in the sun belt, huh?"

"Nah. When I retire I plan on just sitting in front of the fire and staring out my picture window for a while—just smelling Alma's good cooking."

The principal of the school met them at the door, having seen them pull into the parking lot. A short, balding man, he appeared to carry the burdens of educating the younger generations on his tapered shoulders.

"Good morning. I'm Harvey Gates, principal of Oakwood School," said Gates, extending his hand.

"Mr. Gates, I'm Detective Richard Lanslow. This is my partner, Detective Sergeant Dean Brooks."

"Yes, good morning, Sergeant Brooks," said Gates, turning to Brooks and shaking his hand. "Not often, to say the least, that we get visits from the police. A good thing, too, come to think about it." He smiled wanly at both men. "I hope we can be of help."

Somewhere, the sounds of children shouting could be heard, a basketball bouncing, feet running, a shrill whistle. Odors of leather and sweat wafted through the hallway. Brooks, the basketball player, was obviously curious as he looked in the direction of the sounds.

"As I said on the phone," said Lanslow, "we're trying to locate a John P. Matson. We have information that he went to school here. Any information you might be able to provide would be appreciated."

"Come this way," said Gates. "I've had Miss Brown pull what records we have on the Matson boy. It seems he was with Oakwood until age sixteen, tenth grade. I wasn't here then, of course, but from the record it seems the boy was in trouble quite a lot, over and over. When he allegedly attempted to rape a girl, his mother took him out of school and, I believe, placed him in a reform school somewhere. We don't have anything on the boy after that."

Gates motioned the two detectives into a small conference room furnished with a single table and some chairs. On the table there was a stack of yearbooks and a manila folder.

"You can go over the records here," said Gates. He pointed to the manila folder. "That's the boy's records. We've provided some year-books, as well. That's the latest one." He pointed to a yearbook lying off to the side from the others. "If you need any further assistance, just let me know. I'll be in my office just down the hall."

"Thank you. This will do very well," said Lanslow, as Gates left, closing the door behind him. The sounds of the yelling children, the bouncing balls, subsided.

The yearbook lying off to the side was already open. Lanslow pulled it across the table as Brooks sat down and opened the manila folder. Lanslow peered at the open page. Scanning across the page row by row, his eyes alighted on the picture of a young boy, turned slightly sideways to the camera, his hair neatly combed, smiling. Beneath the picture was the name: "John Matson."

Lanslow turned the yearbook toward Brooks and slid it over to him, pointing to the picture. "Here's our boy," he said.

Both men scrutinized the picture closely. The face was vaguely famil-iar to Lanslow, somehow. He searched his memory but couldn't come up with anything.

"He'd be what age today?" asked Brooks.

Lanslow turned the yearbook over to look at the cover. The year was 1975.

"He was in tenth grade here," said Lanslow. "The principal said he was sixteen when this picture was taken ... he'd be about ... forty-something now? About forty-three, forty-four." Lanslow looked at the picture again. "Who would ever think an innocent face like that could turn into a cop killer," he said, shaking his head dejectedly.

"We don't know that he had anything to do with Zeke, yet," admonished Brooks, quickly.

Lanslow caught himself. He'd made an unwarranted leap in fitting the facts to his theory. "Yeah. Sorry. My mistake."

"Anyway, he's gonna look a lot different from this picture," said Brooks. "We can post it, though. Maybe someone will recognize it. We can get forensics to age it, too."

"Anything in there?" asked Lanslow, pointing to the manila folder.

"Nothing I can see right away. Got pretty good grades. Like the principal said, though, he was in trouble a lot. Fighting, mostly."

Gates appeared in the doorway. "Anything you need?" he asked.

"I don't suppose any of these teachers in here would still be around?" asked Brooks, holding up the manila folder.

"No," said Gates. "Those teachers have all retired or left. The boy left in 1975. That's nearly thirty years ago."

"You know if any of them might still be living in this area?"

Gates looked over the names. "I don't know any of these teachers, Detective. I've been here only a couple of years myself."

Brooks nodded. "We'll check," he said. He began flipping through the grade cards and other records again, jotting the names of John Paul Matson's teachers in his notebook.

Lanslow was busy jotting down the names of Matson's classmates. "Would you know if any of these students are still around?" he asked.

Gates looked over the student's pictures, reading the names beneath. "I'm afraid not, Detective. I don't recognize any of them, either."

"One other thing," said Lanslow, rising, "John Matson was only sixteen when he left Oakwood. You say you don't know which reform school he went to?"

"No. I don't know anything more than what's in the record, Detective. Sorry I can't be of more help."

"I forgot to mention it on the phone," said Lanslow, "but Matson had a sister, name of Lee Ann. Would you have any records on her?"

"I'm certain we do. I can have Miss Brown pull her records if you like. Her photo would probably be in that yearbook, too. The grades weren't separated into different schools back then, like they are now."

Lanslow checked through his notes after Gates had left. He hadn't taken any more information than the girl's name. He began to thumb back through the yearbook, scanning across each of the photos. On the page showing the seventh grade he saw a photo with the name Lee Ann Matson under it, a girl with blonde hair and a Mona Lisa smile.

I

"Well, by damn, that turned out to be a lot more valuable than I thought," said Brooks, smacking his gloved hands together as they walked to the squad car, their shoes crunching in the snow. "You're coming along, Richie."

Lanslow smiled in amusement. 'Richie' was what Zeke had begun to call him, after they had been together for a while. "What do you think we should do first? Get this picture to the lab or do a little legwork?"

Brooks glanced at his watch. "We'll do the legwork while we're over here. I've never liked to do it, but it has to be done."

"Getting Matson's juvenile records once we find out where he was sent will require a court order."

"Yeah. And if it's the juvenile system in Wisconsin, it's gonna take a while."

They got in the car. Lanslow sat for a moment. Brooks looked at him questioningly.

"You know, Dean," said Lanslow, turning toward Brooks, "if Matson spent most of his early life in this area, there just has to be some more records that might let us find him quicker."

"County records?"

"Yeah. Birth certificate, marriage license. I'm thinking we might be able to get a couple of addresses, or relative's or friend's names ... ."

Brooks glanced at his watch again. "If we do that, the interviews will just have to wait. I think you're right, though. The county seat for this county is in Hudson. That's south of here."

∎

The St. Croix County government complex sat on a plateau above and a couple of miles east of the town of Hudson. The town itself sat on the banks of the St. Croix river. The road to the complex rose moderately upward to the plateau. They pulled into a large parking lot. The snowfall had been heavier here and the snow in the parking lot had been plowed into long, high rows.

The detectives had to show their badges and tell the clerk behind the counter why they needed to look at the records, and the clerk had to go get her supervisor because, as she said, the records weren't "open to just anybody," and she wasn't sure she had the authority to allow the detectives to see them, especially since they were from Minnesota and not Wisconsin. The supervisor was a tall, brusque, no-nonsense lady, in a dark dress, who knew her business. Again, the detectives had to show their badges and fill out a form the lady produced.

When they had done so, she said "Which record do you want to check first?"

Lanslow and Brooks looked at one another. "How about birth records, to start, then marriages?" said Brooks.

The supervisor turned and disappeared into a room in back.

"The birth certificate will give us his residential address at that time, as well as his birthplace," Brooks said to Lanslow. "Also, we should be able get the father's name as well as the maiden name of his mother."

"What good will that do?" asked Lanslow.

"Just some loose ends tied," said Brooks. "You never know what might come of it."

The supervisor returned a few minutes later bearing a heavy, vinyl-bound volume with maroon colored covers. It was labeled as an index to births in St. Croix County. "What's the name you're looking for, Detective?"

"John Paul Matson," said Brooks.

She opened the book and began going through the many pages. She came to a page and traced downward through the list of names. She turned the book so the detectives could read it. "We don't have that name on our birth records" she said.

Lanslow scanned the page. He looked at Brooks.

"Maybe he was born in another county," said Brooks, shrugging. "Okay. Let's try marriages. He went to school in this county. Maybe he got married here even if he was born somewhere else."

The supervisor returned, struggling with another large volume. She laid the volume down, turning the pages. She turned until she came to the M's, then began tracing downward. She traced all the way through until she came to the name Matzke. She traced back, again, up the page. There were no Matsons listed. "Sorry, no Matson," she said, turning the book to the detectives.

"He went to school here, but he was born somewhere else and he didn't get married here," said Lanslow, more or less to himself.

Brooks took the volume from Lanslow and traced down the lines. He traced through twice, more slowly the second time. "Is the name spelled with two T's or one? ... Hey, look at that" he said. "Do you see what I see?" Brooks pointed at the lines of names, pushing the book to where Lanslow could see. "That one. There."

Lanslow bent over the book, reading down the lines again. He read the name, then looked at Brooks, a puzzled expression on his face.

"Isn't that curious?" asked Brooks.

"I don't see it, Dean, what are you looking at?"

The supervisor was watching this exchange. She looked at the list of names, too, staring, as if it would reveal something extraordinary.

"There," said Brooks, pointing. "Do you see the name there, on the third line from the bottom?"

Lanslow bent low, his eyes moving to the referenced line. The name on the page read "John Paul Matthews."

"I see it," said Lanslow. "What about it?"

"Would that be *the* Professor Matthews?"

"Beats the heck out of me," said Lanslow, still staring at the name. "Is Matthew's name John Paul?"

"I thought you knew him," said Brooks.

"Actually, I don't know his full name. I've always just called him 'Jack,' like everybody else at the college. 'Course, 'Jack' is another form of 'John.' I don't know his middle name, but the initial is P, come to think of it."

"Sure is. P for 'Paul.' I remember because I read his book on gangs several years ago—'John Paul Matthews,' right on the front cover."

Lanslow stared at the name. "That's quite a coincidence. What do you make of it?"

"What the … heck," said Brooks, looking quickly at the supervisor. "Looks like maybe the professor got married right here in St. Croix county," he said to Lanslow, shrugging his shoulders, "or someone with the same name. Wonder if this Matthews was born here, too?"

"I suppose you want to see the birth records again," said the supervisor.

"If you don't mind, ma'am," said Brooks. "We'll just have a look."

28

Matthews had decided to avoid the issue with Luke Tuesday evening, including his decision about Annie, and he had stayed overnight at Maureen's.

"You seem preoccupied," she had said once during their early dinner, and he realized he hadn't spoken for a considerable length of time.

"Sorry," he said, and he tried to give her his full attention afterward. It had been a struggle; and then he couldn't sleep. Staring into the darkness as Maureen slept beside him, he kept going over and over how he could resolve his dilemma concerning Luke.

He still hadn't come to any resolution by morning light and when he got to his office, he was searching for his last ounce of energy and had grown irritable. He plodded through the student's blue books, skimmed through the student's essays, not remembering the paragraph he'd read, having to read it again, having to leave his chair and take walks to relieve the monotony.

At lunch time he went to the cafeteria, intending to get a bowl of soup and bring it back to his office but he spied Harvey Schroedl sitting at a table with Leo Morganthaler. They motioned him over. He managed to delay returning to his office for a half hour, talking about students and grading and what the administration would spring on them next semester, and whether the faculty would get its normal two percent raise against a four percent rate of inflation this year with a Republican governor in office and a Republican-controlled senate. He'd been through these same kinds of conversations for over fifteen years. He finished his soup, excused himself and returned to his office.

He managed with great effort to work his way through several more blue books before having to attend a department meeting. Afterwards, he placed his class lists and the essays into his briefcase to be done tomorrow. He had until Monday to get them into the records office.

Driving from the parking lot, he tried to avoid the broken bottle, standing upright, but he hit it. Nothing happened, at first. He continued out of the college parking lot, turned north and eventually merged onto South Shore Boulevard, skirting the large lake from which the city of White Bear Lake got its name. That's when the tire gave out. He felt the wheel wobble in his hands and then it eventually became almost impossible to steer. He managed to pull the vehicle onto the shoulder. He got out of the car and walked around the front to the right side. The tire was completely flat. He would have to change it.

Matthews boiled. "One damned, stupid thing after another," he said to himself. He glanced at his watch. Half past five and he and Maureen had another dinner reservation at six. "Some yahoo can't even have the decency to keep the damned bottle in the car after he's finished with the damned thing. Has to leave it in the goddamned parking lot!"

He pulled off his topcoat, slung it over the seat, and pressed the trunk latch. He rolled up his sleeves and walked to the rear, beginning to shiver from the cold almost immediately. The spare tire was fastened by a large wing nut. He unscrewed the nut, dropping it to the side of the trunk, lifted the cover and pulled out the small spare. As he did so, a red rag with dark stains fell to the bottom of the well.

"What the hell?"

He picked up the rag. It was stained darkly, and it was heavy—something in it. Carefully, he unwrapped the rag, and there, lying in his hands, was a large knife, and the blade still carried evidence of reddish brown stains.

■

Their drive back to White Bear Lake was taking longer than usual, Brooks having slowed the squad down to a cruise while both men mulled the information they had gleaned from their inquiries. A line of traffic piled up behind them, the drivers fearing to pass and risk getting a ticket.

They had found no record of birth in St. Croix County for John Paul Matthews and had been able to interview only one of the former teachers of John Paul Matson, a very elderly lady who wanted to reminisce but who, as it turned out, couldn't remember a thing about the boy. They hadn't been able to find a single classmate. The light of day had faded to a dark gray. The car's headlights pushed into the dimness ahead.

They had driven several miles and Lanslow thought that for once Brooks was keeping his thoughts to himself. Then Brooks said, "Do you know whether Professor Matthews is from Wisconsin?""

"I never thought to ask" said Lanslow.

"It's funny" said Brooks. "John Paul Matthews's name shows up on the marriage records. Same first and second names. And the marriage took place in Somerset," he added, "and that's where Matson went to school."

"The name Matthews didn't show up on any birth record, though, and Professor Matthews isn't married, now," said Lanslow.

"Oh, yeah?"

"Naw. He and a woman named Evans more or less live together. The woman's last name on the marriage certificate was Garvey."

"More or less?" asked Brooks, grinning.

"They live separately. They just stay over."

"Sounds like a great arrangement."

"If the Matthews on the marriage certificate is the professor, then he's been divorced," said Lanslow.

"Was the Professor divorced?"

"I don't know. Maybe."

"Maybe it is just a coincidence," said Brooks, backing away somewhat from a hypothesis that just seemed too far-fetched. "I've never believed in coincidences, but this ... ." Brooks's voice trailed off.

"This whole case has too damned many coincidences," said Lanslow, "but this has to be one."

"Yeah. Could be someone else with the same name."

"Yeah. Could be. Seems like a pretty common name."

"Even if it is the Professor, that doesn't mean much."

"No. Could be just a coincidence."

"Yeah, that's probably it."

Both men went silent again. Lanslow imagined the wheels turning in the older detective's head, just as they were in his. It was just too fantastic to believe, of course, but the idea kept popping up.

"I've learned a long time ago to expect some twists and turns in murder cases," said Brooks, after awhile, "and I've seen a lot of them when I was with LAPD. But if the Professor somehow turns out to be implicated in Henry Barrows's murder, it will top them all."

Brooks had said it, what they were both thinking.

"Unbelievable," said Lanslow.

"When I was on the gang task force in L.A. I read everything I could about gangs. Matthews's book on gangs ... I read that thing over and over." Brooks shook his head.

"I'm afraid I never read it," said Lanslow. "Before my time."

"He helped win that big case over in Minneapolis, you know, the one where some gang members killed another gang member during a riot? The defense was arguing that the gang members had been caught up in the 'emotional contagion' of the riot. Kind of a temporary insanity type of thing."

Lanslow recalled the case. He'd been in college then, and his criminology class had been following it.

"Matthews was called in as an expert for the prosecution," said Brooks.

The young detective couldn't quite remember that. "How so?"

"Everybody was afraid these punks would beat the rap. Professor Matthews argued that research showed that people keep their judgment about right from wrong, even in riots. The gang members were found guilty and got life. It was a big deal at the time."

Lanslow shook his head ruefully. Despite how preposterous it seemed, he was beginning to consider seriously the possibility that Jack Matthews was somehow involved. "You know," said Lanslow, "White saw the perp at both scenes. He described him as a little white guy. Jack Matthews isn't that big."

"That's true. Too bad we can't find White and get him in here to help ID the photo, once we get it aged. He saw his face, didn't he?"

"Says he did. White is gone, though. We'll be a long time catching him, even if we do."

"If we can age that photo we got of Matson, we'll know whether it's Matthews, anyway," said Brooks.

"Maybe so. People change a lot."

"That's for damn sure," said Brooks.

"Matson was about sixteen when that photo was taken. That'd put him in his early forties now. Wouldn't the professor be about that age, now?"

Both men went silent again.

"You think John Paul Matson and John Paul Matthews are the same person then?" asked Brooks.

"I don't know what to think. There's a lot that fits, here, but how can that be, different names and all?"

"People change their names all the time. "

"Man! I hadn't thought about that." Lanslow began going over his notes again. "According to the principal, Matson was sent to reform school when he was sixteen or so. If Matson and Matthews are the same person, then Matson would have had to change his name sometime between sixteen and twenty-two, which was the age on the marriage certificate. Why would a man that young want to change his name?"

"Who knows? But people who change their names probably do it mostly to hide their backgrounds. Matson was sent to reform school … or at least we're assuming he was."

"Okay ... but ... those records are closed to the public, anyway. So what else would he have to hide?"

"That principal said he'd tried to rape a girl, right?"

"Yeah."

"Maybe that's why."

"But only people in his hometown would know that. And they would know who he is, anyway, even with a new name. Doesn't stand to reason."

"Well, whatever it is, he would have had to change his name between the time he got out of reform school and the time he got married."

"Assuming he did, then he would have gotten out, done something he wants to keep hidden, then changed his name. He's running away from something."

"Sounds plausible. Now, the next thing we've got to consider is motive," said Brooks. "We know why Matson, or Matthews, might want to kill Barrows, but why in hell would Matthews want to kill Zeke?"

"Well, there's one possibility, and this is where it gets weird," said Lanslow. "Remember? I told you that Matthews himself had suggested we have a psycho on our hands and that the two murders might be purely coincidental? He thought the murderer has this psychosis of some kind— that the murderer could have run into Zeke, something happened, and he killed him. Similar stab wounds as with Barrows, but no other connection between the two."

"Holy crap!" exclaimed Brooks, eyebrows raised in disbelief. "I'd forgotten you told me that. You talked to the possible murderer about his own case! Holy crap!"

The incredulity of the situation struck both men. They both were silent again. Lanslow's thoughts whirled, jumbled together like shredded paper. Had he gotten the case off on the wrong track? Maybe his hunch that John Paul Matson had killed Barrows out of revenge was just a wild-assed shot in the dark and had led them to a fruitless nowhere. And maybe Jack Matthews's name on the marriage certificate, if it was him, was merely coincidence. And if that was all there was to it, he could well imagine how Chief Bradbury and the rest of his colleagues would react. He felt the embarrassment creeping up his rookie neck right then and there.

It just seems too impossible, Lanslow thought. Professor Jack Matthews, the Professor Matthews, a psycho cop killer? Diagnosing and consulting on his own case? John Paul Matthews and John Paul Matson just had to be two different people.

▌

The door to Matthews's garage slid open quietly, the headlights of his car illuminating the interior. He drove the car inside, turned off the headlights, shut down the engine and just sat. The knife, wrapped in the red rag, lay on the seat beside him. He had elected not to drop the damaged tire off to be fixed. He wanted to get home, to think.

How had the knife and rag gotten into his car? Why would it be there?

Matthews thoughts focused on Luke. Were the knife and rag connected to the girl's wallet? Was Luke involved in even more than he had begun to suspect? What on earth could Luke have been thinking to have hidden the knife in his car?

He picked up the rag and knife and his briefcase, his emotional burden growing geometrically, compounded by fear and dread for himself and his son. As he opened the door to his house he heard the phone ringing. He hurried to his study and picked it up. Maureen was wondering why he was late. He had forgotten to call her, even on the cellular. And he would have to drive to her house on the little spare tire, or she would have to come and get him.

▌

"I have dinner on the table!"

"I know, hon. I can't help it. I'll be home as soon as I can." There was a long silence. "Laura?"

"Is this what our life is going to be like, Richard? Is it? If it is, then we need to talk."

"Laura, listen. I'll be home as soon as I can. We have a break in the case."

"Zeke's?"

"Yes. We've found a new suspect."

"Who is it?"

"I can't say right now."

"When will you be home?"

"I'm not sure."

Again, a long silence. Finally, "I'll keep your dinner warm, then."

There had been a note of finality in Laura's voice that alarmed him. When he got home a little after midnight, she was in bed, asleep, though he couldn't be sure. He tried to remain quiet as he pulled the plate from the warm oven. There were potatoes, baked, then browned in a skillet. There was shredded beef with the sauce he loved, and asparagus, and a roll. He thought of Christine, planning for the special evening with Zeke that had turned into horror. Being a policeman's wife wasn't easy. Finally, he thought of Sarah Riggs and the delight she might feel at the news that he and Laura had broken up. "Damn!" he said, as he poured himself a glass of milk.

Before he'd left the station, Lanslow had made copies of John Paul Matson's school photo and then driven to the Minnesota BCA to drop off the yearbook they'd gotten from the school. Linda Voiss, the computer technician at the lab, whom he knew and was on good terms with, was still working. He'd tried to impress her with the importance of getting the photo done quickly. "Hey, you think I live here?" she'd said. He had also called the county clerk in Hudson to ask for the records of the court's actions during the 1970s decade. They would have a record of name changes if, indeed, Matson had changed his name in St. Croix County. The clerk's office had been closed, though, and he left a message.

What kept nagging Lanslow was the idea, planted by Matthews himself, that they were dealing with a psychotic personality. He thought back to his and Matthews's relationship over the years. Matthews had some strange ways about him, but Lanslow didn't consider them to be abnormal. Still, he thought, who was he to say who was demented and who wasn't? He knew that psychotics often hid their condition very well, being very good at appearing normal. Most people just couldn't believe it when their next door neighbor turned out to be a serial killer. On the other hand, Matthews often did appear to be forgetful and moody, somewhat stoic, but Lanslow, now that he thought about it, didn't consider that very peculiar. It was obvious that the professor had other things on his mind, but that certainly didn't make him psychotic. Hell, he was to have other things on his mind.

The question was: what would they do should Matthews turn out to be the young man in the photo? Obviously, Matthews would become a prime suspect for the murder of Henry Barrows, but what then? How, exactly, was he connected to Zeke Mallard? Lanslow tried to remember if Zeke had ever mentioned meeting or knowing the professor, but he couldn't recall him ever doing so. Zeke's secret life with Angelena Rosario had shaken his presuppositions about his partner, to say the least. Were there more secrets, secrets involving Zeke and Jack Matthews?

He thought again about his and the professor's past relationship— mentor and friend—and their discussions of the case they'd had. If the professor, indeed, had anything to do with Zeke's murder, it was amazing that the man had been able to carry these discussions off without revealing a single hint of his culpability.

He felt hands around his throat and jumped.

"A little jumpy, are we?" said Laura, her hands slipping up to his hair, over his ears, around his eyes, down to his throat again. He looked up at her.

"We have to talk, Richard," she said.

29

L anslow had not slept well, an indisposition he'd acquired since Zeke
Mallard's death that was only exacerbated by his and Laura's "conversation" which lasted until 2:00 A.M. He had won a reprieve. Keeping
his girl while trying to solve his partner's death at the same time was
turning out to be a hell of a task. He felt tired and listless and his arms
ached. Over and over the facts of Zeke's case and the findings from yesterday's foray into Wisconsin had percolated through his half-awake
mind, even into his early morning dreams, dreams of a wispy figure of a
woman, swaying to and fro, and a shadowy figure of a man, a little man,
following her wherever she went. And he couldn't catch either one of
them.

As he lay there, he tried again to distill the results of his nighttime per-
egrinations. He should concentrate his energies on one thing at a time,
he thought, and for now it had to be his partner's murder.

His investigation of the abused Matson boy had turned out radically
different than he'd expected. There was the possibility that he'd gotten
no closer to solving Zeke's murder— that, in fact, he may have led the
investigation astray. Even if the boy named Matson and Professor Matthews were one and the same person, it meant only that he and Brooks
had uncovered a distant, past association between Matthews and Barrows that yielded a possible motive. Should Matthews, indeed, turn out
to be Matson, what then? CSI's forensic technicians had found zero evi-

dence. A case against Matthews would be nothing but circumstantial. And even if prosecutors could make a circumstantial case stick and get a conviction, there wouldn't be anything to connect Matthews to Zeke's murder other than the fact that the MOs in the two murders were remarkably similar. As far as Zeke's case was concerned, the DA's office, Lanslow knew, would have none of it. They would need more.

Energy ebbed. He sat up on the edge of the bed, retrieved his T-shirt from the edge of the chair, and tried to pull it on. Everything, his T-shirt and robe, his house-shoes, resisted attempts to get them on. He ambled to the bathroom, despairing of the image he would find in the mirror. His despair was affirmed. He could only hope that the warm water on his face, a shave and brushing his teeth, would restore some semblance of his better self.

Laura slept and he eyed her jealously as he sat in the chair beside the bed and pulled on socks, trousers, shirt, belt and sport coat. He avoided ties; he abhorred anything that tightened the collar around his neck.

One shoe on, the other, resisting, dropped to the floor with a thud.

Laura stirred and turned over, her face half submerged in the fluffy pillow and blanket. She looked at him through half-closed eyes. "You're leaving? What time is it?"

"Early. I can't sleep."

"What time will you be home? We have more shopping ..."

"I'll be home as soon as I can. We'll go shopping," he said, curtly, unable to control the testiness he felt.

"Okay, hon. Have a good day."

Laura had missed his sour mood. "You too," he said, closing the door to their bedroom quietly.

▌

Lanslow guided his unmarked car down State Highway 96, turning north on State Highway 61 toward the main part of White Bear Lake. The police station sat on the West side of Highway 61, just behind a new shopping mall housing the usual deli and pizza and Chinese fast food stores, a video store and an upscale coffee shop, among other businesses. The City Hall sat adjoining the mall to the south, directly across from the police and fire stations. Most of the business owners had followed a tradition that had been established in White Bear Lake of stringing various colored lights along their building's roofs, forming an outline of the town. The older part of the city, sitting south of the highway, with its more traditional architecture, was more complex, more interesting.

The station was quiet at 7:00 A.M. Trudging through the parking lot, the temperature seemed to be warming, though the sky was gray and cloudy. Lanslow hadn't paid any attention to the forecasts. Old Man Winter couldn't seem to make up his mind; having a quarrel with Mother Nature, maybe.

The rookie detective checked in, sat down at his desk and tried to think, the activity that seemed to take most of his job description. He had already concluded during his drive to the station that their only recourse was to play out the lead on Matson as far as it took them. The hope would be that they might uncover something that would connect Matson to Zeke's murder.

Should he call the lab? He'd probably only delay the process, if they were doing anything at all. Waves of fatigue washed over him. He rose, plucked Zeke Mallard's case file from the shelf. As he opened the file, the fax-phone rang. He went to the fax machine and watched as the paper rolled out. The first page was addressed to him, from Linda Voiss at the Minnesota BCA and bore a note informing him that the photo of John Paul Matson had been processed. At the bottom she'd written in big letters: "YOU OWE ME!" The second sheet began to feed out, taking an eternity. An image appeared, of a middle-aged man, with an eerie likeness of Professor John Paul Matthews. Lanslow took the image back to his desk, sat down, and just stared at it, trying to absorb its implications.

"That's him, for sure," said Brooks, having moped in a little before eight, staring at the computer-aged image of Jack Matthews over Lanslow's shoulder.

"It's him," said Lanslow. "But it just doesn't figure. How in hell … ."

They were both silent for a while.

"We don't have much, even if we know he did it," said Brooks, finally. "And actually, we don't even know that he did it, for sure. Even if he is this John Paul Matson kid, all we have is a possible motive for him killing Barrows and an MO link to Zeke. That's all we have, and that ain't diddly."

Brooks had merely echoed the flitting, darting thoughts in Lanslow's brain that had kept him awake most of the night.

"There's one more thing, just to tie up a loose end," said Lanslow. "I called earlier and left a message with the county clerk's office in Wisconsin to see if Matson changed his name, even though it's a near certainty he must have." He glanced at his watch. "I'll give them another call, see if they have anything yet." He picked up the phone and dialed the number. The clerk said she'd gotten the message and would get back to him.

About forty-five minutes later the county clerk called and it was confirmed. John Paul Matson had changed his name to John Paul Matthews in January of 1977, three months before he had gotten married.

"Well, that's that. What do we do now?" asked Lanslow.

"We gotta have a little get together with the Chief," said Brooks.

I

Chief Bradbury stared at the aged photo of Professor Jack Matthews in disbelief. "I'll be goddamned," he said. "This is unbelievable." He looked from the photo of the younger Matthews to the older one, and back again, over and over. He read the scribbled Post-It note by Lanslow confirming that Jack Matthews had once been John Paul Matson.

After a time, Bradbury said "Well, okay, there it is." He looked at Lanslow, his lips pressed in a barely visible line, his eyes saddened. "You said before that the reason Matson could have murdered Zeke was just a matter of chance, that he was psycho, that something happened to set him off and he killed Zeke. But Matthews is no psycho, or if he is, he sure as hell has fooled a lot of people around here for a long time. Hard to believe." It seemed almost as though the Chief was attempting to talk himself out of the possibility that Jack Matthews was implicated, despite the evidence he held in his hands.

"It's the only explanation, Chief," said Lanslow, "unless there's something we've missed in Matthews's background ... maybe something between him and Zeke ... that we don't know about. But I don't think so. I don't think Zeke even knew him, or vice versa."

"Well, anyway, Matthews is our only lead," said Brooks. "We have to check him out. The question is how."

"You have no physical evidence linking Matthews to either crime," said Lieutenant Johnson, standing beside Bradbury's desk, "and without it, all you have here is circumstantial, and even that is very weak, to boot. Basically, it's just your hunch, Rich. We have to have more evidence that points to Matthews, like the lack of an alibi for either of the periods of the crime, for example. That'll show opportunity. You have to try to come up with motive and means, too, if you can. You get all that, maybe we can get a search warrant and even make an arrest, or at least bring him in for questioning."

"We'd have to have him tested by a psychiatrist or psychologist to get motive," said Brooks.

"We'd have to give him a lie-detector test," said Lanslow, thinking at the same time that they had a lot more than just his hunch.

"I don't know of any other way," said Bradbury.

"Then he'd know we're on his trail," said Lanslow.

"Yes, he'd know he's under suspicion," said Bradbury.

"He'd know that anyway if we interview him" said Brooks.

"True," said Bradbury.

"Do we want him to know he's a suspect this soon?" asked Lanslow. "What about surveillance?"

Bradbury swiveled his chair to where he could look out his window. After a pause long enough to cause the detectives to look at one another questioningly, he said, "We'll need to set up surveillance, but first try to get as much information as you can. Check his background out thoroughly. See if anything pops out, or if any additional circumstantial evidence might emerge. Check his work schedule, his phone records, his financial situation, and his medical background. It'll be better if we can get all of this before we get a warrant for search or arrest, just to keep some smart-ass lawyer from being able to persuade a judge not to admit it in court afterwards. I don't see any reason to hurry on this as long as we can be sure he's not going to do anything else. Let's get everything together here, then we'll move."

When Brooks and Lanslow returned to their desks, Lanslow's phone rang. Lanslow lifted the receiver. "Detective Lanslow."

There was a pause on the other end. Then Lanslow heard a familiar voice.

"Lanslow, this is Andrew White."

30

Sitting at his office desk Thursday evening, entering the final grades into the computer, depression descended on Jack Matthews like a heavy black cloud. He tried to overcome it cognitively, with the rationality and reason that had served him relatively well throughout his life, but he found he was talking to himself in clichés, metaphors and generalities. So, he was depressed. What of it? Everyone got depressed. Things would probably turn out all right. Anyway, he was probably blowing this thing all out of whack. And, really, what's the worst that could happen?

Well, of course, that was the wrong thing to ask himself. He imagined all sorts of things. His son, involved in drugs or even worse, violence—and, if so, what then? Gangs? The police? A trial? Prison? Maybe, even ... a sentence of death? What in God's name (he realized the irony of this expression) had Luke done?

Events of the day hadn't helped. The weather had turned warm, though cloudy, and it was raining, a slow, cold drizzle that had lasted all day. The snow was beginning to melt, becoming lumpy, exposing the older dirty layer underneath. Rain always brought melancholy anyway, but now it was even more depressing. It seemed to Matthews that it had rained a lot lately. What was the song by Brook Benton? "A Rainy Night in Georgia—It seems like it's raining all over the world?" Those words caught his mood exactly.

Then he'd had to attend one of those silly "Faculty Development" sessions where the faculty and administrators had divided into small groups, with a discussion leader, and they'd had to work up a set of answers to a set of questions the administration thought might unearth what they perceived as low morale at the college. The discussion leader of each group had then gotten up and read what the group had come up with. The administrator in charge of the session had dutifully annotated his interpretation of the answers as they were reported. This was all to show the faculty how much the administrators cared about their opinions. But, of course, that would be the end of it. It was the same, year after year. Nothing changed. All Matthews had wanted to do was finish grading his exams, turn in his grades and go home to confront, again, his situation.

They were finally released around three o'clock and he had machine-scored the final answer sheets, entered the scores into his computer, calculated the breaking points on the distribution, and assigned the grades. The grades were awful. It seemed they got worse every year. It only added to his depression. Resignedly, he signed the grade sheets, placed them in an envelope and carried them to the office of the registrar. He then returned to his office and answered some mail and tied up some other loose ends. He wanted to be completely free of his academic duties over the semester break.

Luke's car wasn't in the driveway when he drove in. It was about seven o'clock. The house was dark. He slid wearily out of his car, inserted the house key into the lock and went in. Where the hell was that kid? They needed to confront this. Once and for all, they needed to talk.

Matthews turned on the light, removed his coat and hung it in the closet.

Dinner Wednesday night with Maureen had been another effort, to say the least. Matthews was again aware of her searching gaze the whole time. He tried to cover the turmoil inside but knew she suspected that something was wrong and she was worried. He didn't know quite why, but he just didn't want to share this with her. He had kissed her this morning with the emotion engendered by his dread of the future and what it seemed to imply—something frightful, something that would be another turning point in his life, and he'd had the feeling that it might be the last time he would ever feel Maureen's soft kiss. Completely irrational, he knew. Nevertheless ...

Depression hung on. He felt pangs of hunger but didn't want to make the effort. He picked up his briefcase and went downstairs to take it to his study. He set the briefcase to the side of his desk, in its accustomed place. His organizer and Glenda Morrison's wallet sat on the top of his desk where he had left them, the desk lamp still on. Just more reminders of his growing forgetfulness.

He sat down, turned on his computer to check his e-mail, and waited for the desktop to load. As the computer screen filled, he surveyed his office where he spent so much of his time. The feeling that something bad was going to happen lay heavy and leaden in the pit of his stomach: he began to think of the futility of his life. Rows of bookshelves lined his office, from floor to ceiling, full of books he'd read: Emile Durkheim's *The Elementary Forms of the Religious Life;* Max Weber's *The Theory of Social and Economic Organization,* Daniel Bell's T*he Coming of Post Industrial Society,* and a hundred more. All for what? What had it come to?

He looked at the drawer to his desk where the knife, wrapped in the red rag, lay. Reluctantly, he opened the drawer and reached in to bring the bundle out. He couldn't find it. He explored every part of the drawer as well as all the others. He opened his briefcase and explored every pocket. The knife and rag were nowhere to be found—gone.

■

Dorian was amazed that Glenda Morrison had not changed her address. He waited back among the trees and shrubs until a car drove into the parking lot, made its way to the underground garage, and the driver used her remote control to open the door. He slipped in unobtrusively as the car entered, moving directly to a car parked in a slot off to the side, as if he was going to use it. The woman's car proceeded on down the driving lane and pulled into a slot. The woman exited the car and walked to an elevator. Dorian waited until she entered and the door had closed, then went to the elevator himself and pressed the button. He exited on the first floor. In the entryway he peered through the glass doors and checked the names on the mailboxes and buzzers and found Glenda Morrison's name on the box for room 308. He had found her. The question now was how to get the job done.

At that moment someone walked up the steps outside and started to come in. Dorian turned quickly, walking to the stairway, his back turned to the person. He stopped and glanced back. Glenda Morrison stood just outside the door, her face stricken with terror. She had seen him. She turned and ran back out the way she had come. Dorian ran after her, struggling with the doors, pursuing her into the parking lot. She had jumped in the passenger side of a car with another woman driver.

Dorian ran to the car, tried to open the locked door, then pounded on the driver-side glass, but the driver jammed the gas pedal down and the car spun out, wet snow and ice flying, covering his jacket, speckling his hair, clogging his eyelashes. He stood there, helpless, and watched the car speed away.

▌

Even though Lanslow tried to convince White he was no longer the number one suspect, White refused to come to the station. He agreed to meet with Lanslow, alone, on the detective's word that he would not be arrested. Lanslow was to use his own personal car and his own personal cell phone and come unarmed. If not, the deal was off.

Bradbury, Brooks and Johnson had been reluctant but in the end had given in. They knew who their main suspect was, now, and they needed White's identification of Matthews as the man he'd seen at Zeke Mallard's home. Brooks would back Lanslow up, sufficiently out of sight so as to arouse no suspicion, but only a call away on their own frequency. Lanslow would carry the police cell phone beneath the car seat. He would also carry a weapon, a .38 caliber, in the small of his back to escape immediate detection. They would install a tracking device on Lanslow's vehicle.

Lanslow convinced White he had to meet him within the White Bear jurisdiction, but White would call and let Lanslow know exactly where to meet him. The detective presumed White would probably be calling from pay phones, or perhaps had stolen someone's cell phone.

White's first call directed him to a restaurant parking lot at an intersection near the interstate highway. Lanslow was to wait there for the next call. On the police phone, Lanslow checked with Brooks to make sure they knew where he was headed, then placed it under the front seat. He drove to the location and waited. It was 6:30 P.M. and dark. The air was heavy and damp, a thin mist forming on the windshield. Thirty minutes passed, during which the young detective assumed White was checking him out, from somewhere. Lanslow spotted a couple just sitting in a car in one of the parking spots. They seemed to be talking about something and not paying any attention to him. But any of the customers in the parking lot, going to the restaurant or leaving it, or just driving through, could be White's lookout.

The next call came. Lanslow answered on the first ring. "Lanslow."

"Lanslow, go on down County Road E to 120. Park in the shopping mall lot. I'll meet you there. You'd better be alone."

"All right, White. Got it."

Lanslow waited until he was on the road before calling Brooks again. He hadn't seen any car follow him. He thought the possibility of anyone seeing him make the call was slim. He got to the mall only a few minutes later. Again, there was a wait. Then Lanslow was startled to hear a tap on the car window. When he looked up, it wasn't White who peered in at him. He was looking into the face of Albert Carter.

The concern on Lanslow's countenance apparently amused Carter. He had a smile on his face. Lanslow hesitated, then rolled down the glass, his hand near his gun at his back.

"What are you doing here, Detective?" Carter asked.

"I might ask you the same thing, Carter," Lanslow replied.

"I thought we might take a little ride, Detective."

"Where's White, Carter?"

"Andrew? Oh, he'll be along. You have to come with me."

Lanslow tried to think. If he went he would lose contact and backup. "No deal, Carter. White said he'd meet me here."

"He won't do it, Detective. Either you come with me or Andrew skips."

"What is this, Carter? Andrew can trust me. I told him that."

"Sorry, Detective. That's it. Take it or leave it."

Lanslow knew it was foolish. Brooks and the others would lose him now, but Andrew White's eyewitness identification would be the key to connecting Matthews with Zeke's murder and would be crucial in the trial. It was the break they needed. Lanslow opened the door to the car and got out. Carter loomed over him. Lanslow had forgotten how big Carter was.

"Back off, Carter," he said. "I'll go along with this but it'd better be good. I can already get you back in prison as an accomplice to a suspected murder." When he said it, he realized too late that this would be all the more reason for Carter to kill him if he was going to.

"Come with me," said Carter.

Lanslow turned back to his car and retrieved the book of mug shots and a recorder he'd brought along.

"What's that?" asked Carter.

"Mug shots. I have to see if Andrew can identify the man we think killed my partner, and it has to be recorded."

Carter shrugged. He turned and walked toward a car. Lanslow followed. Carter got in the driver's seat and motioned for Lanslow to go around to the passenger side. Lanslow got in, an uneasy feeling growing. Carter started the car and headed south, toward I-694. They were leaving the White Bear Lake city limits. At the interstate, he headed down the wrong ramp, going west.

"What the hell are you doing, Carter?" said Lanslow, but he knew.

"Checking to see if your friends are with you, Detective," said Carter, as a car coming in the opposite direction began honking and flashing its lights. Several others did the same, pulling over to the side to let him pass. He finally reached the freeway and turned east, now going in the right direction. Carter had been checking his rearview mirror. No car had followed.

Lanslow had to smile. Carter hadn't even checked him for a weapon, and if the police had wanted, they could have spotted Carter easily going east on the freeway, even after he had gone down the wrong way, and could have radioed his position. The smile faded. The fact was, they had made no such arrangements. Carter would probably take other evasive measures, too, somewhere down the line and, indeed, Lanslow would be alone with Carter and White and God knows who else. Brooks didn't know where he was, even now. He began to regret his impetuousness.

Surprisingly, Carter took no more evasive measures and pulled onto a ramp, then exited into a roadside park. The car rolled slowly to a stop near a cement block building and then Carter flashed the headlights. Moments later, the figure of a small man, bundled in a parka, the hood almost completely hiding his face, emerged from the building and walked toward the car.

▌

Just down the street from Matthews's house, Lanslow sat, still in his own car, again waiting. A slow drizzle of rain tapped on the car's roof. It had been raining off and on all day, a cold, dreary December rain that would turn to snow or sleet and ice as the temperatures continued to drop during the morning. The road fronting the house was a dirt road, pockmarked with potholes full of water. Cars and trucks, moving slowly because of the rough road, jolted by from time to time, water from the potholes spouting. It was nearing eleven o'clock and the occasional traffic was the only thing keeping Lanslow from dozing.

The neighborhood was a relatively old one, the houses of late sixties vintage, mostly ramblers, as they were called in the Midwest, a few with second story additions, one or two colonials. The area was an early development, with one-acre lots still on septic systems and with individual wells. Mature trees lined the streets and crowded round the houses.

Lanslow had been there for about an hour. A single light glinted from what the detective knew to be Matthews's kitchen window. He had been there a couple of years ago at Christmas party Matthews had held for his neighbors and selected other colleagues from the college. Even though Lanslow held a master's degree, he'd felt out of place there, crowded among all the Ph.Ds, talking the finer points of this theory and that. He thought of Sarah Riggs, that her social snobbery might be having an effect on his own psyche.

Lanslow knew that Matthews's home office, or "study" as he called it, was downstairs, in his finished basement, so there would be no light emanating from there, if that's where he was. He was sure Matthews was home because he had called earlier and Matthews had answered. Lanslow had hung up without speaking.

Lanslow's surveillance was unofficial. But after he had talked with Andrew White he couldn't go home—not just yet. White had picked Matthews's age-enhanced photo out of the mug book, somewhat uncertainly. He had passed over it, passed over it a second time, then had returned to it. He had also promised to be a witness, should the need arise. He was to call Lanslow and check from time to time, or if the need arose, Lanslow would put an ad in the Pioneer Press. Strangely enough, White had seemingly acquired some trust of Lanslow as they had proceeded. The detective thought back to the strange scene: White, a small man, nearly swallowed by a parka obviously not his own, in the backseat, going through mug shots; Carter, his huge belly nearly engulfing the lower half of the steering wheel, obviously enjoying Lanslow's precarious predicament; and himself, in the front passenger seat, trying to keep one hand near enough to his weapon, with one eye on Carter and the other on White as he leafed through the mug book. Surprisingly, they had still not frisked him. It occurred to him that they probably suspected he was armed and had simply chosen to ignore it.

After White had fingered Matthews, Lanslow contacted Brooks, and they went back to the station. Brooks didn't chastise him, as Lanslow thought he might. Nor did the others. He'd probably hear about it later.

With Bradbury and Johnson, they discussed obtaining a search warrant then and there. The judge wouldn't be happy about it. He would do it, but it would probably take hours. On the other hand, they had been somewhat uncertain of the grounds for a warrant. White wouldn't be the ideal witness, to say the least, and the circumstances under which Lanslow had obtained an ID might not sit well, either, even though the rookie detective had taken all the usual precautions, reading into the recorder from a prepared statement: "In a moment I am going to show you some photographs ... You do not have to identify anyone ... You should pay no attention to numbers or markings that may appear on the photos ... When you have completed viewing all the photos, please tell me whether or not you can make an identification ... " and so on, and so forth, duly recorded. In the end, Bradbury thought the grounds were sufficient but saw no reason to not wait until the morning. There was no hurry at this point. They would have to take Matthews by use of a SWAT team, anyway, and that would require some planning.

Nevertheless, Lanslow had found himself parked here, the digits on the clock in his car approaching midnight, watching Matthews house, still astounded at the turn in the case, still not quite able to believe how it had come down.

At that moment, a car pulled into Matthews's driveway, and a young man, whom Lanslow recognized as Luke Matthews, got out and ran through the rain to the front door.

31

Chief Bradbury looked up from the daily report form he held in his hand. He was surrounded by Charlie Johnson, Brooks and Lanslow. They had just finished listening to the tape again in which Andrew White had identified Jack Matthews as the man he'd seen at Mallard's and Barrows's murder scenes. They were going over the part where White was saying, "The guy seems a little old. Wait a minute."

Bradbury pressed the stop button. "He wasn't sure?" asked the chief, directing his question to Lanslow.

"He skipped the photo the first time. He went back."

"That's not good," said Johnson. "A lawyer can stomp the crap out of him on that."

The chief pressed the play button again. White's voice was saying, "Yeah, man, that's got to be him. That looks like him."

"That's not real positive, Chief," said Johnson.

Bradbury held up his hand, listening some more. The tape ended. The chief leaned back in his chair. "Charlie is right," he said. "That's not real positive."

"That's all we got, Chief. I think it's enough," said Brooks. "We've got all the other stuff, too ... the MO, the change of name ... and we're working on more."

"You don't have a motive," said Johnson.

"We'll have to get that," said Lanslow. "We'll get it after we arrest him."

Bradbury let his chair come forward. He looked from man to man. He sighed visibly. "Okay. It's weak, but I think it's enough, we'll let the attorneys worry about it later," he said. "We have a witness. Like Rich says, we can get the other stuff. I don't have any doubt that Judge Mason will sign. With that kind of evidence we can go for both arrest and search. Let's get Matthews in here."

Lanslow felt the adrenaline rise. "I'll get the affidavits prepared," he said. "It's the semester break. Matthews should be at home or at the college, depending on whether he got his grades turned in. The faculty had a duty day yesterday, but I think they're free today."

"You and Brooks check his house," said Bradbury. "If he's home, we'll take him. If not, stake it out until he shows up, then call for backup. No use making a fuss at the college. I'll alert the sheriff to get the SWAT team ready when we want to move in."

Lanslow rose from his chair.

"The young man is gonna make a good detective, someday, don't you think, Chief?" said Brooks, clapping Lanslow on the shoulder.

"Good work, both of you," said Bradbury, looking from Lanslow to Brooks and back again. Lanslow said nothing about the apprehension he'd felt these last two days and the relief he was feeling now, even though he had the lingering dread that the lead on Matthews might still turn out to be wrong. White had told him before he'd started recording that both times he'd only gotten a glimpse of the killer. Lanslow didn't mention that to the other detectives.

Lanslow had watched Jack Matthews's house until after midnight. After Luke Matthews arrived, the upstairs living room light had gone on and from time to time he could see what appeared to be Jack Matthews and his son passing back and forth in front of the bow window. They were talking, gesticulating, apparently arguing. Probably not politics, Lanslow thought, and he had wished he could be a fly on the wall to hear the conversation. Suddenly, Lanslow remembered who the photo of the young John Paul Matson reminded him of: none other than Professor Matthews's son, Luke.

I

"You messed it up," said Conrad to Dorian. "Now what?"

"Will the police come to get us?" asked Linda, panic in her voice.

"Shut up, Linda! Let me think," said Dorian.

"That's hardly even a possibility," said Gary, contemptuously.

Dorian wheeled on him, but Conrad intervened. "We can't fight among ourselves," he interjected. "It serves no purpose and saps our energy."

"You're all a bunch of wimps," said Dorian. "I'm the one who has to take care of these things, and I'll do it now."

"What do you intend to do?" asked Conrad, obviously alarmed.

"Linda's right. They'll come to get us. We have to fight them."

"That's always your answer to everything," said Gary. "Your violence is what has gotten us into this mess."

"My violence! My violence!" cried Dorian. "It's always the little man that gets us into these messes!"

"How are we going to fight them? They have guns!" said Linda.

Dorian stood up, an air of superiority about him. He went to the bookcase beside the fireplace, removed some books and pulled out a package. Making a show of it, he reached into the package and pulled out a red rag and laid it on the coffee table. Once again, he reached into the package and, this time, pulled out a gun.

"With these," he said, triumphantly, as he laid the gun on the table and unwrapped the rag to expose a knife.

"Where did you get that gun?" said Conrad, aghast.

"I've had it for a while," said Dorian. "I knew, someday, it would come to this."

I

When they got within sight of Matthew's house, Lanslow noted that Luke Matthews's car was still parked where he had seen it last night. A call to

Matthews's home a few minutes before they arrived had left Lanslow puzzled. The voice had not sounded like the professor's. Pretending to be a telemarketer, Lanslow attempted to verify that Matthews was on the other end. The person identified himself as Matthews, but had said he wasn't interested, and promptly hung up.

"That didn't sound like him," said Lanslow to Brooks.

"Maybe he has visitors."

Brooks, sitting on the passenger side of the vehicle, peered intently at Matthews's house. It was a little after 9:00 A.M. They had just arrived, stationing themselves at a point where they could monitor the house without themselves drawing suspicion. The overnight rain had stopped. It was turning colder. There was a thin layer of ice on the water in the ruts and potholes. The road's surface was a layer of half-frozen brown mud.

"I don't think it was Luke, his son, either," said Lanslow. "Could be wrong, but I don't think it was him."

"I'll give him another call," said Brooks.

Brooks dialed Matthews's phone number. The phone rang five times. A female voice answered.

"Hello?"

"Hello ... ma'am," Brooks said, a startled look on his face. "Could I speak to Dr. Matthews please?"

There was a pause long enough to cause Brooks to think he had not been heard. Then the woman hung up and left Brooks with only a dial tone.

"That was a woman," said Brooks.

Now Lanslow was even more puzzled. "Well, I'll be damned! What's going on? I watched the house last night 'til way after midnight," said Lanslow, noting Brooks's quick look.

"You were here at Matthews's house last night?" said Brooks.

"Yeah, I know. Probably shouldn't have, but I was. I wouldn't have been able to sleep. Anyway, I never saw anyone else in that house last night except Jack and Luke. Seems strange that he could have a house fill up with people between midnight and nine this morning, don't you think?"

"Maybe he had some guests come in on a red-eye flight," said Brooks, doubting his own explanation.

"Maybe," said Lanslow, his brow furrowing. He picked up the cell phone and punched the re-dial button.

"Hello?" said a child's voice.

"Hello, could I speak to Professor Matthews, please?" said Lanslow. Again, a long pause.

"He's not here," said the child's voice.

"Could you tell me where he is?" asked Lanslow.

The voice on the other end changed. "Who is this?" asked the deep male voice.

"Sir, I'm from Brown Associates and I'm trying to reach Professor Matthews," said Lanslow, thinking fast.

"I'm not interested, thanks," said the man, and hung up the phone.

"What the hell … ? This is getting really weird," said Lanslow.

"Was that Matthews?" asked Brooks.

"No. Someone different. A kid answered, then a man with a deep voice, but he acted like he was Matthews."

"You're sure it wasn't Matthews, or the son?"

"I'm certain," said Lanslow. "Something strange going on here. What the hell do we do now?"

"Taking Matthews down could be dangerous," said Brooks. "He's a cop killer. There are women and kids inside. It's time to check with HQ."

■

"They're here," said Dorian.

"Who?" asked Gary.

"The police," said Conrad, returning the phone to its cradle.

"Yes, the police," said Linda. "They're here to kill us, all of us."

"I'm scared," said Brian, tears welling.

"This is it," said Dorian.

32

H e's probably in there, Chief," said Brooks on his cell phone, "But we can't verify it. And there's at least one kid and a woman, as well as maybe a couple of men or more in there, too. We're going to need the SWAT team."

"You two hold on there and keep us informed. I'll notify the sheriff and I'm sending backup now."

Not more than five minutes later, three more squads, their sirens silent, pulled up behind Lanslow and Brooks. The two detectives got out of their own squad, making their way around and over the potholes and muddy ruts, and went back to meet the other six officers.

"Henry, you and Gabe position yourselves down the street about a block, that way" said Brooks, assuming command. "Stop all cars from coming through that direction. Jerry, you and Carl drop back that way, at the intersection, and block this road off. Don't let anyone come through or get out. Art, we need someone at the back of the house. You and Larry sneak on back there and station yourselves in the woods. We want that escape route blocked off, for sure, too. We'll let you all know when the SWAT team gets here."

A short time after the officers deployed, Lanslow saw Chief Bradbury's car turn onto their street. He pulled up beside Brooks's and Lanslow's squad. Charlie Johnson was in the passenger's seat.

Brooks explained to Bradbury what had just transpired. "Got the interior perimeter set, Chief," he said. "All we need is the SWAT team."

"All right," said Bradbury. "SWAT is on its way. We have personnel stationed along the highway and at all the other exits, too. He can't get out any of the roads without being seen. We're evacuating the area, too. Anything else I should know?"

"There's a woman and a kid in there, Chief," said Lanslow.

"Yes, I know. Brooks told me. Can't be helped. SWAT can handle it."

❚

Burly men, swaddled in heavy, bulletproof vests, wearing Plexiglas-visored helmets and carrying guns, piled out of the van and made their way up the drive, in close-packed single file, to Matthews's front door. The man at the front carried a battering ram. Another file of men from the SWAT team had made its way to the back door of the walkout basement. There was no attempt at secrecy now. Police squads lined the street, lights turning and flashing, strobe-like, shielding officers armed with guns trained on Professor Jack Matthews's house.

Even though he had authority to conduct a "no-knock" raid, the SWAT commander, a Lieutenant Ridgeway, yelled "Police. Open up!" and rapped on the door.

There was no response. The SWAT commander nodded to the officer carrying the battering ram.

"We're going in," announced Ridgeway through his mike.

The door burst open on the second try, the man with the battering ram stepped aside, and the men rushed in, shouting, holding guns at the ready. The living room into which the officers emerged was unoccupied. The men fanned out, pairs of officers taking different sections of the house. A door, straight back, opened into what was a hallway to the bedrooms. The commander signaled two of his men to bear left into the kitchen, while he and another officer named Dibruzzi approached the hallway.

Down below, in Matthews's basement, the rest of the SWAT team had entered and their noisy search could be easily heard.

"What's happening down there?" asked the SWAT commander through his mike.

"We're in," said Sergeant Conrad, the downstairs team leader. "No one down here, yet."

"Cauffman and Leonard are at the head of the stairs to the basement," said Ridgeway. "Be careful."

"Ten-four."

From his position out front with Bradbury and Brooks, Lanslow could hear the communications. The team members were both upstairs and downstairs—and no one was there?

"What the hell?" said Lanslow, looking at Bradbury. "He's got to be there, Chief. We just talked to people in there."

"Hang on," said Bradbury, holding up his hand. "It's not over yet."

The upstairs SWAT commander edged down the hallway, flat against the wall. The hallway turned abruptly left a few feet away, leading to a bedroom. A closed door, straight ahead, led into another room. The officer kept his eyes and his Heckler-Koch MP5 SD submachine gun trained on the door. Behind him, Officer Dibruzzi covered the closed door with a shotgun.

Ridgeway stepped quickly into the hallway leading to the left, his gun at the ready. Dibruzzi remained guarding the closed doorway. Cautiously, Ridgeway edged forward, signaling Dibruzzi to remain where he was. The hallway led to a master bedroom, its windows looking out toward the backyard. He spotted two officers just inside the trees that marked the perimeter of the lot. A bathroom, its door open, was on his right. Doors to a double closet farther to the right were open, exposing clothing. Both the bedroom and bathroom were unoccupied. He approached the closet and knelt to peer beneath the hanging clothing; plenty of men's shoes but no feet in them. He poked the barrel of his gun carefully into the clothing, moving the garments to the side, though he was sure no adult person could hide there. There was no one.

Ridgeway made his way back into the hallway where Dibruzzi stood guard at the closed door. Carefully he grasped the door knob and twisted. It was locked. He motioned for Dibruzzi to kick it down.

With a carefully aimed, vicious kick, the door sprung open with a cracking sound. Standing, his silhouette framed against the window, a man had a gun and it was pointed straight at Dibruzzi.

■

The little man could hear the commotion throughout the house, things being knocked over, loud voices, wood splintering. He could picture the men who were tearing the house to pieces at that very moment: large, brawny men, in camouflage, bearing guns, tracking muddy snow all over his carpets.

He had heard the voice again, and several others. For the first time he had talked back to them, and he still couldn't understand what had happened. They were there, inside his head, but not inside his head. They had been there for a long time. They lived in this house, knew most everything about him. They said they had tried for a long time to talk to him, but he hadn't listened. They had told him the police were coming because he, and they, had done something wrong, something terrible. Apparently, he had murdered people; yes, that's what they had said: He, they (for they were all together now), had murdered someone, and they'd even raped a young woman! And now they were going to have to pay for it.

It was beyond him. But the police were here.

Now, all of them—the voices—were afraid they were going to die. It seemed they might be right. And once again, there was this one voice urging him on, telling him it would be better, that there would be no more struggle, no more wondering how he had come to such a strait; just peace, at last ... (Peace at last, peace at last. Thank God almighty, peace at last.)

The thought occurred to him that he hadn't planned his death this way. Then he almost laughed at himself. It was a strange thought, ridiculous. Who ever planned their death, anyway? It was one of his parrot phrases, something he'd heard somewhere. Maybe he hadn't planned his death, but he had thought about it, even at his age; he'd just never imagined it like this.

He shouldn't be surprised. That was the way his life had been ever since he could remember. Random events, unanticipated turns. Yet, when he thought about it, perhaps that was the central tendency in his life, oddly enough. A central tendency of no central tendency; no "best fitting" line, so to speak. It didn't make any sense, but not much of anything else seemed to, either.

He could hear them outside the door now. Stealthy steps, but the floor had always creaked at that particular spot.

His life was hopeless, and had been all along, carried on a trajectory not of his own making. Somewhere along the way, he had lost out, and he still didn't know quite where or how, though he sometimes thought he did. He looked at others and they seemed to be so different from him, so much a part of things. He knew that this was an irrational thought, that he was part of things, too, but he didn't feel it. He had never acquired that feeling, of being a part, of being accepted. Knowing without the feeling wasn't enough.

He saw the doorknob turning, slowly, slowly, as if in a slow-motion movie. Not long now.

He was about to die, and he contemplated what it would be like. He could end it, now, before they did it for him. He had the gun. He consciously focused on its weight and coldness in his hand, a new experience. He wondered how it felt to shoot oneself. Searing pain? A quick loss of consciousness, of knowing and feeling?

He began to understand the serenity of death: no feeling; no worries; no "Being"—in Sartre's sense—because the self had at last surrendered to the abyss of Nothingness. Yes, literally, no thing. (He had long since given up the notion of an afterlife, other than that he would come back as part of a plant, maybe, and then become part of a cow, or some other animal. Ashes to ashes; dust to dust.)

Knowing he would be dead soon, he wondered why his whole life did not flash before him, like he'd heard it did when one is about to die. Not that he wanted it to. It hadn't been much of a life, so why belabor it? And it was another parrot phrase, anyway, nothing to it.

A vision of his dead mother came to his consciousness. He had marveled at how they had been able to fix her up as well as they had, to soften her harsh features, such that he had hardly even recognized her as he had seen her last. Would they be kind enough to do that for him?

At that thought he broke down. He began to sob. And that was when he heard the door crashing in.

∎

"Police!" screamed Ridgeway, "Drop the gun!"

"Drop the gun!" screamed Dibruzzi, "Drop the gun!"

Dorian had jumped up on a chair, the .22 revolver in his hand. He was looking down the barrels of a submachine gun and a shotgun. He held his .22 revolver pointed at the police. For just a moment, Dorian was tempted to pull the trigger, then, slowly, he lowered the gun to his side.

Dibruzzi was on Dorian in an instant, wresting the gun from his hand, pinning him on the floor with his knee, pulling his hands behind his back and slipping on the handcuffs. Ridgeway held the submachine gun on Dorian while this was happening.

"Frisk him," said Ridgeway to Dibruzzi.

This was a cop killer and they spared no sympathy. Dorian's nose, pressed into the carpet began to bleed, and the knee in his back didn't let up. He was jerked to a sitting position, his arms nearly wrenched from their sockets.

"We got one," Ridgeway radioed to the other team, and to the other officers outside. "We got him."

"We got one, too, Lieutenant," said Sergeant Conrad, from below. "We've searched everything down here."

"Bring him up," said Ridgeway.

"Lieutenant Ridgeway, this is Chief Bradbury," said the voice from Ridgeway's radio.

"Go ahead, Chief."

"You have two men? There were no women or children inside?"

"Negative, Chief. We have two men only, one from below, one above."

"Okay, Lieutenant. You're bringing them out?"

"Right now, Chief. On our way."

Outside, Bradbury looked questioningly at Brooks and Lanslow. "You heard him. You said there were women and children in there?"

"No doubt about it, Chief," said Brooks. "I'd swear I talked to a woman."

"And I talked to two men who didn't sound like Matthews at all, and a kid," said Lanslow.

At that moment, the members of the SWAT team who had gone behind emerged from the house. In their midst, another man, small in stature, almost diminutive, walked with them, his hands cuffed behind his back. As they walked him to the van to be brought to the station, a crowd of officers gathered around. Lanslow made his way to the front. Luke Matthews, wearing only jeans and a T-shirt, stumbled ahead of a burly deputy, his face a frozen mask of perplexity.

From the front of the house, Lieutenant Ridgeway emerged, a deputy trailing, and between them, another man, again in handcuffs, followed by Dibruzzi. As Ridgeway and the others passed with their prisoner, the little man looked directly at Lanslow. The young detective stared into the countenance of Professor Jack Matthews, the professor's face, too, nothing but a dazed, blank mask.

33

Dissociative identity disorder, formerly known as multiple personality disorder, or MPD" the woman psychiatrist was saying, " consists of the presence of two or more distinct identities or personalities that can control the individual's behavior at different times." She peered at Lanslow over her reading glasses, lowering the copy of *Diagnostic and Statistical Manual of Mental Disorders* from which she'd been reading.

Detective Lanslow shifted in the chair across the table from the doctor. "I don't quite understand," he said. "You mean Professor Matthews can actually be several different people?"

"Exactly," said the psychiatrist. "We have been able to identify several different personalities so far. There are probably more."

Lanslow still couldn't quite believe what he was hearing, even though he'd heard it repeated over and over in trial testimony during the past several months, a trial that, itself, had been a panoply of disbelief. "I've known this man for a number of years, now, socialized with him. Why wouldn't I know this? He even advised me from time to time on these killings! Is he always the same person with me?"

"In all probability, yes. On the other hand, the changes are sometimes subtle, and ordinarily we wouldn't even be looking for such things, so we can sometimes just be unaware of the switches from one personality to another. The alterations can be quite rapid and shift back and forth. Most people just attribute the personality changes to mood swings, but it's far more than that."

"It just seems impossible," said Lanslow. "You said one of the personalities was a woman ... and one or two children? How can a person be both sexes or different ages?"

"Each personality has its own separate history and name—even its own image and personality characteristics. Of course, a man can't physically be a woman, nor an adult a child, but the particular personality in control, whether man or woman, or child or adult, sees him- or herself physically as that person and behaves as that person. They can see themselves as large or small, fat or thin, strong or weak, regardless of how they actually look to others. Some personalities may be quite outgoing, while others may be extremely introverted. They can even have different tastes in food, different reactions to medications, etc. The personalities develop separately to handle different situations. John's female personality, by the way, is also lesbian." The woman smiled at this, watching Lanslow's face closely.

Lanslow had heard references to this, too, but he shook his head nevertheless. "Yes... well, that explains another thing that had confused us for awhile. We know Matthews raped a young student at the University," he said. "She has identified him. He even had her wallet in his possession. His fingerprints were on her travel bag and his semen was on her ski cap. She said she'd heard the voice of a woman, and believed the woman actually did the raping, but I thought she was just imagining things."

"It's true. That was Linda, with Dorian's 'help.'" The doctor held up two fingers on either hand to signal her quotation.

"Can you tell me more about Dorian?"

"Dorian is the physical protector of the bunch. He has a special hatred of larger men. Dorian was the actual killer of your partner and Mr. Barrows. Your partner offended the 'little man' personality in some way to set him off and Dorian reacted. Your partner and John supposedly met in a liquor store. John, or Dorian in this case, followed your partner home and caught him leaning into his car to retrieve his groceries. That's when Dorian stabbed him."

Lanslow had heard about this during the trial. It was a sensational moment, when everyone in the courtroom had actually witnessed the transformation of John Matthews into the personality known as Dorian. It had probably been the turning point with the jury and had helped to place Matthews in this institution rather than in prison.

"Henry Barrows was killed for molesting John Matthews sexually when he was a child," the psychiatrist continued. "John is the victim of sexual and physical abuse as a young boy. Even his mother was probably responsible for a good deal of mental abuse, if not physical abuse, too."

"You talk like these personalities are in fact different people."

"Well, of course, they're not, physically speaking. Psychologically speaking, however, they are."

"Do the personalities know one another?"

"Some do, some don't. Conrad, Gary, Dorian, Linda and two children, Larry and Brian, seem to be the main alter-personalities. But there are others. These main alters know one another and carry on conversations. Of course, the conversation is really just a matter of the personalities switching control, back and forth, speaking and reacting to one another. When this is happening, from a distance it looks like John is talking to himself, but closer in you can hear his voice changing—even to some degree his physical appearance—as each of the personalities weigh in. The John Matthews personality didn't know of the others, for sure, until the very day he was captured. Apparently they spoke to him then and he heard them and could even see them. But, as far as we know, they all knew of him. To them, though, he was called 'little man' because that's apparently what everyone called John when he was young, although he went by 'Paul,' too. "

"Jack didn't know what Dorian was doing, then?"

"No. John told me that he found the young woman's wallet and the knife and rag and thought that his son, Luke, was somehow mixed up in something. But Dorian had hidden the items. John said he has often lost time, has sometimes found himself in places where he didn't have any idea how he had gotten there. He says he's often found things, clothing, etc., that he couldn't remember purchasing, things, he says, he would never have bought for himself."

Many more of the things Lanslow and the other detectives had been mystified about were becoming clearer, now. Apparently Matthews, the criminologist, knew nothing of what his other personalities had done, hence, incredibly he could provide advice on his own case! And when the police interrogated Matthews, it was as though he hadn't the slightest idea of what they were talking about. He had even passed a lie-detector test. He claimed he'd only recently learned of these "others" inside him.

Nonetheless, they had Andrew White's eyewitness identification and they had found the knife and rag, with Zeke Mallard's dried blood on them, as well as traces of Zeke's blood in Matthews's car. Otherwise, they would have had a very weak case. Probably only a rape case. Matthews had been found "not guilty by reason of insanity" and had been sent to this hospital.

"One other thing, Doctor. Has Jack told you anything about why he changed his name?"

"Oh, yes. His mother, after her separation and subsequent divorce from John's father, had changed her and John's name back to her maiden name, Matson. Sometime later, I'm not sure exactly when, John changed it back to Matthews, the name of his biological father. His father, killed in Vietnam, had become a hero to him by then. He needed to have someone who he looked up to, who he thought was kind and loved him—a normal part of the MPD syndrome. Besides, he had fallen out with his mother by then, for sending him to reform school. John had only seen his mother again once, after she became ill."

Lanslow shook his head again. Listening to what the doctor was saying, he began to feel ambivalent toward the man he once knew as Jack Matthews. He couldn't help but feel rage at Matthews for murdering his partner, merely because of a perceived insult, as the doctor had said. Yet, on the other hand, he had also known the professor, both as academic mentor and criminologist-consultant for the department. Out of those relationships he had developed a great respect and had come to like the man and to think of him as a friend.

Could he forgive Matthews for killing Zeke Mallard? After all, according to this psychiatrist, it wasn't Matthews who killed his partner or the old man; it was Dorian. And if he could ever convince himself that MPD was real, it was Dorian, then, that he should direct his feelings toward, and it was Dorian who should have to pay the price. But, on the other hand, Dorian himself was mostly protecting Jack Matthews, the product of an abusive surrogate father and an unconcerned, neglectful mother who may have been abusive herself.

Lanslow became aware that he hadn't said anything for some time. He looked up and the doctor was smiling at him.

"The human mind is a complicated thing, isn't it, Detective?" she said.

"More than I could have imagined, ma'am," he said, nodding.

"We wear many masks at one time or another."

"Even the mask of a murderer," said Lanslow.

"Yes, that too."

❚

After his talk with the psychiatrist, as he walked down the hall of the dreary institution, its glazed block walls the color of green lemons, Lanslow tried to recollect his thoughts.

It had been left up to him, more or less out of conscience, to deal with Luke Matthews and his sister Annie, who now lived together in Jack Matthews's house. He felt sorry for the brother and sister; they'd had it rough, but they seemed to be pulling through. They were young adults and could take care of themselves. Maureen had sold her condo and was also living in Jack Matthews's house. It had been a different story for Maureen. She had taken it very hard. He had talked with her some during the trial. She visited Matthews often, according to Luke and Annie.

As far as Lanslow knew, Andrew White had disappeared again. According to Angelena Rosario, whom Lanslow had visited at the Val Mart store a couple of times, White had not tried to contact her, probably because he'd learned his lesson and was heeding Lanslow's warning.

And then, there was Christine Mallard. Her newborn son had weighed in at well over eight pounds, the image of his father even at a couple of months of age. Christine had taken the revelation of her husband's affair stoically in public, but had wept in Lanslow's arms in private. The birth of the baby and his resemblance to his father had seemed to mitigate her grief somewhat. Lanslow and Laura had kept up their relationship with Christine, and Laura had taken to the baby, named after his father, obviously in anticipation of their own. Lanslow was certain he'd be throwing a ball to Zeke, Jr. and his own little boy (or, perhaps, a girl) in the backyard of the Mallard home, until Christine remarried. A woman like her wouldn't stay single for long.

As Lanslow walked through the institute's outer doors, he could only wonder at the twists and turns in life, at where justice lay in all of this. Who, of all the personages, was really paying the price for the murder of Zeke Mallard? Henry Barrows had paid the price for his abominable behavior, but the woman who had perhaps started it all, John's mother, had probably escaped unscathed unless she'd have to answer for her deeds in the afterlife. He hoped it wasn't his friend and mentor, Professor John Paul Matthews. But, he supposed, that remained to be seen. The whole thing still left him unsettled. He would go and visit the professor one day, and perhaps find out then, and maybe get a little more closure.

In the meantime, he had a wedding to attend to, with a beautiful woman named Laura Riggs, who had apparently reached some reconciliation to a life that would be lived mostly alone, keeping his dinners warm in the oven, making excuses to their friends for social occasions unmet. Detective Brooks would be his best man ("Absolutely," he'd said). Over Christmas, Lanslow had even managed to get on the good side of Sarah Riggs. He wondered if it would last, or if, under the circumstances, she had just felt sorry for him.